I0747036

NICOLE MACCARRON

Hazel's Mirror

Copyright © 2021 by Nicole MacCarron

All rights reserved. No part of this publication may be reproduced, stored or transmitted in any form or by any means, electronic, mechanical, photocopying, recording, scanning, or otherwise without written permission from the publisher. It is illegal to copy this book, post it to a website, or distribute it by any other means without permission.

Designations used by companies to distinguish their products are often claimed as trademarks. All brand names and product names used in this book and on its cover are trade names, service marks, trademarks and registered trademarks of their respective owners. The publishers and the book are not associated with any product or vendor mentioned in this book. None of the companies referenced within the book have endorsed the book.

Cover art by Sara Oliver at www.saraoliverdesign.com

First edition

This book was professionally typeset on Reedsy.
Find out more at reedsy.com

Dedication

This is for my three sisters, who grew up with a future horror author. Thanks for your support and for helping me grow into the person I am today. I'm sorry for the times I scared the crap out of you.
But not that sorry.

Contents

Acknowledgement

Thank you to my amazing Beta Readers! I couldn't have gotten through editing without you. Special thank you to Amy, whose enthusiasm and demands for more both gave me life and frightened me into finishing the book. Well done, Amy! Another thank you to Cecilia for her Portuguese translations. You gave the dialogue authenticity and accuracy, which I so appreciate. And finally, thank you to Sarah, for your expert polishing of this manuscript!

An Important Update

I realized after publishing Hazel's Shadow that burning sage is a sacred practice for many Indigenous peoples. I also learned that sage is being depleted because it is being mass harvested for the mainstream market. Having Irish heritage myself (where sage is also used for cleansing), I could possibly have gotten away with it, but I didn't think it was responsible. So I asked around and some Indigenous people suggested I switch to lavender, which can be burned and used for cleansing in a similar way, but isn't necessarily sacred. All new editions of Hazel's Shadow have been updated, and you will read about Hazel using lavender in this book as well. If you are purchasing sage for your cleansing needs, please ensure you are obtaining it from an ethical source, such as from your local Indigenous community.

1

Hazel

Hazel had not looked fully into a mirror in almost a year. Now she stood in a dingy rest-stop bathroom, taking deep breaths and searching her own eyes for evil. She could see the tiny reflection of herself in her black pupils and tried not to see a stranger. Her heart fluttered with fear. Did part of her want it to?

Outside the bathroom, the hiss of brakes and the conversation of truckers and passengers went on. In a fit of madness, Hazel flicked the light switch off. Her heart raced, eyes never leaving the pitch-black mirror. Even then, all her pupils did was contract and expand. She leaned towards the glass, concentrating as hard as she could, her hands now gripping the chipped counter.

Just as she began to feel dizzy, there was a knock on the bathroom door, and Hazel jumped back in shock. She broke her gaze with the mirror, then flicked the light back on and snapped back just as fast. In the mirror, her normal reflection stared back. She let out a slow breath.

Last summer, when the Shadow was freshly trapped inside

her, it had surfaced at the slightest scent of fear. Even nerves before a university exam would call up that urge, that call to violence that was not her own. Now there was nothing.

Over the course of the year, Hazel had done her best to stay calm and starve the Shadow. Sometimes she went weeks without remembering she had possession of something hellish inside her. Lately she had found herself drawn to mirrors and resolutely looked the other way. Until now.

The knock came again. "Hazel," said Riva from the other side of the door, "are you almost done? There's a line starting out here."

"Sorry," Hazel said, thumping the soap dispenser so she could speed wash her hands.

Outside in the blinding sun, Riva's dark skin was beading with sweat. Hazel grimaced with guilt.

"You good?" Riva asked.

She nodded. "I'll be in the car."

She crossed the parking lot and weaved her way through the gas pumps towards Riva's borrowed SUV. It was only when she glimpsed her own wide body reflected in the grey side of the car that Hazel remembered the whole point of looking in the mirror. She had been planning on putting on makeup for the first time all year. The girls were heading out of town for the weekend to watch Hazel's girlfriend's basketball playoffs. For two weeks Hazel had only managed to snatch a few moments alone with Jen, and she wanted to surprise her by looking nice for their reunion.

Makeup or no, Hazel breathed a sigh of relief as she settled into the passenger's seat. She had finally stared down a mirror and nothing terrible had happened.

A few minutes later, Riva hopped into the driver's seat and

they pulled out onto the quiet highway. The SUV strained up the inclines and soared down the hills as they followed the road through the lush mountain curves. After a while, Riva tapped the volume button to cut off the music.

"Was this a mistake?"

"What?" Hazel asked, tearing her eyes away from the tree-studded valley.

"You've been really quiet this whole drive."

"I was just thinking, that's all."

Riva hesitated. "Is it Jen?"

"No, no, we're good," Hazel laughed.

There was a moment's pause as Riva waited. Hazel's smile drained away. Riva could always tell when there was more.

"When we were leaving, we drove past the memorial."

Horror spread across Riva's face.

"It's fine," Hazel insisted. "It's just that … I wasn't expecting all the flowers."

It was still almost a week before Hazel would have to face the anniversary of her family's death, of the first time she had ever seen zombies. She had experienced a jolt this morning when Riva drove past the high school and the concrete memorial with a black plaque on its face. The memorial had been erected months ago to honour the lives of those lost to the corrupt. The wreaths and flowers collected at the memorial's base were new.

The high school and the hospital were the two locations of the Shadow's most devastating zombie attacks. Hazel had lost her mom and grandmother at the hospital, but at the high school she had also lost her sister. As the trees flashed past the passenger's side window, Hazel realized she had been ignoring the passing of time. She had been swallowing a lump in her throat nearly the whole drive, trying not to think about her sister's name etched into the plaque among so many others.

Kelly should have been preparing for graduation next year. Maybe by now she would have found herself a date to this year's prom. Was her date alive and missing out on Kelly, or had they died as well?

Left hand still on the steering wheel, Riva reached over with her right and grabbed Hazel's. Hazel's eyes misted over as she watched the sunlight shine through the trees. Riva didn't say any more; she was one of the lucky few whose family had survived intact. Hazel and Derrick, another orphan, had been living with her ever since. It was difficult not to be envious, but Riva's grip was always firm, and she was always willing to follow Hazel into the trenches of loss.

***

The roadsides changed from a deep green to a dry yellow, and when the mountain landscape turned to a riverside city, the girls had finally arrived. In the parking lot of the motel where Jen's team was staying, Hazel curled her eyelashes with the door open. Riva, who was well aware of the reason behind Hazel's aversion to mirrors, waited on the hot blacktop. Then they crossed the heat haze together, flip-flops slapping the pavement. Both girls let out a breath of relief when they passed through a set of tinted glass doors and met the cool air of the lobby.

It was narrow inside, with only a shabby front desk just steps ahead and two tunnel-like sets of stairs going up on the right and left. Hazel grimaced with claustrophobia, but then Jen came flying down the right set. The stairs came alive with a tremendous creaking as Jen's hands swung down the white walls on either side for balance.

"You made it!" she cried, pinning Hazel in a sideways hug.

Hazel smiled. It was involuntary. When Jen smiled, Hazel smiled. Her whole chest warmed up in a way that was far more pleasant than the heat outside. She patted Jen's curls, which were a rich, dark purple, and the only things that her trapped t-rex arm could reach. Jen lifted her beaming face to Hazel's, who saw that Jen was already tanned from the new summer sun. Her dark lips were so close.

"Hi Jen," Riva grinned, and Jen pulled away from Hazel too soon.

Jen and Riva were good friends. During the zombie attack, the three girls and a few other classmates had taken shelter together in Jen's house. Hazel shuffled towards the front desk so they could hug behind her in the tight space.

"Sorry I'm so sweaty. It's so hot here," Riva said. She pulled her long braids off her neck and fanned herself.

"It's stifling," Jen agreed.

When Hazel had her plastic keycard in hand, Jen led them up the right stairwell. Unlike the other two girls, Hazel had to hoist her backpack up in front of her just to fit. She hoped their room was far away from the cracking and groaning stairs, but she needn't have worried. It took three turns down identical hallways floored with paper-thin green carpet before they reached a wall of windows.

"It's just ahead," Jen said.

Sure enough, as Hazel was eyeing up the courtyard pool outside the windows, a door burst open in the adjoining hall. Screams of laughter poured out.

"I'll get the freaking ice, I'll get it!" giggled a tall blonde girl tossing a handful of ice cubes back into the room like grenades.

"Lor!" Jen called to her. "Hazel's here!"

"Aah!" the girl screamed. She shouted into the room, "Hazel's here!"

Cries of excitement sounded from inside, and Hazel looked back at Riva with her eyebrows raised.

"Guess I'm chopped liver," Riva grinned.

Jen didn't hear her. "Come and meet the team!" she said, trying to drag Hazel along.

Hazel held back. She had spotted their room number on the right. "Let me just drop my stuff off first. I'll be right there."

She and Riva ducked into the wood-panelled room with two double beds. An air conditioner was sticking its boxy head in through the window. The room was already stuffy. Riva chucked her duffel bag and purse onto the first bed.

"Okay," she said, bouncing on the balls of her toes a few times as if pumping herself up, "looks like the party's starting now!"

Hazel grinned and switched on the air conditioner. This part of British Columbia's interior was technically a desert. She pulled back the curtain to see nothing but an outside wall. A tiny courtyard down below housed a broom, a bucket, and a lone plastic lawn chair. They were on the second story. She let the curtain fall and turned back to Riva, about to speak, but then swore instead. An old lady had just walked out of the bathroom and now stood at Riva's elbow.

Riva zipped to Hazel's side with her elbows tucked in, staring in the direction of the old woman.

"What? What is it?"

"Visitor," Hazel answered, catching her breath. She groaned. "Great."

The ghost spoke to Hazel, her hands reaching out, but Hazel

couldn't understand a word. It sounded like Spanish. The stocky woman was not transparent like the ghosts in movies. She was indistinguishable from the living. She wore a modest floral dress in faded black, and her thick chin-length hair was wiry and steel grey.

"I can't understand you," Hazel said with a sympathetic shake of her head, but the old woman kept moving closer, talking nonstop. Hazel turned to Riva. "Jen might be able to help with this one. She knows a little Spanish."

"On it. I'll see if I can drag her out of there." Riva skirted the edges of the room, keeping an absurd distance from the ghost she couldn't see. She kept her back to the dresser as she passed the woman, rattling the drawers.

The old lady stepped up to Hazel. She was so close that Hazel backed into the wall.

"I'm going to try to help you," Hazel said as she pressed against the curtains. She gave the old woman a nervous smile, hoping to calm her. "Just give us a minute."

Riva returned with Jen just as the lady's eyes were filling with tears of pain and frustration. Hazel sighed with relief.

"I'm up to speed," Jen said, plopping down onto the end of Riva's mattress, which sagged under her. "But I don't know how much I can help. Mom's the only one who's fluent, and even she's rusty from living with all of us." To the room at large, she sang, "Hola. Como podemos ayudarté?"

The old woman's eyes went wide, and she hurried over to Jen, her hands raised as if she wanted to seize Jen's face. "Você poderia me ajudar?"

Hazel attempted to repeat what the ghost said, gesturing to the old woman so Jen would know where she was. Riva put another step between them.

Jen frowned. "I don't think that's Spanish. It sounds like it might be Portuguese."

"So we're stuck?" Hazel asked, wilting with disappointment.

"Maybe not. They are similar." She sucked in her bottom lip as she thought. To the ghost she said, "Yo hablo español. Queremos ayudarle. We want to help you."

The woman began speaking so fast in Portuguese that Hazel was left completely in the dust, mouth open. When the woman paused to stare back and forth between the silent girls, Hazel grimaced her apology. The woman raised a finger, paced a moment, then slowed her speech down so Hazel could repeat it word for word.

"Por favor, vai a minha casa, pega na concha, e ponha para baixo da árvore grande."

"Okay," Jen said, nodding. " 'Por favor' is obviously 'please.' 'Vai a minha casa.' ... 'Go to my house.' 'Pega na concha. ...' " She paused, frowning again. "Well, it sounds a bit like 'take the shell.' And then I think that last part might have been 'under the big tree.' "

Hazel and Riva waited in silence while Jen pieced it all together.

"I think she either wants us to move a shell to a big tree or take a shell from under a big tree." To the woman, she asked, "Por qué?"

The old woman looked down at the floor and answered in a whisper, "Meu marido," which Hazel repeated.

Jen's eyes glistened. "For her husband."

Riva put a hand to her heart.

"Well," Jen said finally, "we'll need her to show us the way to her house. But we can't do it now; the girls are already waiting for us to go to dinner." To the woman she stumbled through,

"Queremos ayudar pero tendrá que ser esta noche."

The woman seemed to understand. She touched Hazel's chin with upturned fingers, then Jen's, though neither girl could feel it. "Querida meninas. Muita obrigada. Graças a Deus."

"Okay, now come meet everyone," Jen said, bouncing up off the bed with a bright smile.

Riva caught Hazel's eye. "Right back to party energy."

Jen gave Riva a playful glare. Hazel eyed up the tidy beds for a moment, but there was no stopping Jen's energy.

"Come on, it's going to be fun," Jen promised. "They're excited to meet you."

Hazel had met some of the team over the course of the season, but this was the first time they were spending more than quick moments together. Jen's university was the next town over from Hazel's, so Jen spent much of her time commuting, in class, or at practice. She wove her fingers through Hazel's, squeezed, and then pulled her out into the hall.

"See you soon," Hazel reassured the old woman, but the ghost followed along behind Riva anyway.

The team was congregating in the hall outside their rooms, preparing to go out for dinner. At Riva's "I'll drive," there was an uproar of polite arguing over the fact that she had already driven four hours today.

"No, really," Hazel tried, "Riva loves driving."

She exchanged a glance with Riva, who didn't care one way or the other about it. They needed a way to make a pitstop at the ghost's house on the way back without telling anyone about Hazel. No one here knew that last year's massacre was more than a devastating illness, let alone that Hazel had ended it with her abilities.

"It's okay, Hazel," Jen began, but Hazel squeezed her wrist

in warning.

Riva covered the moment, "I like to drive in a new place. It helps me get to know it."

Jen opened her mouth to speak again, and Hazel was sure she was about to tell the truth. Hazel glared her disbelief. Jen gave an amused shrug instead, which made Hazel bristle.

In the end, they climbed into Riva's SUV, but they were saddled with carpooling two of Jen's motel roommates. Lor was the tall blonde girl who had been throwing ice, and Kate was a sunburned goth-type with heavy eyeliner. Hazel watched a smiling Jen squeeze between them in the backseat. She seemed completely unbothered by the complication.

Meanwhile, in the front seat, Hazel stiffened as the old lady ghost followed her into the car and sat, weightless, on her lap. She shot Hazel an arched look, as if Hazel deserved this for not offering her shotgun. Hazel felt the stirrings of panic as she tried to ignore the ghost, think of a way to ditch the girls on the way back, and act normal at the same time.

All throughout dinner, the Portuguese ghost sat at an empty table for two, waiting with her hands folded. Every now and then she caught Hazel's eye and Hazel tried to give her a subtle, encouraging smile. Her stomach squirmed with guilt at keeping the woman waiting. She wished she could muster Jen's nonchalant attitude.

The restaurant was family-style, with a long row of wooden tables pushed together to accommodate the team. Hazel sat near the middle, beside Jen. The other seven players and Riva sat along the row. The team was rowdy despite having already played two games that day.

When Hazel looked up from her most recent exchange with the ghost, Kate was staring at her over a Long Island iced tea.

She tipped her head in the direction of the woman and raised her eyebrows at Hazel. Hazel's insides froze.

"Do you see someone?" Kate asked, point-blank.

Hazel's mouth dropped open. "What?"

A wave of quiet rippled down the table. Hazel stared at all the faces turned towards her, unnerved by the unanimous silence. Jen put her hand on Hazel's arm.

"It's okay," she said. "This is what I was trying to tell you before. I told them about you."

"You told them what, exactly?" Hazel hissed through her teeth.

"You know," Jen said, not lowering her voice, "that you can see ghosts."

Hazel felt the blood drain from her face.

Jen stroked her arm. "Don't worry! Everyone's really interested. It's not a secret anymore, right?"

There were nods and words of encouragement down the table. Hazel sought Riva, who had paused with the straw of her drink pointing at her open mouth, her expression as shocked as Hazel's. Yes, everyone in their hometown knew what Hazel could do, but she still enjoyed anonymity in the world at large. It felt like the room was shrinking.

"Is it the old woman?" Jen continued. "We never did get her name, you know."

Hazel's voice had abandoned her. Heat crept up her neck as the entire table continued looking at her. She fixed her eyes on her plate.

"There was the spirit of an old woman in their room earlier," Jen explained to the table. "But she only spoke Portuguese, so I had to help translate with my Spanish." There was pride in her voice. "We think she wants us to go to her house and move a seashell to send her husband a message. We're going to do it after dinner."

Hazel dared a glance at the faces all around her. The girls were leaning forward conspiratorially, their eyes shining with interest.

"Ooh, can we come?" asked Lor. "That's so exciting!"

At last, Jen hesitated. "Well, we're a pretty big group. …" She trailed off and deferred to Hazel, but Hazel did not oblige. Her teeth felt locked together.

Kate's shoulders slumped, but as she opened her mouth to plead her case, Riva took pity on Hazel and interrupted.

"Yeah, that's too many. We'll be trespassing as it is, it would be hard to hide a whole team." She gave the entire group a threatening look, sparing a little extra venom for Jen. "And it is a secret."

"You can trust us," a ponytailed girl swore, hand to heart. Hazel couldn't even remember her name.

"Yeah, Hazel, we won't tell anyone," another said, nodding.

Jen beamed around at them. She gave Hazel an affectionate nudge and whispered, "You can trust them. Really."

Hazel swallowed back her arguments for the time being. She hated to fight, especially in front of other people. Plus, Jen had been so proud of Hazel for opening up about her abilities to their hometown. It was hard to explain why this scenario was different or why her defenses had come shooting back up.

"So what does this old lady look like?" Kate pressed. "Does she look dead? Where is she, exactly?"

Riva threw Hazel a sympathetic grimace, then pointed to the bathroom, offering Hazel a way out. Hazel shrugged in response. It was too late now. She took a steadying breath, then began fielding questions. She avoided Jen's eye altogether.

***

Silver moonlight lit the way between the apple trees, replacing the headlights Riva had switched off. The driveway was narrow, the trees of the orchard reaching for the SUV on both sides. When the house came into view, Riva parked, not daring to get any closer. They studied the windows to make sure the old lady's husband wasn't looking out. The wind rustled the leaves of the apple trees.

"Can I do it?" Lor whispered from the backseat. "Please? I want to help!"

"You're crazy!" Kate giggled. "My heart is freaking pounding."

"Why not?" Jen said. "What do you think, Hazel? Lor knows what to look for."

Hazel eyed the girls in the rearview mirror, something she would not have done just yesterday. At eighteen, all the girls were of age, so they had enjoyed a few drinks at the restaurant to celebrate winning their first game of the finals.

"I better do it," she said, "in case the lady has more to tell me."

"Then I'll come too," Jen said, pushing open the backdoor and sliding out.

Hazel pressed her lips together and followed suit. At the same time, the old lady stepped off her lap and onto familiar soil. Like most ghosts, she had not yet grasped that the rules of the living didn't apply to her anymore and she could travel without a vehicle.

Hazel and Jen left the doors ajar. The air was still warm on Hazel's arms. They crept up to the house, keeping to the orchard while the old woman marched out into the open front yard. Hazel held up her hand to stop Jen at the edge of the trees but waved the old woman on, nodding her encouragement. The woman climbed the porch stairs and stopped beside a set of heavy, wooden patio furniture to look back.

"Oh man, she wants us to go right up to the front door," Hazel groaned.

"I don't see any lights or movement," Jen replied. "I say we go for it, now."

Hazel nodded, and they sped across the packed earth at a low crouch. She signaled for Jen to wait at the bottom of the steps, then climbed up alone. Hazel kept her feet close to the railing, where the stairs were used the least but still had to endure one loud creak before she reached the top.

She edged along the porch as well. The old lady pointed out a pink conch shell resting on the circular bistro table. Hazel paused to peer into the window just behind it. She thought she could make out a dark TV. There was a prickle of nervous sweat under her arms as she reached across the porch for the shell. She urged herself to take deeper breaths. The last thing she wanted to do was feed the Shadow.

The shell was cold and smooth in her hand. It had been polished with love and was clean despite residing outside. The woman gestured for Hazel to follow her around the back of the house, so Hazel tiptoed back down the porch stairs. She pointed with the shell so Jen knew where they were headed. Jen threw a quick thumbs-up to the girls in the car.

Around the side of the house they went, ears alert for any sound that wasn't crickets. Around a shed and down a sloping hill, the woman finally stopped at the foot of a creek-side weeping willow. Hazel and Jen caught up, both panting. The woman said something in Portuguese and searched the grass for a moment. When she had picked out a spot, she pointed, and Hazel lay the shell down.

"Do you think it's their picnic spot?" Jen asked as the woman knelt low beside the shell and eyed the house.

Hazel watched as the woman nodded her satisfaction and stood back up. She said something to the girls in Portuguese.

Hazel whispered it to Jen, who thought for a moment and then said, "He'll know."

The woman raised her hands, placing them on Hazel's cheeks. She stared with teary eyes into Hazel's for a long moment, and Hazel didn't need to understand the next words to know how the woman felt.

"Obrigada," she said. "Obrigada."

Hazel smiled and pretended to pat the woman's hand on her cheek. It was moments like these when her abilities felt more like a gift than a curse.

***

She and Jen jumped back into the car.

"Go, go, go!" squealed Kate.

Riva backed down the drive, the car making a high-pitched reverse whine as she sped up. Finally, they reached the deserted farm road, and she was able to pull around and speed off in the direction of the motel.

"So?" demanded Lor. "How did it go? You were gone forever. I was sure the old man was going to spot us from the window!"

"It wasn't that long," Jen laughed.

"It felt like it! We couldn't see you at all, and for all we knew, the old man was watching us!"

Hazel turned around in her seat. "He wasn't though, was he?"

"No," Riva answered, but she caught Lor's eye in the mirror

and smiled. "It was creepy though. I kept thinking I saw things move too."

"But you did it?" Kate asked. She was leaning so far forward Hazel thought her seatbelt might snap. "You moved the shell for her? What did she say then?"

"She was really thankful," Jen said with a happy sigh.

"Is she still with us?" Lor asked.

Hazel shook her head. "She'll probably stay home to be there for him when he sees it."

"And then what?" Kate pressed.

"She'll either move on, or she'll come find me," Hazel guessed.

"What happens if she comes to find you?"

"Then I'll have to help her move on."

"How will you do that?"

"Save some of your questions for the rest of the girls," Jen teased. She held up her phone for Hazel to see. "I have eight million messages from them demanding to know what's going on."

"I didn't realize it was going to be this kind of evening," Hazel hinted, but she kept her tone light. Her anger had eased with the rush of helping someone.

In a wise move, Jen changed the subject.

The rest of the team was waiting for them in the parking lot, too excited and impatient to wait upstairs. They cheered when they saw the SUV and came running across the dark asphalt as Riva parked. Hazel climbed out, looked around at their expectant faces, and cracked a smile.

"Mission accomplished," she said.

They cheered again. Hazel had her back clapped by a few of the girls while others expressed their jealousy. Hazel felt like she had just won a game herself. Lor put her arm over Hazel's shoulders like a proud old friend and led the way back inside. Hazel spotted Jen beaming at this sight and let the rest of her irritation slip away. At least just for tonight.

2

Riley

"Riley!" Hands clapped behind Riley, loud and sharp as a gunshot. His chair grated against the floor as his whole body flinched. "I asked you a question!"

Riley's cheeks grew hot when the class turned to stare at him. This was the third time Mr. Lloyd had called on him today, and all three times he hadn't been paying attention. His eyes were itchy from another sleepless night and his brain wouldn't stop following different paths to avoid the teacher's droning. After the second question, Riley had thought he was safe to let his mind wander.

Mr. Lloyd drew level with him now, his face red with frustration. "Show me your notes," he demanded, holding out a hand.

Riley shrunk around his binder, trying to shield it from view. "Now!"

Grimacing, Riley sunk back in his chair, exposing the letters he had been embellishing: Mass Migraine. It was his favourite band. He had been busy shading globs of blood along the letters' edges.

"Do you mean to tell me that doodling a love letter to that angsty man-child is more important than passing my class?"

Riley's face flushed even more as several classmates snickered. He refused to look at Sophie over in the front row, but he could feel her eyes on him.

"He's not an angsty man-child," he muttered.

"He's not Math notes either," Mr. Lloyd snapped. "I'll see you in here for lunch."

Riley opened his mouth to argue, but Mr. Lloyd was already marching away. His eyes met Aaron Pierson instead, whose smirk made Riley want to kick something.

When the bell rang, Riley rushed out the door and let Mr. Lloyd's detention reminder meet only his retreating back. He headed for his locker down the crowded Science wing, but the flood of students pouring out of their classrooms slowed him down. Just as he was reaching for his lock, Sophie passed him, her long bronze curls swaying against her back.

Desperate for some redemption, he called, "Hey, So—"

Smack.

A banana peel slapped against his cheek. It stuck there like a slimy octopus before flopping to the floor. There were gasps and shocked laughter from the students in the hall. Instant rage ignited inside Riley and he looked up for the thrower, teeth and fists clenched. Aaron and Mason were shoving each other to get around the corner first, laughing.

Riley's face burned once again as his eyes darted around to see who had witnessed his humiliation. Sophie had disappeared. He wiped the banana slime off his face with a fist, struggling to keep his face impassive as he wished fiery deaths upon Aaron and Mason. He reached for his lock again, pretending that nothing had happened. The tension broke, and conversations resumed.

Riley's downcast eyes and fuming expression kept questions at bay during his English class. He couldn't stop himself from thinking what he should have said to both Mr. Lloyd and Aaron. He imagined catching the banana before it hit Sophie, then taking on both Aaron and Mason for her. He imagined channelling all his anger into a punch so hard it knocked Aaron off his feet. By the time the lesson was wrapping up, he was just as furious with himself for the missed opportunities as he was with Aaron.

When the next bell finally rang, signaling his detention with Mr. Lloyd, Riley was in such a temper he did something he hadn't done in months. He packed his backpack and walked out. He blended in with the kids who were already making their way across the quiet street to the pizza place for lunch. Ignoring a group who ran past trying to beat the lineup, Riley slipped behind the building. On the other side was the dry, rocky woods.

There wasn't a path, but Riley had used this shortcut home so often he could use certain trees and boulders as landmarks. The upward slope was gentle, but the June sun baked his neck, and his back was soon sweating under his backpack. Just as he was heading left down the steep opposite slope, he realized he wasn't alone.

He stepped lighter, trying to hear whether the follower was the kind who rustled the rocks and dry grass or not. There was a clatter, so it wasn't the dead kind. Blood pulsed in his ears as his adrenaline kicked in. He turned. His pursuers halted on the hill behind him, skidding a bit as they pulled up short.

Mason smirked down at him. "Thought you had a detention, man-child."

Aaron chuckled. "No, it's *angsty* man-child. Right, Riley?"

Riley scowled. "What do you want?"

Aaron gave a casual shrug. "We just wondered where you were going." His tone implied Riley was the one being rude. "You know, when you've got such an important meeting."

Riley turned his back on them and kept walking.

"And," Mason called after him, "we wondered when you're going to tell Sophie you love her?"

Riley's heart stopped in his chest. If they knew, maybe Sophie knew.

Aaron laughed again. "Maybe we should tell her for him. You know, help a little guy out."

Riley riffled through retorts in his head, trying to figure out what response would get them to never speak to Sophie again. It was hopeless. He threw them the dirtiest look he could manage and kept climbing down the hill.

"Hey man, we're talking to you!" Aaron called.

"Man?" Mason echoed skeptically, and Aaron snorted.

There were a few seconds in which Riley knew they were running, but whether to stop him or to hit him, he didn't know. His heart gave a painful lurch as he thought of his dad. Aaron and Mason knew what had happened to him. They knew exactly what they were doing to Riley.

Riley turned and swung his fist just as Aaron caught up. His knuckles collided with Aaron's teeth, which shaved the skin off the back of Riley's hand. Aaron swore so loud that birds burst from the trees. Riley felt a savage pleasure at the sound, but then Mason slammed him into a tree. His backpack protected him from the worst of it, but Mason had the weight of his downhill run behind him.

Before Riley could react, Aaron was back. His punch caught

Riley in the eye, triggering a flash of stars. Mason kneed him in the stomach, and Riley doubled over. The next thing he knew, the sole of Aaron's shoe had slammed into his shoulder and sent him flying over the edge of the hill.

He rolled for powerless, eternal seconds as the world spun around him. Before he could even get his hands up to protect his head, he rolled straight into a patch of blackberry brambles. The thorns tugged at his clothes and slowed him down. He stopped facedown in the middle of the sharp bushes and lay there, stunned.

In the sudden silence, he realized how loud his fall had been. There was a moment when his classmates stayed quiet too, probably fearing they'd broken his neck. When Riley tried to fight the thorns and push his head out of their clutches, he heard their laughter start up again.

"Should have gone to detention!" Aaron yelled, and they left him there.

Five minutes of scratches and swears later, Riley finally wrenched his shoe out of the brambles' grip. He collapsed on the rough ground and stared up at the blue sky over the trees' reaching arms. He could feel his heartbeat in every cut but especially around his throbbing eye. He thought of his dad again, and his heart ached worse than any other wound.

As he raised his bloody hands to wipe his brow, he saw someone watching him by a tree to his right. His heart sent a particularly strong throb through his cuts. He sat up too fast, and the figure blurred as his head spun.

"Dad?" he croaked.

The tall old man drifted closer, revealing flyaway grey hair that was undisturbed by wind; no rocks shifted under the weight of his footsteps. "Sorry, son, no."

Riley choked on his disappointment. Less than a year ago, Liam had died in the woods behind their house. It had been a senseless act of violence. Riley had been looking for him ever since. Here was the perfect moment, and still no Liam. What kind of father wouldn't show up to help his son through a similar plight? Riley wobbled as he got to his feet, abandonment coursing through his veins, dripping down his hands with his blood.

"They'll regret this someday," the old man assured him, "when they've grown up a bit."

Riley spat blood from his cut lip into the brambles, and the green leaves swung with the weight of it. What good was regretting it later?

"You have good reflexes," the man went on. "Got in one good hit."

"Yeah, well ..."

Riley searched the ground for his backpack, which had gone flying off. He backed up the hill a few paces and spotted it in the midst of the brambles. He sighed. His textbooks were too expensive to abandon there, so he set about stomping the bush down so he could climb back in. The old man watched.

When the tattered bag was free, he set off along the base of the hill, clearing a new path. Even though he couldn't hear him, Riley knew the old man was following. Where the blackberry bushes met a crooked white birch tree, Riley was able to climb back onto his usual path and leave the woods behind. They emerged in a wide, unfenced backyard.

"You don't have to walk with me," Riley told the man in a low voice. He didn't want anyone to hear him talking to himself as they made their way past the house and out onto the potholed road. "I'm fine. Or do you want something?"

"A little conversation is nice," the old man said, ignoring Riley's tone. "It's not often people can see me."

"I don't really feel like talking."

"No, I suppose you don't," the man agreed. Nevertheless, he held out a hand to Riley. "I'm George."

Riley raised his eyebrows and George let his hand fall, tucking it into the pocket of his jeans. "Old habits," he explained with a rueful chuckle.

They walked on in silence. Riley wished George would go away.

"What will your folks say?"

"Dad's dead," Riley said shortly. "Dunno about Mom."

"I'm sorry for your loss. Dad's gone on, then?"

Riley shrugged.

George frowned. "Died before you could remember him, did he?"

Annoyed, Riley pressed his lips shut tight, but after a moment he shook his head.

George's eyes narrowed. "Didn't he visit you before he moved on?" he pressed. "Did he know about ... you?"

Riley nodded. His mom and dad had always known he could see ghosts, which made it that much worse that his dad had never bothered to say goodbye.

George's eyebrows, which were much thicker than his flyaway hair, furrowed as they passed the next house. "I suspect you're the expert on death here. I didn't even believe in ghosts until I was one. But was he never a ghost? Is there something that makes some people ghosts and others not?"

"No," Riley said. He kept his good eye fixed straight ahead. The other was swelling shut. "Everyone becomes a ghost."

"Well, shit," George said.

Riley felt a knot of misery in his throat as he dodged a pothole. He nodded again. Now George was getting it.

"I'm sorry, kid. I'm sure he had a reason."

"Yeah, he didn't care about us as much as we thought," Riley spat.

George's voice stayed even and gentle. "That's jumping to conclusions, I think. What happened to him?"

Riley couldn't suppress a frustrated sigh. The sun was beating down on them, he was thirsty, and he had just taken a beating. This was the last conversation he wanted to have right now. His answer was clipped.

"He was killed. Nine months ago. Apparently these two guys thought he was someone else. He was just hiking. They got the guys, though."

"And a lot of good that does your dad, right?" George said.

Riley looked at him in surprise. George bobbed his head in a knowing nod.

"My mother was killed when I was a young man. You're what, sixteen?" He paused for Riley to agree. "I was a good few years older than you then. They got the guy too, but it didn't bring her back. I shudder now to think of her spirit watching the way I took it all. I did some things I'm not proud of, and she wouldn't be either."

Riley knew he should say something comforting, but he was sick of all the phrases people say after someone dies. He couldn't bring himself to say them to George, even if he was starting to think George was alright.

"Well, you can't change the past." George heaved a sigh. "Do you think I'll see her when I go?"

Riley shrugged. "I don't know where we go. But if she's not here, it means she's done saying her goodbyes. So, yeah, she could be in the next place."

He couldn't keep the hope out of his voice. If ghosts went somewhere after they vanished, maybe his dad wasn't lost forever. Maybe he was just in the next place. They turned right. The hill curved with them, houses sitting at its base. On the slopes, the trees grew more thickly, and the yards between the houses stretched for longer distances.

"Have you ever gone home roughed up before?" George asked after a long silence.

"No," Riley admitted. He checked his knuckles, which were a mess of smeared blood and clumped ribbons of dead skin.

"My advice is to slip in, get some ice on that eye, and clean up that hand, quick as you can. Don't let your mom see it at its worst. Spare her that."

Riley nodded. It was sound advice. He knew it wasn't what George meant, but with any luck, he could avoid seeing his mom altogether.

They reached the small, one-story hobby farm Riley called home. From this angle, they could see that the backyard was bursting with chickens, rows of vegetables, and grapevines. Beyond that was the mountain where his dad had died. The forest looked innocent in the sunlight.

Riley turned to his companion. "Well ..."

"Thanks for the company," said George, with a little bow. "You take care now. And cherish your mother."

"Right ..." was all Riley could think to say. "Bye, George. Good luck with ... you know."

They parted at the mailbox. Riley crossed the yellowing lawn, hoping his mom was out back working on the crops as usual on a Friday. He unlocked the front door and slipped inside. It was dark, the living room curtains all drawn to keep out the heat.

He tiptoed down the hallway to the kitchen, peeking into his mom's empty room as he went. She wasn't there, or in the kitchen, so he helped himself to some ice. He tried to spot her with his good eye through the window over the sink. Some movement through the open shed door caught his eye, and he saw his mom was moving tools around. Their dog was sniffing along the ground at the entrance, keeping her company.

Charlie was a cross somewhere between a Saint Bernard and a German shepherd. He had short hair, pointy ears, and was black and white with tan patches. Two of these patches were right above his eyes, and Riley loved how they made it look like Charlie was glaring at you. If he was lucky, both Mom and Charlie would be outside for another hour, and he could pretend he had just arrived after a full day of school.

Riley's bedroom was to the right of the kitchen, on the complete opposite side of the house from his mom's. He managed to stay in there all afternoon before she called from the kitchen that he would be in charge of his own dinner tonight. He snuck out now and then to get more ice, and when it was dark enough, he joined his mom on the couch where she was watching TV with the lights off. Riley smiled when Charlie came and put his head on his lap.

They were halfway through an episode when Riley caught sight of someone in the dark kitchen doorway. He flinched so bad the couch springs squeaked and Charlie jerked awake.

"What is it?" his mom asked before the springs had even stopped bouncing.

She was so quick Riley hadn't gotten a good look himself. It turned out to be the familiar ghost of a little girl who sometimes passed through the house. She never spoke to Riley, just stopped to give a shy smile before running away again. He suspected she didn't speak English.

Riley let out a breath as he relaxed. "Just the little girl again."

His mother's face darkened as she settled back into the couch. Out of the corner of his eye, Riley saw her jaw clench. He looked down at his hands, feeling, as he had so often before, like he had let her down.

After his dad's death, Elisabeth had attached herself to Riley's side for two weeks, waiting for Liam to show up. Each time she caught Riley flinching, her whole body had tensed with desperate anticipation. A tiny piece of Riley's heart broke every time he had to tell her it wasn't Liam; it wasn't Dad. He hated to see the pain in her eyes before she hid her face from him.

Over time, the pair had slipped back into their usual routine and then into the opposite: they spent almost no time together. The constant jumping, the continual letdown—it was too much for either of them to bear.

In the light from the TV, Riley saw Elisabeth's hand tighten around the remote. She was grinding her teeth, and her breath was rapid, like she was winding up to say something. He chewed his lips, waiting.

At last, she paused the TV and twisted in her seat to look at him. Under the glare of her full attention, he froze in place, determined to keep his puffy eye out of sight.

"Has Dad visited you?" she demanded.

"No," he said in surprise. "I told you, it was the little girl."

"I meant ever," she snapped, waving the remote.

Riley shook his head, stroking Charlie's nose and avoiding her eyes.

"You're lying to me!" She sprang to her feet.

Charlie rose at the sudden movement and went to his bed in

the corner, where he could have more peace.

"I'm not," Riley said, wounded.

"Yes, you are!" she shouted, her voice rising dangerously. Riley knew she was winding up to say whatever it was she had been holding in for months. "He wouldn't leave us when he knows what you can do! You've been keeping him from me! How could you do that to me? Look at me! How could you be such a selfish—"

She had crouched down in front of him to force him to meet her eye, and now she gasped. She could see his black eye. She mouthed wordlessly for a moment.

"How?—"

"I got in a fight," he mumbled.

"You got in a fight?"

"I didn't start it."

She grabbed his chin and turned his head this way and that, inspecting him in the dark before flicking on the light and trying again.

"I can't believe you," she hissed. "What were you thinking? When was this? Why didn't you tell me earlier? Why didn't the school call me?"

Her grip pressed a bruise, and he pulled away. "It was at lunch," he lied. "I didn't tell anyone."

Her eyes flashed. "And no one noticed this giant shiner?"

His cheeks flushed.

"You skipped class again!" she accused.

"I was having a really bad day," he tried to explain, but she cut him off.

"I am so sick of your behaviour!" She was upright and yelling again. "First you lie about your dad, then—"

"I didn't lie about Dad!"

"Then explain why he hasn't come to us!" She paced the living room. When she turned back to Riley, her eyes sparkled with tears. "Your father would never do this to me!"

Riley leapt to his feet, done with getting yelled at. "He's doing it to me too! It's not my fault he turned out to be an asshole!"

Charlie barked once, like an admonition. The colour drained from Elisabeth's face. For a moment she looked like she'd like to hit Riley.

Her voice trembling with suppressed emotion, she repeated, "He wouldn't leave us like this."

Riley was shaking with rage at both his parents now. He couldn't believe she was still accusing him when he had done nothing wrong. He had held his breath as much as she had. His hopes had been dashed time and time again, just like hers.

Riley was getting so worked up, a muscle was twitching in his chin. He couldn't express how deep her betrayal cut him. He gave her the dirty look he had so recently used on Aaron and stormed out of the living room.

"We are not done!" she yelled.

Riley ignored her and flew across the kitchen to the backdoor. He jammed his feet into his yard work shoes and threw the door open. It slammed against the side of the house. Elisabeth grabbed the sleeve of his t-shirt, but Riley wrenched away and sped off across the yard. Elisabeth didn't follow him, and he didn't look back.

The corn flashed past on one side, the chicken coop on the other, and before long Riley reached the woods. He stumbled on the pitch-dark trail. Without slowing down, Riley pulled out his phone and turned on the flashlight. The light zigzagged over the rocky, pine-strewn earth.

He hadn't planned it, but within half an hour Riley stood where his neighbours had found Liam's body. He knew it by the short brick well in the middle of the clearing. The well was green with moss and weeds and only came up to his knees. It was a square hole just big enough for a bucket, of which there was none. The front bricks had collapsed into the well and disappeared into its dark interior. His light reflected off a metal sign in the dark. It stood to the side of the well and read, 'Caution, nonpotable water. Do not drink.'

When Riley was a kid, this place had fascinated him. His dad told him there used to be a tiny house nearby, just a cabin, but the woods had long since taken it back. Riley would come here to sit beside the well, waiting for ghosts and imagining how they must have gone about their lives. He had hoped to ask them questions about the old days.

The spirits were long gone; he never met a single one. Then, a week after Liam's death, Riley had come in search of a ghost again. Riley had thought, had hoped, that maybe his dad was stuck here. Now, as his flashlight roved over the clearing, the memory of disappointment bubbled like acid in Riley's chest.

Yet the next time he had visited here was worse. A month or so after their loss, Riley had watched Elisabeth disappear along the trail from where he was working in the yard. He had returned to raking. Sometime later her anguished scream reached him through the trees. His heart had stopped beating in his chest, and he felt like all the blood in his body had drained into the dirt below his feet. Feeling close to passing out, he had forced himself to run the trail with the rake gripped tight in his hands.

By the time he arrived, both palms sweating on the handle, Elisabeth was sitting in the dirt with her back to him, hunched in front of the well. His eyes swept the forest for signs of an attacker, but she was alone. She moaned and rocked, both hands in her hair, and Riley stood frozen. Moms weren't supposed to make sounds like that.

The moan rose and morphed into a scream of rage. She pounded the ground with her fists. In the next second she was on her feet, and faster than Riley could blink, had kicked in the front of the well. The bricks clattered and splashed on the way down. When she started throwing rocks in every direction, Riley had backed away.

Here he was again, and he could still hear the gong-like sound of one of her rocks pinging off the metal sign. The memory prickled; she was not the only one who had suffered. Riley wanted to rage like she had. He filled his lungs.

"daaad!"

If the woods had been quiet before, it was nothing to how they sounded after his echo faded away. Riley's heart ached as he flashed his light into the trees all around him, searching for his father. The light passed over the well. A dark face looked out at him.

Riley went cold. He refocused the light on the well, but the headlike shape was gone. He stared at the mossy bricks, his eyes making up faces in the surrounding leaves. Then, in the broken-toothed front of the well, long black fingers shifted. Riley's whole body tensed, the grip on his phone like a vice.

"R–Riley ...," a voice rasped.

Riley's lungs were frozen. He drew in minuscule snatches of air as he watched the fingers. This didn't make sense. No spirits were ever here, and Liam's body had not been found inside the well.

His voice came out low and weak. "Who's there?"

"Riley …," the rasping voice called again, a little stronger this time.

The well's echo distorted the sound. Riley couldn't tell if it was male. Yet there was something familiar in it.

"Dad?" he whispered.

Plaintive and pained, the voice spoke again, "Why … did you … leave me?"

Riley gasped. He choked out, "I didn't! I didn't leave you!"

"Come … back …"

Wracked with guilt, Riley threw himself down before the well, wondering what hell his dad had been trapped in all this time. He looked down into the narrow, dark pit.

The head made of shadows tipped slowly to leer up at Riley. Its abnormally long and skeletal limbs were folded in a spider-like pose as it clung to the ledges. Riley knew a second of sheer horror before the shadow launched from the well, wrapping its sickening limbs around him.

3

Hazel: The Mirror

They were eating at the same family-style restaurant as last night, but the energy had shifted. The table was heaped with scrambled eggs and coffees as the basketball team fought off their hangovers. The teams' eyes kept drifting towards Hazel. She kept her own gaze down. There was more skepticism in their looks today than there had been under yesterday's moonlight.

Hazel played with the crust of her toast. Her shoulders slumped with disappointment, but she was not altogether surprised.

Kate had seated herself opposite Hazel again. She set down her coffee with a satisfied sigh and asked, "Are we clear today? No ghosts?"

Hazel frowned at her toast and shook her head no.

"Does that mean the old lady moved on?"

"It's possible," Hazel mumbled.

"But you don't know?" Kate asked, oblivious to Hazel's short answers.

"Not unless she comes to see me."

"Hmm," Kate said. "That's a lot of uncertainty."

"Do you know where your acquaintances are at all times?" Hazel snapped, shooting a furtive glance at the eavesdroppers down the table. Riva and Jen had both gone to the washroom, leaving Hazel alone with the team. She gave the bathroom door a glowering look before fixing her eyes back on her plate.

Kate looked startled. "I'm sorry. I just thought it might bother you, not knowing."

There was a twist of guilt in Hazel's stomach. Kate sounded genuine.

"It does," she admitted.

Kate followed Hazel's quick gaze to the other girls and finally lowered her voice. "Don't worry about them. They're just worried they got carried away last night. I believe you, though."

Hazel raised her eyes and studied the sincere face under Kate's dark makeup. "You didn't see much proof," she pointed out.

Kate shrugged. "You don't seem like the attention-seeking type. And I know ghosts are real. I've seen things myself."

Hazel stilled. "You have?"

"Sure," Kate said with another shrug. "I mean, not as clear as what you see. But I've seen shadows move out of the corner of my eye."

A chill washed over Hazel.

"What?" Kate asked, pausing as she picked up her fork. "Shadows? Like people-shaped shadows?"

"Yeah. What's so weird about that?"

Hazel shook her head and said a little too quickly, "Nothing."

A smile crept up Kate's face. "Me seeing ghost-shadows is weirder than you seeing actual ghosts?"

Hazel struggled to return the smile. "I've had bad experiences with shadows." She straightened a napkin on the table, thinking. "Do you feel like the shadows were … good?"

"I don't know," Kate said. "I assumed they were … neutral. I sometimes wonder if one was my old friend who died when we were kids."

They both looked up as Riva returned from the bathroom and bounced into the empty seat beside Hazel. She plucked her mug from the messy table and asked, "What are we talking about?"

"That I can see shadows sometimes," Kate supplied.

Riva choked on her coffee. Heads turned towards them as she hacked into the crook of her elbow.

"I don't think it's that," Hazel whispered undercover of all the coughing.

Riva gave a thumbs-up to say she was alright but had to excuse herself from the table again. Kate's eyes were alight with interest and alarm. Before she could ask any more questions, Lor began rallying the team to pay their bills and head out.

Jen swooped in to give Hazel a swift surprise-kiss. "See you at the game," she said, squeezing Hazel's shoulders. "I'm so happy you came."

"Good luck," Hazel returned, warmth jumping to her cheeks.

The team trooped out, leaving Hazel alone at the table. She and Riva had some time to kill before they needed to join the spectators. She shredded the edges of the napkin she had just straightened and wished for more than stolen moments with Jen.

Riva plunked back down beside Hazel.

"What the hell was that about? Kate can see shadows?"

"Ghosts in the form of shadows," Hazel corrected.

"Is that possible?"

Hazel shrugged and said the very words she had always feared and hated, "Could be her imagination." She scrunched up her face like she tasted something bitter.

"But ...," Riva said, "what if it's not just ghosts? What if it's really shadows?"

"I'm sure it's not," Hazel lied, ripping the shredded napkin she was holding in two. She dropped the remnants onto her plate and pushed it away.

Riva looked uneasy. She leaned in and whispered, "If there was one, there could be more."

Hazel shivered and met Riva's eye. "I think about that all the time."

***

The team won their first two games. With still one more game to go after dinner, Jen decided that she needed a nap, so Hazel and Riva found themselves killing more time.

Bored of the motel, they took a walk through Main Street to stretch their legs. The tiny shops spoke of the old west with their flat facades and trusting sidewalk displays, but the two girls passed most of them by.

Outside a card-and-knickknack store, a little boy was opening and closing the door to set off the tinkling bells. Riva winked at him as they passed.

"Don't encourage him," Hazel teased when they were out of earshot. Living with Riva's kindergarten-aged siblings made Hazel retreat to the quiet of her bedroom most evenings. She had watched Riva's patience with the twins and Derrick with growing admiration all year.

"He's not hurting anyone," Riva answered with a smile.

Hazel bumped Riva with her shoulder. "You're going to make

a great teacher."

It wasn't until they spotted a thrift store that they left the hot sidewalk. They emerged carrying dining chair cushions in the hopes of making the bleachers more comfortable at the next game. For the rest of the hot, uphill walk to the motel, they beat each other with the seats.

By the time they arrived, sweaty and flushed, the team had already left to begin their warmups. Riva flopped onto her bed to catch her breath and began scrolling through her phone. Hazel picked up a brochure she found on the nightstand. It boasted of the town's amazing seafood restaurants thanks to the high Portuguese population. Hazel looked up to tell Riva about a restaurant they should try but shrieked instead.

"What?" Riva screamed, fumbling her phone onto her face. She swore as it hit her teeth. "Is it a visitor?"

Then she spotted it too, and within seconds she was standing on her bed. A spider the size of Hazel's entire palm had darted out of the bathroom. It skittered towards them before Riva's sudden movement sent it veering under the closet door.

"Ew, ew, ew, ew, ew!" Riva squealed, her elbows tucked in just like when the ghost had appeared yesterday.

Hazel had a full-body shiver. She jumped onto Riva's bed and the girls clutched at each other.

"What do we do? That thing was massive!" Hazel cried.

"My shoes are in there!" Riva moaned.

"Should we kill it?"

"How? That thing was as tall as I am!"

Hazel grabbed Riva's new seat cushion.

"Oh yeah, that'll work!" Riva yelled, smacking Hazel's arm and wresting her pillow away.

"Well, what? Do we call someone?"

"We can't call someone to come kill a spider!"

"Do you want to kill it?" Hazel countered.

"How did the maid service not kill it?" Riva asked. "How clean is this place if something that enormous can run free?"

"Do they have poisonous spiders here?" Hazel worried.

Riva shrugged helplessly, eyes still on the crack under the closet door. Hazel moved to the corner of Riva's bed and tried to reach for the closet handle. The bed sagged and she almost fell, her heart thudding in her chest as Riva caught her arms.

"Nope, I can't do this!" Hazel cried with another full-body shiver. "It's freaking me out too much, and I can't get freaked out!"

Riva sobered up. "Right. You're right. Let's just ... breathe for a second."

They sank down onto the bed. After a minute, Riva gave a rueful smile and said, "You know, that Shadow's a great excuse."

Hazel cringed an apology. Riva steeled herself. In one move, she lunged across the bed, wrenched the door open, and tore back to the bed again. Hazel's eyes darted around the closet floor.

"I don't see it."

"Oh god, it's in my shoes, isn't it?" Riva moaned again.

Feeling guilty, Hazel insisted she and Riva check the shoes together this time. They grabbed hangers from the closet and began flicking over Riva's sneakers. Their shrieks and hysterical giggles echoed off the walls.

"Nope, not in there," Hazel finally concluded.

They rattled the doors and double-checked the dress and jacket Riva had hung up, but still there was nothing.

"I don't see where it could have gone," Riva said. "It

definitely went in here, right?"

Riva climbed onto the mattress and dipped her head over the edge to check under the bed. She came back up shaking her head. Their eyes swept the floor.

"Can we switch rooms?" Riva asked at last. "I will never be able to sleep knowing that thing's on the loose."

Hazel was glad Riva said it first. They packed in a hurry. Although switching rooms brought them some peace of mind, they wound up close to the noisy stairs and late for the game.

"So," Riva said when they settled onto their new cushions at the top of the bleachers, "do you think the Shadow cared about the spider?"

Hazel gave her a one-shouldered shrug. "I thought it would, but it didn't feel like it."

Riva kept her voice low. "Do you think it's dead?"

Hazel watched Jen finish off her water bottle at the edge of the court before shrugging again. "I think I would feel it if it died. Relief, or something."

"Hmmm," Riva said, staring at the players with glazed eyes.

For the rest of the game, they stared at their phones, laughing and shuddering as they tried to identify the spider from photos. It turned out poisonous spiders did live in the area, namely the dreaded Black Widow. Luckily, the motel spider had long, brown limbs that looked more like those of a brown recluse or a giant house spider.

The girls were horrified to learn that the giant house spider species once held the record for fastest spider in the world. A few heads turned their way as they clutched each other, crying with laughter and disgust.

The buzzer blared at game's end, and they rose to applaud another win. The bleachers emptied around them, and Hazel and Riva slumped down the steps at the back of the crowd. They waited near the exit as the team retreated to the locker rooms. The downside to winning meant they had to sit through more games tomorrow.

It was after 9:00pm and the light was fading outside, but the dry heat remained. In a few minutes, Jen strode across the gym to join them. She was still wearing her sleeveless jersey. She had tucked the front into her matching shorts.

"Good game!" Riva called, grinning.

Jen nodded her thanks. "Can I talk to you privately for a minute, Hazel?"

Hazel raised her eyebrows in surprise. "Yeah, sure."

"Good idea," Riva said.

Hazel turned her surprise to Riva, but Riva didn't meet her eye. Hazel followed Jen into the shadow of the bleachers.

"Congrats!" she said when Jen turned to face her.

Jen folded her arms across her chest. "Did you even watch?"

"Of course I watched," Hazel said, taken aback. "You won!"

Jen pressed her lips together for a moment. "Every time I looked over at you, you and Riva were looking at your phones and laughing."

"Oh, yeah," Hazel giggled. "Wait 'til you hear this. We had to switch rooms because this huge spider—and I mean huge—"

"That's why you were late?"

"Yeah," Hazel said again. "I was hoping you wouldn't notice. We had to—"

"Because of a spider?" Jen persisted.

Hazel paused, realizing how bad it sounded. A sinking sensation started in her stomach. "You don't understand, this spider was—"

Jen waved her hand to stop Hazel, her voice rising in anger.

"I played really well, you know. And you didn't see any of it!"

"Of course I did—"

"And what did Riva mean by, 'Good idea,' when I said I wanted to talk to you?"

Hazel raised both palms, "Nothing! I don't think she meant anything."

The hint of tears was starting in Jen's eyes. Concern swelled in Hazel's heart. She reached out for Jen's arm, but before she could speak, the rest of the team swarmed around them.

"Make way for the MVP!" Lor called, grabbing Jen's arm and raising it into the air. She led Jen outside, leaving Hazel to follow in the team's wake.

A tight sensation of guilt compressed Hazel's throat as she stepped out into the dry heat. She couldn't swallow it away. Jen was so rarely fazed by anything.

***

Some of the girls were planning to use the hot tub before bed to ease their muscles. Since Jen was among them, Hazel struggled to catch her alone. She tried to show her the new room, but Lor followed.

"You're so far away from us now!" Lor pouted.

Hazel stole a glance at Jen's face, which was stony. When Hazel excused herself to change into her bathing suit in the bathroom, the other three went on ahead. That heavy sensation tugged at Hazel's stomach again. She hated fighting with Jen.

As she began pulling her arm through her sleeve, the mirror drew her eye. Her face was rounder; she had put on more weight since starting university. It was no surprise. Hazel couldn't find time for her runs and hadn't bothered to join a wrestling team. She sighed. If she had joined a team and made it to finals, she knew she would have expected Jen to be there cheering her on.

Knowing she was in the wrong did nothing to cheer Hazel up. She splashed cold water on her face too aggressively, and droplets splattered the counter.

"Jen hasn't been perfect either," she consoled herself out loud, thinking about Jen sharing her secret without asking.

Hazel leaned on her arms, droplets of water rolling down her neck. It was the stupid spider's fault, really. She would have been watching the game as usual if it hadn't come prancing into her room in all its disgusting glory. She wished she was afraid of snakes instead, or something uncommon at least.

"Are you even there?" she snapped at the Shadow.

Goosebumps ran up and down her arms. It was a bad idea to tempt the Shadow forward. Hazel dried her face on a towel and tossed it to the floor. She was so exhausted from constantly wondering. Was it there, or was she safe to feel fear like a normal human? If she just knew, one way or the other, she could relax.

Seized once again by recklessness and desperation, she turned the lights off and crossed back to the mirror. She leaned across the countertop until she was nose-to-nose with her dark reflection. Then she held her breath until she felt dizzy.

When still nothing happened, Hazel let it out in a disappointed gust. She threw the elusive Shadow a dirty look, but the flare of anger quickly burnt out. In its place was a pit of aching loneliness. Unable to watch her eyes fill with tears, Hazel bowed her head, and her forehead touched the glass. Or it should have.

A cold sensation cupped her brow, like the mirror had molded to its shape. She jerked her head up to look. The mirror was flat and placid. Yet her heart pounded. Hazel tipped forward again, testing the surface, and the sensation came again. She pushed her face forward, eyes fixed on the glass as her blue irises came closer and her nose disappeared into the surface. She gasped and froze, her nose in some other world.

She stayed like that until her arms began to shake from holding herself up, and the liquid silver mirror began to freeze the tip of her nose. She was equally terrified of what might happen if she carried on and of never knowing if she backed away. She might never get another chance to find out. Hazel set her jaw, sick of not having answers. Breathing hard, she thrust up onto her toes. Her eyes hurtled towards the pupils of her reflection. They closed for a split second as if submerging in water, then she forced them open.

The chill soaked into the orbs of her eyes like ice cubes pressed against the delicate layer of skin. She fought to keep them open. She was in a dark bedroom, but not a bedroom in the motel. The twin bed was unmade with dark blue blankets lumped at the foot. Clothes sat in piles around the floor, and bowls of unfinished cereal covered the nightstand. A poster on the wall showed a screaming male guitarist. Black makeup deepened his eye sockets.

Movement to the right made Hazel start. A boy of about sixteen was shuffling through the clothes on the floor of the closet.

She almost drew back then, but paused at the sight of a white frame before her hands. She was looking at him from inside his mirror. She raised her hand to touch the surface, but then snatched it back, afraid she would enter his room and not be able to return to hers. She studied the back of his head. The hair at his neck was short and bristly, but it grew long and wavy on top. In the dark, she thought it might be a sandy blonde. He froze with an ear tipped towards the door, and Hazel realized he was packing a bag.

Whatever he heard made him speed up. He stuffed a few more items into the bag and slung it over his shoulder. Hazel couldn't hear anything at all, apart from her own blood rushing in her ears. It was like watching a silent movie. Ice crystals crept across her eyes, clouding her vision. Just when Hazel couldn't bear it anymore, the boy turned and saw her. Hazel flinched as the blood drained from his cheeks. The look of sheer terror on his bruised face made her apologize aloud.

"Sorry!" she gasped and pulled herself backwards out of the mirror.

It was like fighting against the strong suction of an ocean undertow. Her palms found the bathroom counter and pressed against it until her head pulled free. She stumbled back until she hit the door and sank to the ground. The room felt off-kilter as the shadows in the bathroom darted and ducked around her. Hazel fumbled the door open and retreated in a frantic crawl, slamming it behind her.

4

Riley: The Woods

Riley woke up shivering on the forest floor. His body ached all over from the fight with Aaron and Mason. Stars sprinkled the black sky between the silhouetted treetops, which swayed in a hypnotizing rhythm. Then Riley remembered why he was in the forest, and he jerked upright, twisting around to check the well.

He had been lying right beside it. He scrambled backwards, leaves and rocks whispering beneath him. His eyes roved the broken bricks, searching for the black fingers at the well's base. All he could see were shadows.

Riley's fingers danced over the rocks and soil in search of his phone, his eyes never leaving the well. His pulse beat loud in his ears as he searched in vain. When he could stand to stare into the depths no longer, Riley pushed himself, trembling, to his feet. He ran and didn't dare look back.

When he arrived home, it was with more bruises than he had started with. Lungs burning, he tucked himself behind the screen door and finally looked back. The rows of corn shifted in the wind, but nothing pursued him between the stocks. Riley entered the silent kitchen and shut the night out, turning the lock for good measure. The sensation of being watched did not leave him.

There was a low growl. Riley jumped and spun towards the hallway on weak legs. Charlie was glaring at him from the darkness.

"It's okay, Charlie," he whispered, sagging against the counter. "It's me."

The clock on the stove said 2:07am, but a blue light was still coming from the living room. He slipped off his shoes and tiptoed to peek inside. Charlie backed away, his hackles up. The TV was still paused where they had left it. His mom had fallen asleep waiting for him, her phone in her hand. Riley reached for a blanket, but hesitated. He didn't want to wake her and risk another fight. He crossed the hall to his room instead, Charlie backing farther away with each step.

Wet with sweat and covered in dirt, Riley collapsed on his bed. His heart was still pounding. He didn't understand what had happened to him. In his mind's eye he saw the creature in the well grinning up at him and lunging faster than he could react. His fists clenched the bedsheets. Today was near second place for the worst day of his life. Maybe he had blacked out from the weight of everything and there had never been a creature in the well at all.

As his heart finally slowed, Riley began shivering with the cold. He climbed under the blankets, dirt and all, and slept with the light on. Charlie never left the doorway.

***

The sun streaked through his curtains with the power to blind. It was already noon. Groaning with pain, Riley limped to the mirror over his dresser and inspected his eye. The swelling had barely retreated, and the skin under his eye was turning purple. He sniffed his armpit. He smelled worse than his eye looked, so he opted to shower over icing it.

Peering out the bathroom window, Riley searched for his mom in the yard. She was pulling weeds in the shade of the chicken coop while Charlie dozed beside her. It occurred to him that maybe she was so angry she had let him sleep just to avoid him. He felt a stab of annoyance when he realized he would have to pass her later to go find his phone.

Kill her.

It was a whisper in the back of his mind, but the intensity drained the blood from Riley's face. Where had that come from? It was disproportionate to the anger he felt towards his mother. He shook himself mentally. He needed breakfast, and he needed it bad.

In the interest of easing his guilt, Riley remembered to wash the pan after cooking his scrambled eggs. His mom hated when he left it in the sink. Then he put on his shoes, which she had returned to their proper place beside the door, and stepped out into the hot sun.

He almost chickened out and went through the corn just to avoid Elisabeth, but at the last second he took the main path. He stopped behind her, watching the chickens waddle around in the shade. Charlie's hackles rose at the sight of him. Riley frowned, offended by the unusually cold welcome.

"Do you need me to do anything today?" he asked, hoping that offering an olive branch would smooth things over.

Elisabeth paused with a handful of weeds. She didn't turn around for a long moment, and he feared she was going to give him the cold shoulder. Then she said, "The carrot patch needs weeding."

Weeding was best done in the morning, when it wasn't so hot, but Riley supposed he deserved the heat for sleeping in.

"Okay," he said. He waited.

Elisabeth looked round at Riley, and the sadness in her eyes chilled him. She simply looked and looked.

Riley bit the inside of his cheek. Little as he wanted to bring up last night or stoke her anger, he admitted, "I have to get my phone first. I lost it in the hills."

Her gaze finally dropped. She spotted a weed at his feet, plucked it, and added it to the growing pile beside her.

"Okay," she said at last and carried on with her work.

Riley moved on too, his stomach contracting with guilt. Up at the well, birds chirped from the safety of the surrounding trees, unaware that anything strange had happened. He returned home half an hour later with a dead phone. Riley never wanted to see the well again.

When the vegetable patch was clear of weeds, Riley had a long drink of water and decided to get away from the house for a while. Elisabeth had left to run some errands, so he was free to wander. He thought he might visit Sophie's neighbourhood to see if she wanted to get an iced drink with him. He pulled a ball cap low over his forehead to hide his eye. He would decide what to tell Sophie about the bruise along the way. If he was feeling brave enough, he thought he might tell her his feelings. Before Aaron got the chance.

Charlie refused to come inside when Riley called, but he was a good dog, and Riley wasn't worried about him running off. He locked up the house and headed in the direction of the school. Sophie lived behind the school, but he didn't have to go that far to find her. As he cut across the soccer field, he spotted a lone figure reading in the dappled light under a young maple tree.

She looked up as he approached, and he saw her expression grow wary.

He lifted his hat so she could see who he was and purposely messed up his hair in the same move. "Hey, Sophie."

"Oh. Hi, Riley." She frowned, bookmarked her page, and set the book down on her lap. "What happened to your eye?"

"Aaron Pierson," he admitted, shrugging like it was no big deal. "What are you reading?"

"*Endless Mountain*," she said. "It's a survival story about a couple of teens who got lost while hiking." Riley's stomach squirmed as an enthusiastic smile spread across Sophie's face. The smile faded too fast as she circled back to him. "But why did Aaron ...?"

Riley squinted up at the maple tree. Her gaze was like a spotlight he couldn't look at for too long.

"Actually—" This time his stomach wriggled with nerves. "—I was wondering if I could talk to you about that. But I was thinking maybe we could get a drink? It was a long walk from my place and I'm dying. I'll pay."

He chanced a glance at her face, hoping he hadn't overexplained. Sophie looked down at her book, and Riley didn't miss the regretful purse of her lips. He had never felt more jealous of an inanimate object. He wanted to blurt more reasons she should come with him, but she spared him the embarrassment by stowing the book in a tote bag.

"Sure," she said, rocking to her feet.

They crossed to the front of the school and tread the usual path to the corner store. Riley latched onto Sophie's book for conversation but found he couldn't take in much of what she was saying. He had stuffed his hands into his pockets but then realized he could communicate his feelings without talking if he just reached for her hand. He took his hands out, but his heart raced so fast he stuffed them back in again.

When they reached the store, Sophie said, "Isn't that Aaron right there?"

Riley's steps faltered. Aaron and a group of his friends were heading to the corner store from the opposite direction. Sophie took one look at Riley's face, grabbed his elbow, and steered him through the side parking lot and behind the store.

"Thanks," Riley said, relieved.

"What happened between you two?" Sophie asked as she stepped into the shade of the white concrete wall.

Heart still racing, Riley eyed up the green dumpster next to them. He didn't want to tell Sophie under these conditions, but he supposed he had no choice. It was better that it came from him.

"To tell you the truth ...," he started, "I think Aaron likes you. He and Mason attacked me in the hills yesterday. ..."

He paused as two conflicting emotions crossed her face. Riley thought he knew what the first one was.

"They didn't ...," Sophie whispered. She knew about his dad. It had shaken everyone in their small town.

Riley shrugged, folded his arms, and stared at the ground. "Well, they're assholes. ... I mean, if you like him back," Riley floundered, "that's fine, I'm sure he's—"

Sophie shook her head. "How could I possibly like someone who'd do that?"

Riley had to fight down the relieved smile creeping up his face.

"But ..." Sophie hesitated. "Why did they attack you?"

Riley's breath caught in his throat. Again, he found he couldn't look at her. "I think because ... I like you."

"Oh," she said.

Now Riley's eyes darted to her face and away again, like he would get burned if he looked for too long, but he had to know.

"I don't really know you," she said, blushing.

"I know," Riley said. He continued all in one breath, "I mean, I don't expect you to like me, I just thought maybe you might want to hang out together and see if, later on, maybe you might want ..."

Before Sophie could answer, Aaron and his friends came around the corner clutching slushies and chip bags. Riley broke off and turned his back so they wouldn't see his eye, but it was too late.

"Is that Banana Face?" Aaron called, delighted.

It was like he had turned on the stove and Riley's stomach was a bubbling pot of water. He threw Aaron a venomous look over his shoulder, keeping the bruise on the other side hidden.

"Is he confessing his love to you, Sophie?" Aaron asked.

"No," Sophie shot back, and the defensive note in her voice pleased Riley even as his face burned.

Aaron didn't seem to hear her. "This is a really romantic spot you picked. Love that dumpster. Great smell."

Riley scowled as Aaron's friends chuckled.

"Let's go," Sophie said, leading the way around the store.

"I'm only joking, Sophie," Aaron called after her. He clamped a hand on Riley's shoulder as Riley made to follow. "We're friends, right Riley?"

He twisted Riley around so his friends could see his face. They gasped and jeered at the sight of his black eye. The pot of water boiled over. Riley threw off Aaron's hand and punched him in the face. Aaron went down backwards.

In a split second three guys descended on him, but Riley

dove under their arms and managed to wrap his hands around Aaron's neck. He squeezed so hard Aaron choked, but the next second they had wrenched Riley back and pinned him to the ground. He could hear Aaron wheezing before his friends' sunk their fists into Riley's stomach. He writhed against their grip, trying to get back to Aaron.

Then Sophie was there, shoving them back by the shoulders and screaming at them to stop. She was making ground, but then a stray elbow knocked her in the mouth, and she tripped backwards, landing next to Riley.

"Sophie!" Riley gasped.

His sudden, searing rage vanished in concern. One arm protecting his stomach, he inched himself closer to her with the other. Pained tears sprang to Sophie's eyes. Her teeth were bloody. Whoever had hit her was apologizing, and it seemed to take the steam out of the others. They backed off. Sophie slapped a proffered hand away and stumbled to her feet, clutching her mouth. Riley scrambled up after her.

"Grow up, all of you!" she yelled. "Riley, let's go!"

She snatched up her tote bag and stomped away. Riley limped after her, struggling to keep up. When they had taken the corner and traveled a ways up the street, she rounded on him.

"I'm not interested in stupid stuff like that," she said. "I'm going home."

"But—"

"Do you know how many fights I've been in, in my entire life?" she interrupted. "Do you know how many times I've wanted to hit someone, and didn't?"

"I didn't want a fight—"

"You hit him first!" Sophie said, throwing up her hands in exasperation. "I saw it!"

"He hit me first yesterday!"

Even as he said it, Riley realized it wasn't true. Yesterday he had acted first, but in self-defense. Today he had lost control.

Sophie took a breath. "I hope you figure it out. I do. But I'm not part of it."

She walked away. Disappointment splashed over Riley like a bucket of water. Then the injustice of it all set the pot in his stomach to bubbling again. Without planning it, he turned back, fists clenched and ready to tear Aaron a new one, when the voice spoke again.

Kill him.

Riley slowed to a stop. Panic coursed through him. He had definitely heard a voice. He waited, nerves jangling, for the voice to speak again. His eyes roved the street. Apart from a plastic bag rolling along the curb, there was no other noise. The voice could only have come from one source.

As he stood there waiting, Riley realized Sophie had been right about one thing: his anger had been different today. He felt as if someone had egged him on, stoked the flames. He hadn't just punched Aaron and left him on the ground, he had tried to strangle him. He had wanted him dead.

Not trusting himself to walk past the corner store, Riley sped the long way around the block, fighting to stay calm. He had never gone to see the school psychologist after his dad's death. He could see now he should have. He darted across the main road and made his way through the hills, constantly looking over his shoulder. He was no longer afraid of attack, but of doing the attacking, and of what might happen then.

He jogged through the trees on the hill, their branches waving in a warm wind. Riley's throat was parched, but he didn't stop until he saw the crushed brambles he had destroyed just yesterday. He suddenly wished George was around to talk to. He stopped to catch his breath, wondering. He called George's name into the forest.

"Help me!" came an echo in response. It was a glitching sound, like a radio station that wasn't quite in range.

Riley frowned, unnerved. "George?"

There was silence across the sloping forest. Then George's figure flashed right in front of him. Riley yelped in alarm. Terror twisted the calm old man's face. He strained against a slimy green rope that protruded from his chest, dragging him towards Riley. To Riley's horror, the other end extended from his own chest. Before Riley could tear at the end of the rope that plunged into him, George flickered away with a lingering scream.

Riley stood petrified in the empty forest, both hands still groping at his sternum, trying to find a rope that didn't exist. He stood there, breathing heavily, for several helpless minutes, hoping he was going crazy. The alternative, the existence of that horrifying creature from the well and what he had just seen it do, was so much worse.

"George?" he managed to whisper.

Only the warm breeze rustling through the branches answered.

***

By the time Riley got home, he was hungry, thirsty, and miserable. He guessed his mom had come and gone again, because she had locked Charlie inside, which was making life difficult. The second Riley opened the door, Charlie's hackles went up and he charged with the vicious growl of a guard dog. It was the first time in his life that he did not greet Riley at the front door with a series of happy barks.

"It's me, Charlie!" Riley cried, even as he backed out of the house.

Charlie barked. Fearing those sharp teeth, Riley slammed the door just as Charlie lunged. He felt a stab of deep hurt, followed by anger. All he wanted was a drink of water in the cool interior of his own home. He stomped around back to the shed, then approached the kitchen door with a shovel in his hands. As soon as the screen door opened, Riley heard Charlie's nails tearing along the hallway floor. His bark echoed through the empty house.

"Shut up, Charlie!" he roared. "Leave me alone!"

He unlocked the main door, set his feet, and raised the shovel. Just before he turned the handle, Riley realized what he was doing. With a gasp, he let the shovel clang to the concrete step. Charlie went berserk at the sound. Riley stumbled backwards down the stairs. He collapsed onto the grass, staring, appalled, at the shovel.

That settled it. Riley loved his big, goofy Charlie so much it pained him sometimes. Never had he ever dreamed he might hurt him. He was not going insane; a creature had possessed him at the well, and it was manipulating him now. It had even done something to George, something he couldn't understand. It might be able to hear his thoughts even now.

Feeling light-headed, Riley crawled to the garden hose and drank straight from the pipe. Then he sat with his back against the house, hidden by a rhododendron bush, and looked out at the crops. He had to get rid of the creature. He had a sudden vision of himself walking into a church and demanding an exorcism. They'd send him to a psychologist, he knew. He wondered what a priest in a movie would do.

In his firmest voice, Riley shouted, "Get out!"

Charlie started barking like mad again. The creature didn't respond. Riley recited a Hail Mary prayer for the first time in a long time. Then he tried three more times. He didn't feel any different.

He tried shouting again. "Get out! Leave me alone! now!"

No.

Just like up at the well, the voice was so much like his dad's, but deeper, and twisted up with another, higher voice. Riley's skin prickled. He wanted to tear at himself to get at it, this evil sliver under his fingernails, this creature hiding behind his eyes, just out of reach.

"What do you want?" Riley half-sobbed.

More ... came the answer. There was a hesitant pause, as if the creature was thinking hard. Then, *More George.*

Riley's mouth fell open in shock.

"What did you do to him?" he whispered.

The voice didn't answer this time. Riley put a hand to his chest again, where that rotting rope had come from, reeling George in. If he hadn't called for George in the forest, maybe this wouldn't have happened to him. Riley pressed his face into his knees, clutching his hair in anguish.

After a few minutes, Riley jumped to his feet. He couldn't stay here. The little girl's ghost could come running through the house at any minute, and he couldn't let the creature reel her in like George. He would have to stay away until he was rid of it. That would keep Charlie and Elisabeth safe from his fits of rage as well.

His phone was still locked in the house, charging, so he would have to find some other way to convince his mom he was safe. He hurried to the shed, where he found a short pencil his mom used for marking length on wood she needed to cut. Then he went round to the mailbox and jotted her a note on a piece of junk mail.

"Staying overnight at Wyatt's. No phone. Still charging."

He tucked the envelope under the door so it was still visible and hoped she wouldn't question it. He hadn't spent much time with Wyatt since his dad died.

It wasn't Wyatt's fault. People without tragedy hanging over their heads always acted in the same three ways when faced with someone else's. There was either pity, awkwardness, or pretending nothing had happened. Riley's own mood about it changed so frequently, he couldn't tell which option he preferred. So he just avoided Wyatt altogether.

Note complete, Riley stood on the step with Charlie barking away and wondered what to do next. He knew he would need clothes and food. He had his wallet, a little cash, and some savings in his bank account. If only Charlie would let him in long enough to pack a bag. He snuck over to his bedroom window. It was open a crack, but the screen was behind it. Then he heard a car coming and ducked beside the hydrangea.

It was Elisabeth. She pulled into the driveway, and he watched her unload and carry groceries to the door. She stooped for a moment and stood up with the note in her hand, reading it for longer than necessary. Her lips made a grim line at first, then her shoulders relaxed. She went inside. Charlie didn't throw a fit over her.

***

Riley whiled away the evening as far from his family, people, and animals, as he could. He got food in town, mindful that his savings weren't going to get him far, and ate it alone in the hills. He planned to go home in the evening to sneak in and pack a bag. In the meantime, he replayed either the mistakes he made with Sophie or the disturbing appearances of the creature. Neither train of thought gave him any comfort.

It took forever for the sun to fade from the sky. It was well after 9:00pm by the time it got dark. From the road, he watched a flicker of light appear between the living room curtains and knew his mom had turned on the TV. He took that as his cue.

He snuck to his window, which was already open a third of the way out. He tugged on it, seeing if he could get the casement to budge, but it barely moved. It would be harder to squeeze through than he thought. He pushed one edge of the screen until the whole thing popped out of the frame. Catching it in a tenuous grip at the last second, he guided it to land on a pile of clothes, then waited, listening.

He couldn't hear the sound of Charlie's nails ticking down the hallway, so he heaved himself through the crack. His stomach ached as it took his weight on the ledge after getting punched so many times today. He wriggled his way inside, scraping his shins on the way.

The first thing Riley checked was his phone. Its battery was weak. He decided to take it and the cord anyway. He dumped out his backpack, stuffed in some fresh clothes, then knelt in the closet to fish through piles of worn jeans and shorts.

He heard his mom get up and enter the kitchen. He kept as still as possible, listening as Charlie ticked along behind her. It was time to go. He threw the bag over his shoulder and turned to leave.

That's when he saw someone in his mirror. All the muscles in his body seized up like he was turning to stone. The girl's skin had a jaundice-green tinge and under her staring eyes were dark circles that spoke of impending death. She looked about Riley's age but heavier than him by a fair deal. With a lurch of his stomach, Riley knew that if he looked behind him, no one would be there. More terrible still was her hand. It was raised like she was about to beckon him forward, but it was the dark aura around it that chilled him. Her hand was swathed in the long, dark fingers of the creature from the well.

In mere seconds he had taken this all in, then she let out a gasp that sent a jolt of fear through Riley.

"Sorry!" she mouthed, and her hair suddenly sprang around her face like she was falling backwards. She was gone.

5

Hazel: Cords

When the Shadow was free last year, it had appeared in mirrors to terrorize Hazel when she least expected it. Now, as she paced the narrow motel room, Hazel half expected the bathroom door handle to turn and the boy, or worse, the Shadow, to follow her out. She strained her ears for sounds of movement inside. Her limbs felt weak and jittery as she debated running out of the motel room and never coming back. The air conditioner in the window hummed to life, and she jumped clear off the ground. All the paranoia she had endured last year during the Shadow's attack had come roaring back, crashing down on her like a tidal wave.

Tears sprang to her eyes as she suffocated in the tiny room. When she couldn't endure the silence any longer, Hazel seized the handle and flung the door open with a little scream.

It banged off the wall and shut in her face, but not before she caught a glimpse of herself in the mirror. There was no boy looking out at her. No Shadow. Just Hazel, looking like a frightened fool. Light-headed with relief, Hazel reopened the door with a trembling hand and flicked on the bathroom light.

"It's just you," she whispered to herself, feeling ill. "You're safe."

She had tried to block out the memories of last June, hoping they would fade. Now, in an instant, they were fresh, and sharp, and physical. It was too easy to imagine the leering face staring out at her, the dual voice that was both witch and demon.

As she took a tentative step onto the linoleum floor, another memory came back. She was in Jen's house, at the barricaded window. She was listening for the sounds of the corrupt outside, the quiet minutes dragging on. It took her days to learn the waiting was more frightening than the seconds it took to actually peer out and check.

With that in mind, Hazel blew out a shaking breath and summoned her courage. She strode across the bathroom and smacked her hand against the glass. It was solid. Next second, she was throwing up into the sink. She sunk to her knees, wondering what was wrong with her and barely mustering the strength to reach for the tap and wash away the vomit.

Her sister, Kelly, had always said Hazel was brave. She had endured the hell that was last year, and this year, Hazel had learned to stay calm in the face of both fear and anxiety. She thought she had mastered the skill, but here she was crumbling, her body reacting outside of her control.

Hazel crawled to bed and drew the blankets up to her chin. Her eyes found the reflective TV on the opposite wall, and she wished she had covered it. She shivered with fever as she stared into its depths and lost track of time.

It was the sound of the keycard sliding into its slot that jolted Hazel out of her trance. Riva emerged from the dark hallway wearing her bathing suit and towel.

"Hey," she said, her voice low. "You okay?"

Hazel didn't know how to respond. The air conditioner filled the silence.

"Jen seemed off this evening too," Riva said as she turned the knob on the bedside lamp and sat down on the bed across from Hazel. Her tone of voice changed with the light. "Seriously, are you okay? You look sick."

Hazel found her voice and croaked, "I threw up in the sink."

"Oh no," Riva groaned. "Was it something you ate?"

Hazel shook her head. A lump climbed her throat. She dreaded breaking it to Riva that life was not back to normal after all.

"Is it the flu?"

"I went into the mirror," Hazel whispered.

Riva leaned closer to hear her. "You what?"

A tear slid down Hazel's cheek. "I traveled through the mirror, Riva. Like the Shadow used to do."

Riva stared at Hazel for a long time. When she finally spoke, it was with a reserved, "Tell me more."

Hazel explained how she had touched her forehead to the glass, and about the boy, and how he had seen her through the mirror.

"I don't like that at all, Hazel," Riva said.

Hazel worried the blanket between her fingers.

Riva stood up, sat back down, then stood again. "I was planning to shower, but ..." She trailed off with a shudder.

"Oh!" Hazel cried, making Riva flinch. "Sorry. I just remembered there's a lavender braid in my backpack."

Hazel usually burned the little bundle to keep ghosts out of her room and secure herself some much-needed privacy. Riva's family now used it regularly throughout their house to give Hazel some peace. It was even on the chore list.

Riva fished the lavender and a lighter out of Hazel's bag, lit the end, and disappeared into the bathroom. She returned in her pajama shorts and t-shirt, smelling of clean smoke. Hazel breathed easier. Still shivery, she watched Riva throw her towel over the TV, then pull a bottle of oil from her travel bag. She sat on her bed and began massaging the oil into the ends of her many braids.

At last, Riva said, "So the Shadow must still be alive then. If you can use its ... ability."

"I guess so," Hazel agreed, rolling onto her side to face Riva.

"You're going to have to be so careful about fear."

Hazel nodded and sighed. "Same as ever."

"No," Riva said, and the sharpness of her voice surprised Hazel. "Not the same as ever. What if traveling through mirrors feeds it? And don't pretend it didn't just scare the shit out of you! You just gave the Shadow a feast! You'll have to be really careful for a while. You can't give it a drop more."

Hazel gave the cream-coloured pillowcase a mutinous glare. It wasn't like she had fed the Shadow on purpose.

"What are you thinking?" Riva asked point-blank. "You're not going to mess with this again, right?"

Hazel closed her eyes for a moment. She hadn't even thought of that yet. She shook her head. "I'm so tired of it all." She looked over at Riva, whose expression was serious. "It's like a weight, you know? I wish it would just die already. But Riva, what if it never dies? What if I die—of old age, say—and the Shadow just goes free again?"

"Can't say I like the sound of that," Riva admitted, continuing to work the oil into her hair.

"But then again ...," Hazel mused, "what if the mirror is part of the deal? I mean, the Shadow wanted to possess me so it could use my abilities. But I possessed it instead. So don't I get to use its abilities?"

"But you're not a Shadow. What if this mirror stuff can kill you?" Riva asked, looking alarmed. "And then the Shadow would be free to start again and kill all the rest of us!"

Hazel pressed her lips together. She knew Riva had a point, but, as usual, Hazel had more questions than answers.

"Who was that boy?" she asked.

Riva twisted the cap back onto her oil. "Someone near a mirror at the same time as you?"

The conversation lulled as they each became lost in their own thoughts. Hazel's eyelids grew heavy. Riva finished getting ready for bed and climbed in, but still neither of them spoke. They fell asleep with the light on.

***

Hazel opened her eyes again at noon. The air conditioner was still humming away, but the light and heat managed to blast through the crack between the curtains. Hazel grabbed her phone to check the time and swore. She had a message from Riva, which said, "I told everyone you got sun stroke yesterday. Call me when you wake up." She had also missed a message from Jen last night and another from this morning that could be either innocent or ominous. It said, "Let's talk soon."

Hazel threw some clothes on and put Riva on speaker as she brushed her hair into a ponytail, all in the main room. She was back to not looking in mirrors.

"I can't believe you let me sleep this long," Hazel said as soon as Riva answered. "Jen's already mad at me for not paying attention to the game yesterday, and now I've completely missed one!"

"I tried to wake you, actually," Riva returned. "You were

out."

Hazel groaned. "How did Jen take it?"

"I told her you threw up last night, which is why you didn't come down. No one can stay mad at someone who's that sick."

Hazel grunted her appreciation. "I hope you're right."

"She'll understand even better when you tell her the truth. I thought it better come from you, and not before the game."

"Smart. And how did they do?"

"They lost. They'll be playing for third place this afternoon."

Hazel groaned again as she shoved her feet into her sneakers. "I hope I didn't throw her off."

"Not everything is your fault, Hazel," Riva said. "Anyway, how are you feeling today?"

"Well rested," Hazel said dryly. When Riva laughed she added, "I'm totally fine. The sleep did help. Where am I meeting you?"

The team was heading to Main Street for lunch, so Riva said she'd swing by the motel to get Hazel along the way. Hazel made her way down the narrow, creaking stairs to wait in the lobby, which was cool and empty. Looking out at the sunbaked parking lot, she realized she hadn't been lying to Riva. Despite the looming conversation with Jen, she felt awake, well rested, and even somewhat lighter. Not even the thought of the big spider on the loose bothered her too much.

When they had parked outside a little bistro on Main Street, Hazel and Riva joined the end of the long lineup. Riva nudged Hazel and pointed to the tables. The largest ones only seated four.

"Now's your chance. Go grab a private table."

When Jen turned around with her food, Hazel was already seated and waving her over to a table for two.

"Hey," Jen said as she set down her tray. She looked Hazel up and down. "You're feeling better?"

"Yes," Hazel said. She grabbed Jen's hand as she settled into the wooden seat.

Jen paused, surprised. "Look—" she began, but Hazel cut her off.

"Sorry, but I have to tell you what happened last night while everyone else is busy."

She launched into the whole story while Jen stared, her food untouched. Hazel only stopped once as one of the girls catcalled them from across the bistro. Jen smirked and rolled her eyes but kept her focus on Hazel as she wrapped it up in a hushed tone.

"The thing is," Hazel said, "I feel better today! And I mean better than I have in a long time. I think the mirror thing might have sapped the Shadow of some of its … I don't know, some of its life force or something."

Jen gawked. "You can't be thinking about doing it again?"

"Maybe!" Hazel admitted, nodding. "Maybe this is the thing that really kills it! I've been depriving it of fear, sure, but that's not sustainable! Everything makes you feel fear. It's always going to have just enough to survive. But if I make it expend energy—energy it doesn't have—" Hazel brushed her palms past each other like she was dusting them off to finish the sentence.

This time Jen reached across the table to take Hazel's hands. "That sounds dangerous, Hazel. I don't want you to get hurt."

"I know," Hazel said, but before they could continue, the other girls rose from their chairs.

"We're going to check out the shops," Kate called. She had reapplied her makeup after this morning's game and had paired the heavy black liner with an opposing flirty pink dress. The pink illuminated her sunburned cheeks. The mismatch reminded Hazel of someone. Kate adopted a deep, seductive tone. "Are you two coming or should we leave you alone?"

Hazel caught Riva's eye just as her stomach growled. Riva was holding up Hazel's breakfast burrito. She hadn't eaten yet. Neither had Jen.

Jen scooped up her food. "We're coming."

They followed along at the end of the pack. Riva passed back Hazel's burrito like a baton, and she and Jen ate outside under faded red-and-white striped awnings while the others dipped into shops.

"The other thing is," Hazel said when she had finished and stuffed the tin foil wrapper in a garbage bin, "I want to know who that boy is. Riva figures it was random, but that seems unlikely to me."

"You think the Shadow led you to him?" Jen asked. She was leaning against a shop's red brick wall.

Hazel joined her. "No. It didn't feel like the Shadow was there at all."

"So you have some kind of connection to him then?"

Hazel's jaw dropped.

"What?"

"I can check for cords. I hadn't thought of that."

As a ghost, Kelly had shown Hazel that the sisters were connected by a blue cord. Hazel was able to sense it more than see it. The Shadow, on the other hand, had ugly, rusting hooks attached to its connections, its prey.

Jen's eyes lit up. "Good idea!"

The girls came out then, and Hazel searched the crowded street for somewhere private she could go.

"I need a washroom," she said when she came up empty.

"Let's try there," Jen suggested, pointing to a music store.

At the sight of the huge record collection, Kate cried, "Oooh!" and bounded inside.

Hazel made her way to the back, where an arrow on the ceiling pointed to a single-occupant restroom. Inside, she refused to look at the mirror. She lowered the toilet lid and sat down, letting her breath out to a four count. The mirror was making her jumpy, so she was forced to close her eyes to relax.

In such unideal conditions, Hazel didn't expect to feel a connection so fast, but Jen's blue cord leapt to her mind's eye. She smiled. The blue cord stretched from Jen's heart to Hazel's. A sense of peace washed over her just by acknowledging its existence.

She continued searching. There were many other cords, but it was sometimes difficult to know where they went. She tried each one, trying to get a feel for the person accompanying it. Finally, she reached a cord that she couldn't name. It struck her that this one was new. Her heart leapt with excitement.

The cord faced south, heading out the front of the store. There, Hazel lost the visual in her mind. She opened her eyes, disappointed. It was possible the connection had nothing to do with the boy, but for a moment she had felt sure. She grasped the cord again and tried to send a message down its length. *Who are you?*

With no answer, Hazel re-emerged and shook her head at a disappointed Jen. She looked around the store for the first time and started with surprise. There was a rack displaying posters, and it was open to a familiar screaming guitarist. She weaved through the displays to get a closer look. Splashed across the bottom of the poster were the words 'Mass Migraine.'

"They're not too bad," Kate said over Hazel's shoulder. "Are you a fan?"

Hazel smiled an apology. "I actually haven't heard of them. They just look familiar."

"They're Canadian," Kate told her, "and pretty new. But they have a weird mix of sad songs and heavy metal. It's kind of like they haven't made up their mind."

Hazel made a mental note to try the band out later. Maybe she could get a better feel for who the boy was.

An hour after that, they were back in the university gym. Hazel made a point to keep her eyes on the game this time, only talking to Riva in short snatches. When the coach blew the whistle for a time-out in the second period, Riva seemed unable to wait any longer.

"So did you and Jen figure everything out?"

"No!" Hazel laughed. "You think she's a Shadow Whisperer or something?"

Riva rolled her eyes. "I didn't mean the Shadow. I mean, did you two talk it out?"

Hazel pressed her lips into a sheepish line. Riva groaned but bumped her with a sympathetic shoulder.

"I know I've neglected her this weekend," Hazel said. "I'm trying to make it up to her."

Riva was quiet for a moment as the teams took their places on the court. "And are you okay with her telling everyone about you?"

Hazel was able to catch Jen's eye and give her a big grin.

"It's done," Hazel said. "Not much I can do about it now."

Riva was quiet again as she readjusted her cushion. At last she said, "You won't lose her if you talk to her. It's the couples who don't talk you have to worry about."

They stood to cheer as Lor managed a breakaway and got a basket. Hazel didn't answer.

***

The team won third place in the tournament. They were a little disappointed, but Hazel, for one, was glad to be done with the gym. No more games meant the rest of the weekend had opened up for her to spend time with Jen. To her dismay, a few of the girls wanted to stay and find out which team would take first place. Hazel and Riva exchanged glances, both fidgeting on their bruised backsides. Jen noticed.

"Just go," she said, flat but understanding. "I'll hang out with my friends, and we'll catch up with you later."

"Are you sure?" Hazel asked, scrutinizing Jen's expression. "We came here to hang out with you."

Jen nodded. "You came here to watch me play, not a bunch of strangers. I get it. I'll see you after."

Relieved, Hazel and Riva said goodbye to everyone and returned to the motel, where they spent the rest of the sweltering afternoon loosening up their knotted muscles in the pool. They ordered pizza for dinner, which they ate in their air-conditioned room with the TV on while Hazel checked in with Jen via text.

Their rivals had won first place, and now Jen and the girls were eating fast food so they could spend the rest of their money on a celebratory night out. The older girls who had played in this tournament last year knew of a bar that wouldn't card the underage players. Win or lose, this night was always meant to be the highlight of the weekend, which is why they had all booked Monday off. They would sleep it off Monday morning, then drive home in the afternoon.

Riva clapped her hands together once and bounced off the

bed. "Alright! Time to get fancy!" She fished out a sexy black dress with red flowers and a pair of shiny black high-heels. "What are you wearing?"

"Nothing that good," Hazel admitted. She could picture just how nice Riva's curves would look in the tight-fitting dress. She dug in her bag and held up a wrap-around dark purple dress that tied on the side.

"That looks perfect," Riva encouraged. "What shoes?"

Hazel held up a pair of boring black flats. "I'll never do heels again," she admitted. "They hurt, for one, but I can't shake the thought of the corrupt attacking and catching me in heels. At least I can ditch flats and run barefoot."

Riva nodded. "That occurred to me too. But I'm going to wear heels tonight because we survived and you stopped the Shadow, so screw that evil bastard."

Hazel grinned. "Fair enough."

Shortly after, there was a knock at their door.

"It's me," Jen said, popping her head in to say hello.

"No!" Riva cried. "You'll see Hazel's dress. Out, you!"

Jen laughed as Riva shooed her away, trying to block Hazel from view. "Alright, alright, I surrender! I just came to tell you we're leaving in an hour. We'll meet you two in the lobby."

Hazel, who was likewise trying to see Jen, stopped craning her neck when the door closed and Riva turned a suspicious glare on her. She held the bathroom door for Riva in mock politeness.

They shared the bathroom mirror, neither voicing how much better it was to stand together rather than be creeped out alone. Hazel concentrated on her makeup and curls, then got out of there as fast as possible. Hot from having a curling iron so close to her head, she turned up the air conditioner in the main room.

The lights flickered. There was an ominous powering-down sound and then everything shut off.

"Ah!" Riva cried, sticking her head out of the dark bathroom. "What happened?"

Hazel cringed and pointed to the air conditioner.

"What do we do now?"

Hazel went to the door and peered through the peephole into the hallway. It was dark out there as well. She grimaced. It looked like she'd shut down power for the whole motel.

"I'll got tell reception," she said. It was the least she could do.

With no windows in the hall, Hazel had to use the light from her phone to see where she was going. Heads poked out of other doors as Hazel passed, and she found herself following another guest who was on her way to complain. Wondering if she should just retreat, Hazel descended the rickety stairs at a safe distance from the woman. Then a jolt went through her. Looking up at her from the bottom of the stairs was the boy from the mirror. The other guest stepped right through him.

He was staring at Hazel. His eyes were plaintive as he extended one hand. His fixed attention was unnerving, but it was his mouth that raised the hair on the back of Hazel's neck. His lips were moving like he was speaking fast, but no sounds were coming out. A wave of nausea passed over Hazel. The boy put one foot on the stairs.

"I can't hear you," Hazel choked, shaking her head more to dispel the disturbing image than to communicate with it. She took a step backwards.

He advanced on her, closing the distance between them. It didn't make sense. Hazel could always hear ghosts. And just yesterday she had seen him lifting a backpack, something a ghost could not do. Was he dead, or was this boy something else? He was gaining speed as his silent mouth continued to move, his gaze never wavering from Hazel's face. She turned on her heel and ran.

Hazel slammed her room's door and dove for her backpack. She dumped everything on the ground, scattering the contents until she found the remaining lavender.

"You scared me!" Riva gasped. She was sitting on the end of the bed, attempting to finish her makeup using her phone's camera. "What's the matter?"

Hazel flicked her lighter too fast, the sparks igniting and dying three times before the lavender caught fire. She hurried to the door, waving the smoke from top to bottom. Riva abandoned her blush compact and phone to follow her.

"What's going on?"

"I saw the boy, but something's not right," she said in a rush.

"What do you mean?"

Hazel continued to waft the smoke over the whole space, everything from window to closet. "He was talking to me, but I couldn't hear him. I don't think he's a ghost. He's something else."

Riva paled. She trailed Hazel around the room, helping to spread the smoke with her hands. "What else could he be?"

"I don't know. That's why I'm worried."

"But what does he want?" Riva asked.

"I don't know," Hazel repeated.

Riva sank back down on the bed as Hazel finally stopped. She set the remaining lavender down in front of the TV and stared at the door to the hallway, wondering if he could just walk right through it. Riva leaned forward to stare as well. The girls stayed like that for a long minute.

The power hummed back to life. Children's laughter sounded in the hallway, followed by the patter of feet as they ran back to their rooms. Hazel and Riva exchanged a look. Light was not like lavender. It would not protect them from a ghost or monster.

"We can't stay like this forever," Riva said at last, chewing on her thumbnail.

Hazel, wringing her hands, nodded. She approached the door and grasped the handle. With a steadying breath, she turned it.

Her heart lurched. The boy was still there. He was kneeling on the floor in a posture of despair, his head bowed. He was transparent, like the stories of ghosts that Hazel had always thought incorrect. He looked up at her then, and his mouthed words were unmistakable.

"Please help me."

Then he vanished. Hazel slowly closed the door.

"Nothing there, right?" came Riva's nervous voice over Hazel's shoulder.

"He was there."

"And?"

"He's gone now."

Riva whacked Hazel's arm.

"I think he asked for help," she elaborated as she sunk onto the end of her bed. An idea struck her and she sat up straighter. "Hold on a second."

She closed her eyes and felt for the cord she had discovered earlier today. It leapt to her call, but to Hazel's surprise, the cord was divided. Even as she sensed the split, it began knitting itself back together. She opened her eyes in wonder.

"I have to try the mirror again," she decided.

"No," Riva said at once. "You can't!"

Just then, Hazel's phone buzzed. Distracted, she read aloud, "The cabs will be here in ten."

"Oh no!" Riva groaned, her hands flying to her unfinished hair.

Hazel teetered on the verge of checking the mirror. She still wasn't sure mirror-travel was safe. Plus, if it made her sick again, she would have to bail on Jen for the biggest night of the weekend. On top of that, the boy might be some creature trying to lure her in with a plea for help. She dropped her phone on the bed. Now was not the time.

"How can I help?" she asked.

6

Riley: Who Are You

Riley crept around the church, trying doors. All of them were locked. He had last been here for his dad's funeral, a thought he avoided the same way he skirted the pools of light coming from the outside sconces. Moth wings made the light flicker as he approached an addition on the left side of the church: the priest's quarters.

It was with mingled relief and nerves that he found the front door open. Inside, the hall light was on, and dishes rattled in a room at the end. To the right was an inner door to the church. Riley stole towards this door, floor creaking, and found that it too was unlocked.

In the shadows, Riley squinted at the narrow wooden room leading to the nave of the church. It was full of robes on hooks. He bumped up against a life-size candelabrum with his backpack and almost sent it clattering to the ground. He set it back on its feet with his heart in his throat, then scurried from the booby-trapped room and emerged onto the altar.

Moonlight through stained-glass windows bathed the first rows of pews in dim colour. He remembered the coffin moving up the centre aisle on the shoulders of his dad's friends. He looked up at the high, peaked ceiling instead, which disappeared in shadow. The whole place had a forbidden feeling, like it knew more than one reason why Riley shouldn't be here.

At the nearest side door, he found what he was looking for: a small bowl attached to the wall by a brass bracket. Inside was a soft rectangular sponge soaked in holy water. Riley squished it down until his fingertips were wet, then made the sign of the cross by touching his forehead, chest, and both shoulders. He waited with bated breath. Nothing happened.

Riley sighed, but he wasn't sure if it was with relief or disappointment. A part of him had expected to feel the water sizzle against his contaminated skin. He plucked the sponge out of its bowl and wiped it all over his face for good measure, letting the water drip all over his chest. All he achieved was a soaked shirt.

It appeared holy water wasn't going to help him. Slumping with weariness and disappointment, Riley stared at the wooden pews. They looked stiff and uncomfortable, but he didn't know where else to go for his first night on his own. At least here, there was no one for him to hurt.

Dreading the abrupt wake-up call of the priest kicking him out, Riley collected a few of the long robes to sleep under. He found an outlet to charge his phone behind them, then he picked out a pew in the middle of the church, out of sight.

With his backpack as a pillow, Riley stretched out on the bench and stared up at the heavy ceiling beams. The disturbing image of the girl in the mirror kept coming back to him. He couldn't help but imagine her standing at the foot of the aisle, staring down the row at him. If the floor wasn't stone, he might have hidden under the pew for peace of mind. He couldn't tell if the shadow creature was messing with him by sending her image or if she was one of its victims pleading for help.

In time, Riley slipped into short, feverish dreams featuring the shadow creature in the well, George and the slimy rope, Charlie and the shovel, and the girl in the mirror. Then there was a loud clang, and Riley jerked awake. The sun was shining through the stained-glass windows. He clutched the robes around himself, listening. Someone was readying the church for the early morning mass. Riley slipped off the bench and crouched down, pulling on his backpack as he went. Over the top of the pew in front of him, he could see a man at the altar.

He waited, and as soon as the man went back into the robe chamber, Riley ran out into the aisle, robes in hand, to follow. Peering around the doorway, he saw the man go straight through and disappear into the priest's quarters. Riley wrenched his phone and cable from the outlet, threw the robes back on a random hook, then slipped out the priest's front door.

He ran all the way down the street and around the corner before he felt safe enough to sit on a curb. Beyond relieved at having made it through the night without incident, he took a deep breath of the fresh morning air, then checked his phone. The battery still wasn't holding a charge. At least there were no messages from his mom yet, which meant she didn't suspect anything. He turned off the location setting for when she realized he was gone.

Riley felt sick with exhaustion, but at least in the daylight his problem felt more practical. He needed to leave town so his mom couldn't find him and drag him home. His debit card would be traceable, so he needed to get money out and use cash for as long as possible. He needed breakfast.

He stopped at a quiet Tim Hortons with only one other customer dining in this early in the morning. Coffee made Riley more alert but also jumpier, so he wolfed down his food and hurried to the bus station. By the time he was on a bus with a wallet full of money, more people had begun spilling onto the streets and going about their days. He turned his face from the window to hide, wishing his phone had enough juice for Mass Migraine to distract him. He only relaxed when the bus finally rumbled to life and pulled out of the station. He fell asleep as soon as they passed the 'Now Departing' sign.

***

"Who are you?"

Riley awoke to a voice and vibration in his chest. At first he thought it was the bus, but that vibration remained in his feet. The question seemed to come from inside his heart. He opened his eyes and, for a second, saw a blue rope extending from his chest with a faint glow. Then it vanished.

He sat bolt upright, thinking of George and the slimy rope. His eyes darted around the bus, but there were no ghosts, and no one had noticed his sudden movement. He touched his chest and found nothing.

The voice had not sounded like the creature. He thought it might have been a girl. He wanted to grab the rope and shout a message down it like a kid playing telephone with paper cups and string, but he didn't know how. He waited, hoping whoever it was would speak again, but after a few minutes he slumped back in his seat, disappointed.

Still, the voice had not been inside his head, like when the creature spoke to him. Nor was the rope the disgusting green one that dragged George. With a leap of heart, Riley realized someone had reached out to him. Maybe there was someone out there who could help him. He wondered if it was the girl from the mirror. Riley located the sun and used it to determine that the rope had come from the west. When the bus stopped, he would get on a new one going that direction.

Unfortunately, changing to a bus heading west meant Riley had to spend a boring two hours wandering an indoor mall awaiting its arrival. He sat in the air-conditioned food court and listened to a mother and teen daughter have a dull conversation about school. He wished he had Sophie's book to read, then they might have something to talk about if she ever forgave him.

He let his forehead rest on the table as the seconds trickled by, annoyed at the delay. The shadow creature stirred inside him, eager for annoyance to swell into anger. Riley jumped up in fright and left the mall immediately, not bothering to tuck in his chair. He wasn't about to hurt innocent people for the creature's pleasure, and certainly not out of sheer boredom.

Dinner on the bus consisted of an apple and a bag of chips. That's when the dreaded message from Elisabeth arrived.

"Where are you?"

Riley wondered if he should lie or ignore her. If she eventually got the police involved, his text might give them a clue about his location, even without that feature on. He decided to put her at ease with a lie and trust that the bus was already taking him away from this spot anyway.

"I'm going to stay at a friend's for a few days. Figured we could both use some space."

He hadn't even set his phone down before she responded. "Wyatt's? Is his family okay with that?" Then another message followed that said, "You have to ask me before you do things like this."

Annoyance was back, and with it the dark presence of the creature, as quick to lap up the emotion as a dog slathering over a treat. Riley couldn't help it. He felt even more annoyed at its intrusion.

Yes, the shadow hissed in his ear.

Riley cringed and rubbed at his ears. *Get lost*, he thought back to it, clenching his teeth.

I'm home, it taunted.

A chill went through Riley. He stared at his phone, not knowing what to say to either of them. He closed his eyes for a minute.

When he was a little calmer, he typed, "Just trying to help. They said they'll take me to school. My phone is busted though, it might die."

Then he turned it off. He would pretend the battery had failed. She might see through it, but it was the best he could do. He sighed and settled back into his seat. The sun and shade flashed red and black over his closed lids, making him flinch. Realizing he was far too edgy for that, Riley watched the trees flicker by as the bus wound through a mountain pass instead. The changing scenery was hypnotizing, and Riley stared at the valleys and hills for a long time. The shadow creature stayed silent.

Just as he was wondering if the bus might drive right by the owner of the voice he was searching for, Riley saw the blue rope reflected in the window. He had conjured it up by thinking about her. Excitement bounced through him, and the rope dimmed.

He forced himself to calm down. It responded to his heart rate, glowing in the window. He didn't dare look at it directly in case it vanished again, so he stared out at the trees, keeping the reflection in the corner of his eye. It extended from his chest and plunged into the trees. He got the impression it didn't end nearby. Riley closed his eyes and imagined he was following it, pulling himself along the rope.

He was lighter. Hand over hand, Riley passed through a blur of evergreen trees and soared through small towns before finding his feet in a parking lot. Everything went so fast he should have been dizzy, but he found the rope grounded him. He looked up at a large building with words over the door. Everything was blurry. He thought it read 'The OK Motel.' He frowned at the strange name, but the rope led inside, so he drifted through the doors without opening them.

Straight ahead was an empty reception desk. Narrow stairs led upwards on his left and right. It was so dark compared to outside that he needed a moment to adjust. A woman descended the right set of stairs. The rope flowed through her chest, and Riley opened his mouth to speak to her.

She stepped right through him. Stunned for a moment, his eyes lit on another figure up the stairs. He gasped. Peering down at him from the top was the heavy girl from the mirror, but she didn't look ill at all. On the contrary, he could see even in the dark that she was healthy, even rosy. She was wearing a dark purple dress with a bow tied to one side, and her hair was curled like she had somewhere nice to be. Even better, there was no shadow drifting around her like an aura.

With a surge of excitement, Riley saw the blue rope end where it connected with her chest. Not only that, but the girl was staring right at him.

"It's you!" Riley called up the stairs. "I saw you in my mirror yesterday, and then I heard you today: you asked me who I was!"

She continued to stare. On closer inspection, Riley saw her eyes were wide and petrified.

"You did come to me ... didn't you?" he asked. He raised his hand like she had in the mirror. "You had shadows all over your hand. I recognised them! They were just like the fingers from the creature in the well."

He put a foot on the stairs, so eager was he to speak to her. She took a step back, her mouth moving.

"What?" he asked. He climbed the stairs towards her.

It was a mistake. She turned on her heel and disappeared into the hallway above, leaving only the glowing blue light behind.

"Wait!" he cried, running after her.

She ran so fast she was gone by the time he made it to the top, but the blue light showed him exactly where to go. She had shut him out behind a wooden door. Riley tried to knock, but his hand sank into the wood. He realized he could walk right through, but he hesitated.

The girl obviously didn't want to see him after all. Disappointment washed over Riley. He remembered seeing the girl in the mirror and how messed up she looked. Maybe that's what he looked like now. In fact, he had a black eye to top it all off. He couldn't blame her for running.

The sensations of his body returned then. He was light-headed, exhausted, and even short of breath. His emotions were no better. Riley had clung to the idea of the girl so he wouldn't feel alone in this. Now that hope was gone. She had no answers for him, and the problems he faced came rushing back to him, overwhelming in their number. How could he get rid of a monster he had never heard of? How was he supposed to do it all without hurting someone else when the monster was inside him, goading him into it? And how could he manage it all while keeping his mom in the dark? He sank to his knees, tears welling in his eyes. He couldn't.

The thought of going back to the bus felt almost as bad as going home. At least here, in this blurry place, he felt light, like there was no creature with him. But even as he lingered, Riley began to struggle for air.

The motel door opened. He looked up to see the girl peering down at him, shielding herself with the door.

"Please help me," he begged on empty lungs.

He took a huge gasp of air back on the bus. It was like he had stretched a bungee cord to its utmost extent and then been yanked backwards by the rebound. It all happened so fast his senses struggled to catch up. One hand had jumped to the window to brace himself, and the other clutched the neighbouring seat. It was lucky he wasn't sharing his row with anyone.

Riley gulped the air, his lungs burning. When his mind had stopped reeling, he realized his lips were tingling. He caught a glimpse of himself in the window. His lips were blue. He had been suffocating. If he had stayed any longer, he might have died. Riley shuddered, feeling feverish.

As far as he could tell, the shadow creature had not noticed his mental absence. Maybe it had gone to sleep as Riley stared at the landscape. He was glad. He didn't think it would be smart to introduce the creature to the girl. Riley stiffened as a thought struck him. Maybe seeing the girl in the mirror was a premonition, a warning. Maybe he wasn't supposed to expose her to the shadow or she'd wind up possessed by it and made to look all sick and green like in the mirror.

As an orange sunset flared over the tip of a mountain range, Riley obsessed over why he had ever been drawn to this girl. He didn't know what made her special or whether his guess about premonitions was right, but he needed answers. Riley set his jaw. His next destination was The OK Motel, wherever that was. But he would think very carefully about how to approach the girl without the shadow knowing.

<h1 style="text-align:center">7</h1>

Hazel: Avoidance

By the time Hazel and Riva descended the awkward lobby stairs, they were running late. Riva stepped down first, her thick braids twisted into a simple low bun. She navigated the narrow stairs like a baby deer in her high heels, but the girls at the bottom cheered her on with wolf-whistles. Hazel was glad most of the attention was on her.

Lor held up her phone to take a picture, and Riva snapped into a model's pose on the last step. Hazel had only a second to think of her own pose before Riva stepped aside, so she raised a cheeky eyebrow and gave the middle finger. The girls laughed, and Hazel grinned. Their disbelief in ghosts aside, Hazel was determined to have fun tonight.

She spotted Jen. She was wearing a low-cut shimmering silver dress that flared at the waist and stopped above her knees. The material was thin and light, and Hazel wanted to touch it. The top half of Jen's hair was in a thick twist, while the purple bottom layer curled around her shoulders. Like Hazel, she had opted for flats.

They drifted towards each other, smiling a little too big.

Hazel gestured to Jen's dress but couldn't find the words to describe how Jen looked. They both blushed, and Jen giggled, slipping her hand into Hazel's. Jen touched one of Hazel's curls, and Hazel thought her heart might float away.

"We're on the move lovebirds," Kate teased, holding the door open to the heat of the night.

The bar was top-to-bottom dark wood. They spent the first few hours trying each other's drinks in the round blue booths while the team hailed opposing players across the bar. Everyone seemed to have forgotten their sudden distrust of Hazel. She forgot too. She found herself enthralled by the way Jen's laugh displayed her perfect teeth and felt lucky to be at her side. She didn't want to bring up Jen's betrayal, no matter what Riva might say. It was most unlike her, but Hazel discovered there was one person she would rather keep more than her secret.

The town might be small, but it was still a university town. The music was new, the DJ was decent, and thanks to the cheap Sunday drink special, the dance floor was crowded, if a little sticky. Under the flashing purple and blue lights, Hazel danced until she couldn't breathe. Her cheeks ached from smiling, but she kept an eye open for the opportunity to dance with Jen alone.

When the moment came, she grabbed Jen's hand and spun her so that her hair and dress twirled around her. Then she pulled Jen face to face with her. Empowered by the anonymity granted by the press of bodies around them, Hazel kissed her. She knew by the mischievous glint in Jen's eye when they pulled apart that Jen wasn't finished with her yet. Just then, Lor arrived with glasses of water.

"You'll thank me tomorrow!" Lor shouted over the music,

winking and raising her own glass.

Hazel and Jen didn't break eye contact over their cheers.

When Hazel stumbled into the tiny bathroom for the third time that night, she paused to check her reflection. Her hair was stringy now, but her cheeks red, and her eyes alive. She realized with pleasure that in all her bathroom trips this evening, she hadn't given a single thought to the Shadow. Over her shoulder, a woman with auburn hair was leaning against the cramped wall by the hand dryer. She was smiling about Hazel's smile.

"Good night?" Hazel asked.

The woman's smile slid into an *o* of surprise.

"The music's pretty good, don't you think?" Hazel said as girls emerged and disappeared into the stalls.

One of the toilets flushed and Kate bounced out. She looked into the corner and back at Hazel. "Oh, are you talking to me?"

Hazel looked back at the woman, who had uncrossed her arms and was looking stunned.

Hazel burst out laughing. "Oh, I thought you were alive!"

"Are you talking to a dead person?" Kate gasped. "That's hilarious!"

A girl with a paper towel in her hands gave them a weird look before moving on.

The woman in the corner cracked an incredulous smile. "I came for one last dance. I can't believe this!"

"Well, I hope you have a hell of a time then," Hazel said, grinning.

Kate danced out of the bathroom, a delighted grin on her face as she led Hazel back to the dance floor. The ghost woman joined them. She danced with such abandon that, had she been alive, she would have spilled drinks. Hazel threw back her head and laughed up at the flashing lights. This woman was going to make it count. Hazel decided to follow suit.

***

The next day she woke to the sound of Riva running to the bathroom. Lor was right. She was glad she switched to water last night before it was too late. She rolled over and groaned. The room was too bright. Hazel squinted at the clock on the nightstand. It was almost 10:00am. They had to check out in an hour.

Something black on the floor slid under Riva's bed and Hazel sat upright. It felt like the whole world was sitting up with her and she had to stabilize herself with the headboard.

"Hazel ...," Riva moaned from the bathroom.

"What?" Hazel croaked back. She cleared her throat and tried again. "What?"

"Can you bring me a glass?"

Hazel spotted a glass of water on the nightstand that she didn't remember pouring. She downed the rest of it, then brought it to Riva. She was too hungover to care if the spider had found them again. She would have laughed if she had the energy. She needed some fortifying food and coffee; she was not herself.

She found Riva huddled by the toilet, her back against the tub, and her head between her knees. Hazel filled the glass at the sink and took in the tangled mess that used to be her hair. Her dress, which she had slept in, was also hopelessly twisted. She handed Riva the fresh water and sat down in the doorway.

"Maybe you'll feel better after breakfast," she said.

Riva paled at the idea of food. Hazel beatboxed a song from last night, and Riva gave a weak laugh.

"I need to shower," Hazel commented, smelling her armpit.

"I need to not move," Riva returned.

"Perfect," Hazel joked. "I don't want to be alone with this mirror anyway." After a moment of silence, Hazel sighed and said, "I don't know the last time I had so much fun."

To Hazel's surprise, tears sprang to her eyes. She wiped them away before Riva could notice.

Later, Hazel threw on some clothes in the main room while Riva took her turn showering, then checked her phone. Jen had sent a message that said, "Ughhhhhhhh."

Hazel chuckled, but her smile vanished when she saw the date. Her stomach dropped so fast it was like she had swallowed a giant ball of heavy lead. This day last year, Gran had died and the Shadow had started its rampage. Shortly afterwards, though she didn't know when for sure, her mom had died as well. The next morning had been Kelly's turn. Hazel felt a flutter of panic. She didn't want to go home and face everything.

"Are you going to be okay to drive home?" Hazel called to Riva, half hoping the answer was no.

Riva either didn't hear her or didn't have an answer yet. Restless, Hazel decided to go check on Jen. She wound her way through the hallways until she found Lor and a few of the others congregating outside their rooms.

Lor gave Hazel a warm smile. "Looks like you're feeling better than your other half." She gestured with her thumb at one of the rooms. "We're checking out of this one, but if Jen doesn't hurry up, she's going to get charged another day for hers. Maybe you can hurry her along."

Jen's room was a touch larger than Hazel and Riva's and included a small alcove with a short old armchair under a mirror. Hazel found Jen in the bathroom doing her makeup.

More worrisome was the lumpy figure of Kate still buried under her covers.

Hazel leaned against the bathroom door frame. "You're going to be late, you know."

Jen managed a weak smile. She finished her mascara before replying. "Actually, we have a little wiggle room there."

"Oh?" Hazel raised her eyebrows.

Jen turned to face Hazel, her expression serious. "Do you know what day it is?"

Hazel's smile dropped like a ball of lead in her stomach.

"I thought you might." Jen took her hand and gave it a squeeze. "Riva and I booked an extra day in case you wanted to stay a little longer."

Hazel opened and then closed her mouth. Relief, gratitude, and pain vied for her attention. She couldn't speak. Jen pulled her into a tight hug.

Into Hazel's shoulder she said, "I'll go tell the girls we're staying." She gave her an extra squeeze before pulling away and looking over at Kate's motionless form. "I don't think Kate's up for leaving today though. Do you mind if she stays too?"

Hazel still hadn't found her voice as she shook her head. Jen squeezed her shoulder one more time and left the room. Hazel was left staring at a new mirror, alone. She saw the tears pooling against her lower eyelashes for the second time that morning and brushed them away. Her heart was aching, and she couldn't bear it.

She checked over her shoulder. Jen had gone. If she listened, she could hear Kate's slow breathing. The bathroom light sparkled in the mirror. Hazel strode up to the glass and touched her forehead to the surface, thinking about the boy; the boy, and not her family.

The cool surface cupped her forehead once again, and rash excitement rushed through her veins. Hazel sunk into the mirror, opening her eyes to the inside of a truck. She was looking through the rearview mirror, her range of vision small. To Hazel's dismay, the truck was empty. The sun was pouring onto the dusty blue seats even as Hazel's eyes chilled with the mirror's ice.

Then the driver's side door opened. A heavy old man in a baseball cap hauled himself up into the cab, setting down a white takeout bag in the middle seat. The truck swayed as he settled in and reached to close the door. Something moved in the truck bed.

A head peeked up at the driver, then ducked back down. Oblivious, the old man started the truck. In one fluid movement, the boy in the back rolled over the edge of the truck, adjusted his backpack, and walked off down the road. The driver pulled away from the curb and the boy disappeared down an alley.

Hazel scanned the surroundings for a clue on the boy's whereabouts as the driver accelerated. She squinted at a street sign as the truck rounded a corner. She managed to read "Bellevue" before the sign was out of sight. Hazel retreated.

Again, she felt the sucking sensation like she was pulling her head out of a strong current. She clutched the counter for support, the shadows around her dancing away as she reoriented herself. She gasped in shock when she saw a pale face in the mirror over her shoulder.

Hazel and Kate stared at each other for a beat, neither girl sure what to say. Kate looked white enough to faint. At last, she broke the silence.

"What just happened? Do I need t-to call an ambulance?"

"No," Hazel said, whirling around and waving the idea away. "No. I'm fine."

The girls stared at each other a moment longer in a standoff over who would give more information first. Kate broke the silence again.

"You were gone for a full minute," she whispered. "Is that normal?"

"What do you mean?" Hazel hedged.

"I was talking to you," Kate said, and her voice shook. "And you didn't react at all. I was scared you were having a seizure or something."

"Oh." Hazel toyed with the idea but knew the lie would inevitably get back to Jen. "Listen," she said instead, "it wasn't a seizure, I promise. But Jen doesn't approve of what I just did. Can we keep this between us?"

"Keep what between us?" Kate asked, bewildered. "What happened?"

Hazel shut the bathroom door, keeping one ear alert for signs of Jen's return.

"I recently figured out I can use my abilities to ... connect with people. Through the mirror. That's what I was doing. But Jen is scared I'm messing with something I shouldn't. Please don't tell her."

"You're connecting with ... dead people?"

Hazel hesitated. "I'm not sure."

Shock and confusion mingled on Kate's face, and Hazel couldn't help but take pity on her. "There's this boy. I saw him the first time I used the mirror, but then he showed up here, at the motel, like a ghost. I was worried he died or something. So I was just checking on him."

"And was he okay?"

"He seemed fine," Hazel admitted. "Same as before, any-way."

The door to the motel room opened with a clatter, and Hazel shot Kate a pleading look. Kate gave her one curt nod.

"We're moving you in!" Jen called.

Hazel met her in the hall. She was carrying Hazel's backpack on her shoulder, with a groaning Riva just behind her. When she spotted Kate, Jen said, "Oh good, you're up! We need to get breakfast before I pass out. Want to come?"

Kate nodded, this time to Jen, and left the bathroom without a word. Jen didn't seem to think her silence was weird. Since the mirror-sickness was starting to return, Hazel decided to use the hangover card too.

They returned to the same bar as last night, which served late breakfasts for low prices. Sweating perhaps more than the heat demanded, they plonked themselves down in a booth and ordered coffee and water. All four of them disappeared into their phones, so Hazel took the opportunity to look up Bellevue.

When she found a local Bellevue Street, Hazel swallowed her excitement. There were probably plenty of Bellevue Streets in the world. She searched for the street view. The Bellevue she saw in the mirror had an alley. The buildings around it were short and brick, like old offices or banks. It had definitely not been busy. It was hard to tell, but from a certain angle, Hazel thought the street on her phone might actually be the same.

She racked her brain for more details. The driver had put a white takeout bag on the middle seat. The top of the bag had been rolled down, and there was a red circle with some kind of mascot in the middle. It was a meager description to go on, and it turned out there were hundreds of restaurants and fast-food chains with similar designs. Scrapping that idea, Hazel searched Bellevue Street restaurants. She found a small bistro called Sara's Subs. The logo showed a cartoon woman holding out a plate while the restaurant name encircled her in red lettering.

Hazel paused to sip her creamy coffee. Logic said it was unlikely for the boy to be so close. Maybe she was deluding herself. But yesterday he had come to find her as some kind of spirit, so he clearly knew where she was. It was possible he might try to find her in person. She shivered at the thought and checked over her shoulder. He wasn't there of course, and she had to hide her smile behind her coffee cup.

After picking at her breakfast for an hour, Hazel began to feel a bit better. Riva and Jen were both chatting more, and even Kate had regained some of her colour.

"Thanks for letting me stay with you," Kate said as they settled their bills. "I didn't mean to intrude on your day."

Hazel didn't miss the glance Riva and Jen shared over the debit machine in Jen's hands.

"It's no problem," Riva said to cover the moment. "I wouldn't feel up for a long drive today either."

Hazel pretended to study her bill. It appeared Riva and Jen had plans to get Hazel talking about last year. She felt a wave of relief to have Kate as a buffer and sent her a welcoming smile. She wished they could stay all week with Kate blocking the topic of the anniversary. She didn't want to go home until all the memorials had wound down.

With a twinge of guilt, Hazel knew people would be seeking her out, trying to contact the spirits of lost loved ones. Most of the dead had already gone on, like Kelly, and Hazel had helped many of them do it with their living families at her side. The problem was the families whose dead had never connected with Hazel.

She knew exactly where those dead family members were but couldn't bring herself to share it. She could picture the families' repulsed, horrified expressions if she admitted the Shadow inside her had eaten their loved ones' souls. Far worse was making them feel the fierce, hollow ache that plagued Hazel whenever she thought of her mom or Gran.

"I still feel like a slug," Riva said, snapping Hazel back to reality as they stepped out of the bar into the bright sunlight. "Do you guys want to just lay by the river today and not move?"

"That sounds perfect," Kate sighed.

Jen looked at Hazel, waiting for her go-ahead. Bellevue Street nagged at her, but Hazel was weary just from walking to the door. She put the street and the grieving families out of her mind, deciding to insist on some exploring when the weather cooled in the evening. She nodded to Jen.

As she hid behind her sunglasses, Hazel reflected that it could be worse. At least the mirror-travel had not made her throw up this time. Maybe she was getting better at it.

8

Riley: The Orchard

When the bus reached the end of its line, Riley picked up a late dinner of fresh fruit, packaged jerky, and a bottle of water from a roadside fruit stand. They hadn't stopped in a town, exactly, but at a collection of roadside stands that formed a sort of farmers' market. The farmers' houses were set far back behind their orchards.

Riley wondered where all these people went for groceries and supplies; he needed somewhere to plug his phone in to look up The OK Motel. He blamed Elisabeth for his phone's death. The second he had turned it on, the phone flashed missed calls and messages until it powered right back down again.

Another bus wouldn't be arriving for hours, so Riley forged along down the dusty road by foot. He left the fruit stands behind, letting the blue cord guide him as the sun burnt his neck. Cars flew past at speeds that vibrated Riley's entire body. He tried not to think about getting hit and counted the rows of trees in the orchards instead.

The sky took its time turning dusky, but Riley trudged along all the while. He had finished his water and was sucking on a cherry to relieve his dry mouth. The cherry didn't stop a pounding headache though, and with the headache came irritability. He felt the shadow creature stir. The irritation was like a cherry of its own. A measly cherry, it was true, but a morsel to suck on nonetheless.

Riley grew worried as the sun set in earnest. A car could easily hit him in the dark, and at this rate he was going to have to sleep on the side of a road. He sighed and raised his thumb. He had never hitchhiked before. It was illegal, for one, and people could be dangerous, for two. Then again, Riley could be dangerous. He gave a weak chuckle at the irony. If anyone wanted to hurt him, they were likely in for a well-deserved surprise.

It was full dark before someone pulled over, the wheels kicking up dirt as Riley trotted over to the window. The driver was a man in his early 20s who took pity on what he assumed was a runaway teen. They drove together for an hour. The driver, Jordan, told Riley all about his adventures in hitchhiking. Riley drank all Jordan's water and convinced him to check out Mass Migraine.

They finally parted along a stretch of moonlit orchards just after the next town's welcome sign. The blue cord directed Riley into town, while Jordan continued along the deserted highway. Riley yawned as Jordan pulled away. He needed a real meal, but he was grateful Jordan had spared him such a long walk. Their conversation had been fortifying, and Riley felt like he could handle this part now. Besides, he needed time to figure out how to keep the girl a secret from the shadow creature.

As he hitched up his backpack and continued down the road, ideas eluded him. Riley realized what he really needed was another conversation with the monster. He needed to know what it knew. Goosebumps lifted his hair at the idea. Before he could talk himself out of it, Riley slipped into an apple orchard for privacy. A few rows in, he sat down among the roots of one of the trees and rested his back against the bark. He eyed the green apples above him. They wouldn't be ready for another few months.

A bird rustled its feathers somewhere among the silvery leaves. Riley listened because he didn't know where to start. It wasn't like the shadow creature had a name. He closed his eyes and tried to relax before he dared whisper aloud, "Are you there?"

There was no answer, but Riley could feel a certain alertness in that heavy, new part of himself.

He went on. "Do you know where we are?"

Again, no answer. He would take that as a no.

"Did today ... Was today a ..." He had to start over, shaking himself. "Did you get what you wanted today?"

Hungry.

The answer was hissed, angry. Riley's skin went cold all over. He wanted to back out now, but what he really needed to know was how much access the creature had to his thoughts.

"Is that why you were so quiet today? There was nothing to eat? Were you sleeping?"

There was a long pause, but Riley knew the shadow creature was still there, thinking. He suddenly wondered if it was difficult for it to talk. Maybe it was learning.

"Do you know where I'm going?" he asked, slow and clear.

There was silence again.

"Where are we going?" he repeated.

Away ... from Mom.

Well, it was smart enough to figure that part out. If it still thought that was the only plan though, Riley was in luck.

"What am I thinking right now?"

He felt the creature bristle with annoyance, and Riley's breath quickened. But he needed to test it. The creature had been quiet during the car ride, so Riley thought about Jordan. There was no answer apart from the creature's growing irritation. Riley started to get scared. He concluded that it didn't know about the hitchhiking, which meant it did sleep and couldn't hear thoughts when it was dormant. He decided not to push his luck.

"Okay, I'll leave you alone."

Just then, something moved on Riley's left. He ducked down on instinct. Through the tree trunks he could see a grey-haired old woman in a black dress. She was picking her way through the rows straight towards him. He had been spotted. Riley couldn't tell if she was a spirit or human, so he scooped up his backpack by the top strap, ready to apologize for trespassing.

The creature inside him went stiff and menacing, like a mountain lion. Before Riley could question the sudden change, he saw the woman cry out and fall to her knees.

"Are you okay?" he called, hurrying to help her.

She flickered, and Riley stopped midstep. His stomach did a sickening twist. This was no heart attack. In a flash she was much closer, dragged on her knees, fighting against the rope that tethered her to Riley.

"No!" he gasped.

"Socorro, ajude-me!" she screamed, tearing at the rope with her nails.

Riley didn't know what she was saying, but her scream ripped through him. Knowing he could not touch the rope, Riley dropped his bag and ran. All he could think to do was put as much distance between them as possible, but when he looked over his shoulder, she had flashed right up to him. There was a split second when he saw tears spilling from her eyes, and then, at the moment when they should have collided, she was gone.

Riley stumbled to a halt and collapsed to his knees. The orchard was silent again, apart from the distant sounds of a passing car. He could feel the shadow creature's satisfaction, could almost hear it smacking its lips. Riley wrapped his arms around his abdomen in horror. He let his forehead meet the dirt and broke down into the earth.

***

He stayed there all night. Halfway through he shivered his way over to his backpack and wrapped himself in an extra sweater. Even then Riley couldn't get the woman's face out of his dreams. The creature kept calling the feelings of the scene forward, Riley was sure of it. The dreams became a mess of frustration and even rage until he felt like he might snap.

The shadow wanted him unstable, Riley concluded. He ground his teeth as he huddled against a tree. If there were no spirits around, it needed someone to create them. In fact, if Aaron were around, Riley would have been hard pressed not to strangle him again. He was scared. His own anger was frightening. On top of that, he was exhausted, dejected, and hungry. In other words, an easy target. It was lucky he was so far from other people.

Riley's miserable night ended in a predictably miserable way. He had finally fallen into a deep sleep just as the sky turned pink, and he remained that way as it shifted to blue and the morning air turned warm. Then there was a hissing sound, and he received a face full of water. His head snapped up and he threw his hands over his face to stem the flow. It was the orchard's sprinkler system.

Jumping to his feet, Riley yanked his backpack out of the stream and jogged through the trees until he found a dry patch. He cursed. His pant legs were drenched. The sound of bird song and the warmth in the air disoriented him as much as the water. His eyes found the sun, which was creeping up the eastern corner of the sky. He guessed it was around 10:00am.

A door shut in the distance. Riley stood on his toes to peer through the branches. An old man with a potbelly and ball cap had emerged from the orchard's farmhouse and was descending the porch steps. He moved with purpose, like he had already been up for hours. With a twinge of guilt, Riley wondered if this was the old woman's husband. He couldn't ask this man for help.

In the driveway was a rusting blue truck. The man set a few objects down in the cab, including a thermos, then returned to the house. Riley made his move. He raced through the trees, the sprinklers thwacking against his pant legs. He dashed across the driveway and crouched down on the hidden side of the truck, all before the man came back.

Riley tried to quiet his breath, but he was panting from his sprint and had to cover his mouth with one hand. The farmer climbed into the front seat. Keeping his head low, Riley used the back tire as a step and hauled himself into the truck bed. His foot made a light thud on the metal surface, but the man closed his door at almost the same time, and it went unnoticed.

Riley crawled towards the cab and lay down under the back window so the man wouldn't see him in the mirror. He hugged his backpack close. The bed vibrated beneath him, and the truck lurched off down the driveway.

"Please, please, please," Riley begged.

At the end of the driveway, the man turned right and Riley got his wish. They were driving into town. He exhaled.

The drive was far from comfortable. The floor was ridged beneath him, and every bump sent his elbows slipping into the dips. The wind paired with his wet clothes to make the drive just as cold as last night. Riley watched insubstantial clouds drift across the blue sky and consoled himself that soon he would be too hot.

It was Monday. Today was the first day Riley was truly crossing a line. He wondered if his mom knew he wasn't at school yet, or if she would be waiting there to accost him. He didn't have much time to worry though, as a few minutes later they stopped at a red light and Riley considered jumping out. The roads were quiet, but if they kept stopping at lights, someone was bound to see him sooner or later. Before he could decide, the truck accelerated, and Riley groaned. His opportunity was lost.

At last, the driver pulled over on a road lined with shops and got out. Riley froze, but the driver went around the cab rather than the bed. A shop door opened and closed. Riley clutched his backpack, trying to muster the nerve to run for it. He didn't dare travel farther in case they went too far.

Just as he was about to hop out, the shop door opened again. Riley cursed himself and sunk as low as he could. The old man must have been a regular. He felt the truck take the man's weight and did a quick check through the rear window. The driver was distracted. Now was the time.

Riley tossed himself over the edge of the bed as the engine came to life. He drew on his backpack as his feet hit the pavement and walked away like nothing was amiss. His heart leapt in a quiet victory as he listened to the truck driving off behind him. For the first time in days, he smiled.

9

Hazel: The Boy

After smothering herself in sunscreen, Hazel passed out on the beach for two hours. She woke up to whispers and a towel covering her face, presumably Jen's attempt to shield her from the sun. She breathed in the scent of pool chlorine that still clung to the towel as she tuned in to the voices.

"At some point she needs to talk about it," Riva was saying.

"I know, but we can't just tell Kate to get lost." There was a pause. "She talks to you about it."

"She used to," Riva admitted. "She says less and less lately."

The wind picked at the corner of Hazel's towel, but dread swirled in her stomach like a whirlpool. The silence went on.

She heard Jen shifting on her own towel, the pebbles and sand whispering beneath her. "Maybe you and Kate can go for dinner? We can say Hazel and I are having a date."

"That sounds like Kate and I are the ones having a date."

"I know," Jen sighed, "but I don't think Hazel will talk about it without privacy."

"Well, you can't blame her," Riva said. "At least we didn't lose our families."

Hazel could feel their eyes on her, and she tried to keep her breathing slow.

"Maybe we should just tell Kate why we're still here. I'm sure she'll understand."

"I don't think Hazel wants anyone else knowing her business," Riva said, and there was a slight edge to her voice.

The insinuation made the next pause tense. Hazel decided to intervene. She stretched and pulled the towel off her face.

"Looks who's finally back," Jen said, flashing her a smile. "Good nap?"

"Yeah, I was dead to the world," Hazel said. She retrieved her sunglasses from the pebbles and spotted Kate sitting in the river. "It's so hot."

"You should go for a dip," Jen suggested.

"I think I will. I'm melting."

She left the two to their plotting, hoping she had moved them past the sticky moment. She picked her way through the sand and smooth river stones to join Kate and do some plotting of her own.

"Hey," she said, wading into the cool water.

Kate grinned up at her from her seat in the shallows. She was wearing a plum-coloured bathing suit with a sequined white skull on the front. "How was your nap?"

"Pretty great," Hazel said, sitting next to her.

The water pooled over her bare thighs, and she breathed a sigh of relief. Looking out over their peaceful spot on the river, Hazel again noticed the weight that had lifted off her shoulders. Just like her last excursion in the mirror, a good sleep had left her feeling lighter than before. She was more convinced than ever that mirror-travel was a good thing.

"I need another favour," she said to Kate, ready to tackle her other mystery.

Kate raised her eyebrows as if to say, 'Oh?'

"I want to find the boy I was telling you about. When I saw him this morning, he was on a street called Bellevue. I looked it up, and there's a street in town with the same name."

"Ooh," Kate said, scooping some cold water into her hand and pouring it down the back of her neck, "how exciting!"

"But it'll be hard to find him without telling these two what I'm up to." Hazel jerked her head in Jen and Riva's direction.

"Ah. Gotcha." Kate nodded. "So we need an excuse to go there and wander around. Are there any shops we could pretend to be interested in?"

Hazel grinned, glad to have such a ready co-conspirator. "Well, there's a sandwich shop, but I don't know if it's any good. I'm not sure what else."

"Hmm." Kate stood up. "I'll go look it up." She winked at Hazel and waded back to shore without another word.

Hazel smiled at the opposite bank, where thorny blackberry bush tendrils dangled over the water. She had realized who Kate reminded her of: Alexis, Derrick's sister. Alexis had been quick to believe that Hazel could see ghosts. She was a small girl who wore fashionable skirts and wasn't afraid to pair them with sneakers. Best of all, she was braver than she looked, risking her life for the group on more than one occasion. Alexis had almost made it out alive.

Hazel felt a terrible pang in her heart and suddenly wanted nothing more than to hug Derrick. He was in good hands with Riva's family, but she knew his pain better than anyone. She felt like a coward, hiding from him like this when they should be in it together. She raised her sunglasses to the top of her head and splashed water on her face to chase away the tears.

Kate wasn't gone long. In a few minutes she treaded back into the water, plonked down beside Hazel, and said, "Here's the plan. Those two are going to set up a surprise for you at the motel. They want me to keep you distracted for a while. They're going to pretend they need a nap, so play along. I suggested we'd do some exploring. Then, if we need more time, we'll just be late and I'll pretend I couldn't drag you away. How's that?"

Hazel stared for a moment, then laughed. "You're a sneaky genius."

Kate tipped her head and batted her eyelashes in a coy 'thank you.' Hazel laughed again and swatted water at her.

"So tell me what this boy looks like so I can keep my eye out for him," Kate said.

Adventure shone in her eyes, and Hazel felt a little spark of excitement herself. Later, when they crossed the sand, both Riva and Jen feigned yawns. Kate gave Hazel a knowing side-eye, and Hazel fought to keep a straight face.

***

The two girls went up and down Bellevue Street, then through alleys and parking lots. They tried the streets that the alleys joined and even went into the sandwich shop to ask about the man with a truck. The boy was gone, and their questions earned them confused looks from the staff.

Out on the scalding sidewalk in front of the shop, Kate pulled strands of dark hair off her sweating forehead and said, "I don't think he stuck around. What else do you know about him? Where might he go?"

"There's one thing, but I don't think it helps. Remember when you told me about that band? Mass Migraine? He had their poster in his room." She shrugged. "Otherwise he seemed like a regular kid—a runaway—with a black eye."

"Okay, so where would a little emo kid run away to?"

Hazel shrugged again and sat against the brick lip of a window. "Probably to a friend's house. He'd need somewhere to sleep."

Kate raised an eyebrow. "Like a motel maybe?"

Hazel paused, then shook her head. "Where would he get the money?"

"He could have a part-time job. Or savings. If he was mad enough to run away, he could have stolen it from his parents."

"Hmm," Hazel said. Having grown up without much money to spare, the motel hadn't occurred to her. "You might be onto something."

"How many motels are around here?" Kate asked, looking around at the short office buildings.

Hazel took a long drink from her water bottle before offering it to Kate. "Let's find somewhere shady to look them up."

They crossed the road and trudged around the block to a bench shaded by a young maple tree.

Kate pulled out her phone as she collapsed onto the bench. "Jen texted. She says they should be ready in half an hour."

"That's not enough time," Hazel said, a little too fast.

Kate arched her eyebrows. Hazel felt her cheeks grow even hotter.

She slumped back against the bench and confessed, "I don't want to go back yet. Jen wants me to talk about last year." She hesitated a moment before adding, "You know. The sickness."

Comprehension dawned on Kate's face. Her hands stiffened around her phone, and she and Hazel both stared at it rather than each other.

"Jen told me you lost your family when that all went down," Kate said, her voice low. "I'm really sorry, Hazel."

Hazel nodded and looked across the quiet street at the windowless back of a realtor's office.

"Jen's just trying to help," she said at last. She took a deep, shaky breath. "But I really hate talking about it. I'm tired of even thinking about it. It just makes me feel like—" She waved her hands, struggling to find the right word. "—like shit. I'm tired of feeling like this."

It was Kate's turn to nod.

"It's just, I've never been left behind before," Hazel went on, and her voice cracked. To her dismay, her eyes filled with tears. She seemed destined to cry today. "I've helped so many ghosts leave, but it was never me who they left. I mean, I knew it sucked to lose someone, but I didn't know how bad it hurt. I didn't know it would never stop hurting." The tears spilled over her cheeks.

Kate fished around in her purse and pulled something out. "I don't have any tissues, but you can wipe your eyes on this panty liner if you want."

Hazel stared at the pad in Kate's hands. The corner of Kate's lip quirked up, then both girls burst into laughter. Hazel took Kate up on it and used the liner to wipe her nose. Kate doubled over on the bench.

"Thank you," Hazel said as they sighed together. "I needed that."

They watched a starling land in the maple above them, then Kate said, "You know that friend I mentioned who died when I was six? I talked about her nonstop after I heard the news. For weeks. And eventually everyone got tired of it. They didn't say so, but I could feel it. So I stopped talking about her at all. I know they were hurt too, but ... I just felt so alone."

She met Hazel's eye.

Hazel nodded. "I'm lucky to have Jen and Riva."

"You are," Kate agreed. The bird flew off to join a group of its fellow starlings. "But on the other hand, have you considered *they* might be the ones who need *you* to talk about it?"

Hazel watched the birds twist and swoop together as she thought over Kate's words.

"I'm sorry about your friend," she said after a while, turning back to Kate.

"Thanks," Kate nodded. Then, gently, she added, "I don't think about her much anymore."

Hazel understood. One day, the pain would visit less. It was both a comforting and terrifying thought.

***

They had come up short on their search for the boy at every turn, and it only made sense that they try the motel next. When they had entered under the Okanagan Motel sign, Hazel went straight to the counter to inquire after him.

"Yes, I think I know who you mean," the girl said when Hazel described his black eye. "He checked in early this afternoon." Her fingers hovered over her keyboard. "What's his name?"

Hazel hesitated. Kate stepped up to rescue her.

"My brother," she said, with a long-suffering sigh, "likes to use fake names when we go on vacations. Just to make things difficult. We'll find him, but thanks anyway. Come on, Hazel." She made to leave.

"I think he was on the second floor," the attendant offered, pointing to the same flight of stairs that led to the girls' wing.

Kate smiled. "Thank you."

At the top of the creaky stairs, Hazel jostled Kate with her elbow and whispered, "Sneaky genius."

Kate grinned. "Now what do we do? Go door to door?"

Hazel grimaced at the suggestion. "I'll start knocking on doors; why don't you try the pool?"

Kate agreed and hurried down the hall towards a window overlooking the pool. Hazel ducked around the corner, closed her eyes, and reached for the cord she suspected belonged to the boy. When she found it, she followed it with her mind's eye down the hall she and Riva had relocated to after the spider incident. The cord wound around the corner at the far end. She followed it to a door just two rooms from the corner. She heard a puffing sound and turned as Kate jogged around the corner.

"He's not at the pool," she panted. "You didn't do all these rooms that fast, did you?"

Hazel shook her head and pointed at the door in front of her. "I think he's in there."

Kate flashed Hazel a fascinated expression, then mimed knocking. Hazel swallowed and stepped up to the door, studying the brass number 72 fastened to the wood. She raised her fist, feeling nervous, and knocked three times. Kate bobbed up and down on her heels as footsteps approached from the other side. There was a pause, then the door flew open.

The boy's light brown eyes flashed over Hazel and landed on Kate. He held out something to her without a word.

"Hi," Hazel started. "I'm—"

Kate took whatever was in the boy's hand, and he slammed the door before Hazel could say another word. Hazel mouthed wordlessly for a moment.

"What the hell?" she asked the door, shocked and offended.

Kate unrolled the tiny note in her hands. Hazel leaned in close to read it.

My shadow is watching.

10

Hazel: The Date

It was like all the blood in Hazel's body had stopped pumping. He couldn't mean what she thought he meant. Kate flipped the note over. On the other side was a phone number. She glanced up at Kate, who looked delighted. Hazel ushered her away down the hall.

"What the heck does this mean?" Kate whispered, brandishing the note as they made their way back to their own room. " 'My shadow is watching.' It's like a secret code!"

"I know," Hazel agreed, but her mind was elsewhere.

"But why bother coming to the motel if he isn't going to talk to you face to face?"

"For the bed, I guess," Hazel said, her thoughts not on her own words. She took the note from Kate and studied it.

"You're going to call him, right?" Kate asked.

"Oh yes, of course." That much Hazel was sure about.

Kate grinned. "I can't wait."

They stopped outside their motel room, where Hazel had first seen Lor throwing ice chips at the other girls. Kate held up a hand to prevent Hazel from opening it with her new keycard and knocked instead. There was a flurry of movement inside, then Riva squeezed out into the hallway, keeping her hand on the door handle behind her.

"Hi," Riva said in a voice higher than usual. "How was exploring?"

"Very enlightening," Kate replied.

"Do you mind if I borrow Kate for a minute?" Riva asked Hazel.

"Sure," Hazel said, trying to ignore the barely suppressed smirk on Kate's face.

"See you in a minute," Kate said, throwing Hazel a wink as she and Riva retreated down the hall.

Hazel pushed open the door and stepped into cool air conditioning and soft music. She found Jen standing at the end of the beds. She had pulled a nightstand between the two mattresses to use as a table and had filled the table with take-out containers.

"Surprise!" Jen smiled, gesturing to the meal. Her lips were a bright red, and she wore a pretty sundress for the occasion.

Despite her dread about the coming conversation, Hazel felt a rush of warmth at the sweet lengths she and Riva had gone.

"I can't believe you did this," she said.

Jen beamed and waved Hazel to her seat on the bed. Hazel scraped her knees on the nightstand's drawers but kept her mouth shut as Jen took her place opposite Hazel.

"Riva and Kate are going out for dinner tonight, so we have the place to ourselves for a while," Jen said. "It's finally just the two of us."

Hazel picked out a bottle of cider from amid the containers and raised it for Jen to clink. "It's been too long."

Hazel chatted between mouthfuls, steering to safe topics

while her eye kept drifting to the note hidden in her left hand. The thought of another shadow kept sending chills up and down her arms. When they finished their meal, Jen brought out rich individual brownies for dessert. It was 6:30pm. She had already kept the boy waiting for an hour.

After their first bites, Jen finally dared to broach the topic Hazel had been dreading. "Do you mind if we … talk about your family?"

The brownie went sour in Hazel's mouth. She swallowed with difficulty. "Why don't we just enjoy each other's company and forget about everything else? I've missed you. I've been looking forward to having you to myself again."

A little crease appeared between Jen's eyebrows. "I've missed you too. And I still think you should have been enjoying your own team while I was playing." They had had this conversation about the wrestling team before. Hazel was ready to go with it, but Jen refocused, not to be distracted for long. "But I'm here now. Talk to me. How are you feeling?"

Hazel met Jen's pleading eyes and thought about Kate's words. In a way, Jen had suffered Hazel's loss too. They might suffer more if there was another shadow down the hall.

"I—" Hazel tried. Then she shook her head and shrugged. It was too hard to say anything that wouldn't lapse into a long, painful conversation.

"It's hard to believe it's been a year," Jen supplied.

Hazel nodded and checked the time on her phone. Without thinking she said, "Sometimes that disgusts me."

"What do you mean?"

Another shrug. "I don't know. Time's a bastard. It keeps taking me further away from them."

Jen nodded and waited.

"I miss our house," Hazel said in another attempt to skirt the subject. To her surprise, voicing the thought backfired and brought a solid lump to her throat.

"A lot changed really quick," Jen whispered.

"Don't get me wrong, I love Riva's family," Hazel amended, forcing herself to take another bite, "but it's their home, not mine."

"Maybe ... Maybe we can live together soon," Jen said. At the same time, Hazel checked the time again. Jen paused. "Why do you keep doing that?"

Hazel dropped her phone but wasn't quick enough.

Jen's mouth fell open. "Do you have plans?"

"I didn't mean to make plans," Hazel said quickly. "Someone else sort of ... forced it on me."

Jen stared, her face hardening.

"The boy from the mirror," Hazel went on, speaking fast. "He's here. He gave me a note." Hazel pulled the now crumpled message from her hand and watched Jen's face go pale at the mention of a shadow.

"Don't do it," Jen said at once. "Then he'll have your number! I know it's a bad idea. It's a trick."

"Why would he want to trick me? He doesn't know anything about me."

"He knows exactly where you are and that you can travel through mirrors! And if he knows all that about you, he could know more. I know it seemed like everyone back home was keeping your secret, but maybe something slipped out after all! Maybe he picked at a rumour, found the truth, and decided to use it against you!"

That was a bit rich coming from Jen.

"But why would anyone want to do that?" Hazel asked. "No

one who believes in the Shadow would want to mess with it!"

"Let's go confront him," Jen said, and she jumped up from her spot before Hazel could object.

Alarmed, Hazel scrambled after her, scraping her knees on the nightstand again and cursing at it for slowing her down. By the time she was out of the room, Jen was already marching down the hall with balled fists. Hazel ran to catch up, grabbing Jen's wrist. Jen yanked her hand free and stormed on.

"Which room is it?" she demanded.

"Stop!" Hazel insisted. "You haven't even considered if he's telling the truth!"

"If he's telling the truth, he can convince me himself," Jen replied.

She was getting close to the boy's room. Hazel felt a thrill of panic in her chest. She grabbed Jen's wrist more firmly this time, yanked her around, and pinned her to the wall with her free arm.

"Hazel!" Jen gasped.

"If there's another shadow, I will *not* have you on its radar!" Hazel said.

They glared at each other, Jen's chest rising and falling under Hazel's forearm. After a long moment, Jen finally lowered her gaze.

"Alright. I won't go talk to him. But for all you know, calling him is putting *you* on *its* radar. And maybe *I* won't have that."

Hazel released her. "So what are we supposed to do then?"

They stood there glowering and catching their breath in silence for a minute as other guests entered their rooms.

"Team meeting," Jen said at last. "We call Morgan and Di, and get Riva back here, and we decide together."

Hazel hadn't thought of that. It was a relief to remember she hadn't been the only one trapped in the house with the Shadow last year. Maybe the other girls could offer more insight.

"He's already been waiting a long time," she said. "And what about Kate?"

Jen gave her a look. "I've told you all along we could trust her."

Hazel sighed. "Alright then."

She held out her hand for Jen as a peace offering. Jen took it with a grudging smile, then warned, "I haven't forgotten the moves you showed me last year."

Hazel tried to suppress her smile.

***

Riva and Kate came bursting back into the motel room at ten to seven. Jen was holding her phone aloft to fit both herself and Hazel into the video call. Kate bounced onto the bed behind them.

"Riva filled me in on everything," she said, her eyes full of awe as she looked at Hazel. To the camera she waved and said, "Hi, I'm Kate. What's everyone thinking?"

Morgan gave her a mistrustful, "Hey."

Di, whose sightless blue eyes stared out at them, said with much more warmth, "Hello."

Di had been Kelly's best friend. A certain redness around her eyes when she answered the phone had given Hazel another twinge of guilt.

Riva crawled onto the bed to look over Hazel's shoulder. "Hey, you two." For Di, she added, "It's me, Riva."

"What do you think about this, Riva?" Morgan asked. She had cut her hair since Hazel had last seen her. The black locks were precision-straight and hovering over her collarbones.

"I want to know more," Riva answered. "But honestly? I feel

like the smartest move is to get as far from this kid as possible."

"But he tracked her down," Di argued. Her hair was the opposite of Morgan's, the wild, white curls filling her side of the screen. "He could just find her again."

"I think he needs help," Kate said. "If he's got a black eye, it sounds like he's in trouble."

"Or he is trouble," Jen said.

"He said, 'My shadow is watching,' " Di quoted. "That sounds like he doesn't have it under control. I agree, I think he needs help."

"Or the Shadow's controlling him," Morgan said.

The group sat in indecision.

"Here are our options," Morgan said in her classic, business-like style. She counted them out on her fingers, "Run somewhere safe, go knock on his door, call him ... or use the mirror."

"No mirror!" Jen said at once. "We don't know how dangerous it is."

"But I've done it twice now and it seems fine," Hazel said, intrigued by Morgan's idea. "I could check him out, make sure he's an okay guy."

"We know running would keep everyone safe," Riva pointed out, "but the mirror is still an unknown." The way she chewed her lip suggested she still wasn't sold on running.

"What if he dies without our help?" Hazel asked.

"What if you die?" Morgan returned.

"I don't like any of these options," Di said. A dog barked on her end, and she disappeared for a minute to quiet it down.

"I would like to axe running," Hazel said. "I'm for using the mirror. I've done it twice. What's once more?"

"One minute to seven," Riva said before the room could dissolve in arguments. "How long can we expect him to wait before he shows up as a ghost again?"

Everyone looked towards the door as if he was about to walk through it.

"I want to do the mirror," Hazel said again, standing up. "Let's see what I can find out before we decide what to do. Everyone on board?"

There was a smattering of reluctant assent. Hazel looked at Jen, who shrugged one shoulder to show she didn't like it, but she wouldn't hold Hazel back. Hazel squeezed her hand, then went to the bathroom. The girls followed, Jen propping up her tired phone arm with her opposite hand.

Hazel looked at them all in the mirror behind her and said, "Be right back."

She took a breath like she was about to dive into deep water, then pressed her forehead to the glass, concentrating on the boy. She opened her eyes to the unnatural chill. The boy was standing right in front of her. She yelped in surprise. In his identical bathroom, he jumped too. He wore the same clothes from this morning, but the purple of his eye had started to turn yellow.

He recovered fast, raising a hand in greeting as he leaned towards her, and Hazel saw his mouth form the word, "Hi."

She pointed at her ear and said, "I can't hear you."

His eyes fixed on her hand, then he seemed to shake himself. He held up both hands to request she wait and hurried out the door. Hazel was left to stare at the bathroom. There were no personal items on the counter, not even a toothbrush, but he returned in seconds with a large notepad and a pen. He scribbled something, thought for a moment, then scribbled some more. He held it up for Hazel, who squinted to read the writing.

"I'm Riley. I think I'm possessed. I can only talk when it's sleeping."

Hazel met his eyes and saw the desperation there. She looked him up and down. His clothes were wrinkled and there were dark shadows under both eyes, not just the bruised one. He looked the same age as Kelly was when she had died. Just like that, Hazel's heart went out to him.

She put her hands together and rested her cheek against them like a pillow to ask if the shadow was sleeping now.

Riley nodded, then flipped the page and scribbled some more. Hazel's eyes were freezing. He held up the page again. The message read, "If we text, I can reply whenever it's safe."

Hazel mulled it over. It would be easier to communicate if they used their phones, and his motivation in asking seemed to be for her safety. She gave him a thumbs up. He tucked the notepad under his arm and pressed his palms together, mouthing the words, "Thank you." There were tears in his eyes. Hazel gave him a reassuring smile, then backed out. She felt the now familiar sucking sensation and pushed against it until she was back in her own bathroom, gripping the counter to regain her balance.

"She's back," Riva said to Jen's phone. At the same time, Kate said, "Trippy."

Jen stepped forward with concern, but Hazel, who was getting used to the mirror-travel, felt better than ever.

"I'm fine," Hazel promised. Then she laughed out loud. Their worries seemed silly now. The sound echoed all over the bathroom walls, and the girls looked alarmed. "He was there. He wanted to give me his number to keep me safe from his shadow," she said. "I think he's alright."

She typed the number into her phone without further explanation and sent, "I'm Hazel."

"What's going on?" Di asked into the quiet.

"We couldn't hear each other in the mirror, so I'm texting him," Hazel explained.

Her phone buzzed. Everyone leaned in.

She read aloud, "Hi. Do you know about shadow creatures? Can you help me?"

"Wait," Morgan said before Hazel could text back. "Are you sure you can trust him? What if he's, like, an undercover reporter sent to find out what really happened last year?" At this, her eyes darted to Kate and back. "You could be exposed as a medium—or as crazy, depending on who's reading."

Hazel's mouth opened and closed. That had not occurred to her.

"He's only, like, sixteen," she said at last. "Besides, if it's real and I don't help him, maybe there will be a whole new 'sickness' to write about."

"Ooh, don't even say that," Di said with a shiver.

Hazel read her text aloud as she wrote, " 'I can try. Is it safe to meet now?' Send."

Jen and Riva both gasped.

"Hazel!" Riva said. "What if you're texting with his shadow and it's trying to lure you in?"

Jen folded her arms. "I'll go instead of you. I know about shadows too."

Before Hazel could argue, Riley texted back: "It would be easier in person, but it might be dangerous for you."

Hazel looked up at the others after reading it to them. "He's worried about me," she said. "I told you he seems decent."

"Let's all go meet him," Jen suggested. "Together." When Hazel began to argue, she said, "He says it's sleeping. If that's safe enough for you, it's safe enough for us."

Hazel couldn't think of a good counterpoint to that, and the others were already agreeing.

"Wait," Hazel said. She didn't try to dissuade them. "If he has a shadow, we can't scare him. Let me warn him we're all coming."

Jen was putting on her shoes. "Hurry up then."

11

Riley: Useless

Riley's stay at the motel had not been peaceful so far, and the room reflected it. Hazel had texted back that she was bringing some friends over, so Riley surveyed the mess and rushed to pick up the clothes he had abandoned everywhere.

When he had first arrived, Riley paid for his room in cash, then hurried straight to the room where he had vision-visited Hazel. He knocked with sweating palms only to find a middle-aged woman vacuuming. His disappointment had been crippling.

The second he arrived at his own room, he had collapsed on the bed and counted the dead flies in the light fixture, at a loss about what to do next. In time, he plugged in his phone to see a veritable tsunami of new messages and missed calls from his mom. She knew he wasn't at school. Riley hadn't responded.

Instead, he showered and dressed in the fresh but wrinkled clothes he had been using as a pillow the last few days. He didn't bother to clean up after himself. He lay despondent on top of the covers and listened to his stomach growl. In his hurry to get to the motel, he had skipped breakfast and lunch.

He must have fallen asleep because the sound of the door smashing against the wall made his eyes fly open. His mom burst into the main room, bags under her eyes and her hair a flyaway mess. Riley jerked upright.

"Mom?"

The look she gave him was withering. He shrunk under its glare.

"I'm sorry, I had to—" he began, raising his hands. He wasn't sure if the gesture was to stop her from getting closer or to show her he had no weapons. He stammered his apology like a frightened child.

"How did I get stuck with you?" she interrupted, advancing on him.

The hollow thud her words delivered to his abdomen felt exactly like Aaron's punch to the stomach. The silence that followed seemed to echo louder and louder around the room as she ignored the chance to take it back.

"I don't know why I bothered to worry about you," she said. "But I did. You dragged me all over the province trying to find you, and here you are, lying in bed like a lazy ingrate. I should have known. I should have spared the energy."

Riley's throat had closed up. He couldn't speak.

Her nostrils flared as she stared down at him. "You're a selfish, useless parasite, Riley."

"Mom!" he choked out, wounded. "I had to—"

"I wish they'd killed you and not your father," she whispered.

Riley gasped, and the tears that had been threatening to fall slid down his face. He stared into her eyes, searching for a remorse that wasn't there.

"How can you say that?" His voice was nothing but a rasp.

She brought her face down to his level. "Because it's true."

But there was something wrong with her face. In the seconds their conversation had taken place, it had changed. It was insubstantial, somehow. As Riley stared into her furious eyes, he realized he could see through them to the bland abstract painting on the wall behind her. He raised a hand in front of her face, but she didn't swat it away. She opened her mouth, fuming, but Riley pushed his hand through her nose. It went straight through. She disappeared.

Riley sat there with his hand still raised, his breathing shallow. He searched the silent room, expecting her to reappear at any moment.

"Why did you do that?" he breathed.

The shadow creature didn't respond. Riley retreated to the head of the bed, curling up in a small ball under the blankets, trying to shake away the terrible words.

"Aw," a mocking voice said, ringing through the room. "Is the little man-child sad?"

Riley didn't emerge from the blanket. He covered his ears to block out Aaron's voice, but the taunting continued as loud as ever. It was inside him.

Sophie's voice joined it. "I can't believe you thought I'd like you."

The two went on and on, their voices rising as they yelled insults at him until he couldn't take it anymore.

"shut up!" he roared, throwing the blankets off.

There was triumph in their jeering faces. They had already been fading like his mother, but they shone stronger again at Riley's words. He backed away until he was sitting against the headboard on the opposite side of the bed. They crawled onto the bed towards him like predators creeping through the woods. He slipped off the other side and paced the room, wondering if he should just run. They stalked him from either side, trapping him in front of the TV, evil grins on their faces.

"Get away from me!" Riley yelled, swiping at Aaron.

Riley's fist went through him, just as it had with his mother. Aaron, however, did not disappear. He leaned in close to Riley and whispered in his ear. His mouth made a wet sound that made Riley cringe.

"Useless," he said.

"I am not useless!" Riley shouted, and he stormed right through Aaron.

He seized the TV remote off the dresser and threw it at the bed. It flew into the air and broke apart on the floor, the batteries spilling out. He hadn't meant to do it, but it was satisfying to see them rolling away. He could feel pressure on his ears, like he was too far underwater, the anger coursing through him.

Someone knocked on the wall from the room next door to tell him to be quiet. He seized his backpack and threw it through Sophie. It spewed its contents through the air and hit the wall behind her. He seized a pillow and punched it with his right fist, over and over. Then he slipped down to the floor, covering his face with his hands. He wanted to scream into the pillow.

"All tuckered out after that nice temper tantrum?" said Aaron's voice.

Riley didn't open his fingers. He knew Aaron was right in front of his face. He could feel his presence like a shadow standing over him.

"Guess who's next door?" Aaron whispered.

Riley clenched his teeth and tried to ignore him.

"You're in luck. Who else would bang on the wall at a time like this? Come and tell me off," he cajoled. His words spilled over Riley, faster and faster. "You can hit me in person. I'll never see it coming, I would never expect you to show up here. Come on, I deserve it. Get back at me. Give me a black eye to match yours. Show me you're not such a useless coward."

Riley's fingers had parted without his noticing. Aaron smiled and vanished. Riley could feel his presence on the other side of the wall. He got to his feet.

"You owe me," Sophie said, and blood poured from her lip, far too much blood for such a little cut. "Hit him for me. Look what he did. Hit him for me, Riley. You owe me!"

Riley went to the door. A mixture of excitement and anger was churning in his stomach. This was his chance. He grasped the cold metal handle. The sensation made Riley freeze. There was no way Aaron was next door, yet he could sense him there, and he yearned to hit him.

"No," he said out loud.

Shaken by how far he had gone, Riley turned around. Sophie was in his face, and his remaining anger turned to horror. Blood was pouring from her mouth now, and her face twisted in an expression of bloodlust. He threw up his hands to fend her off, but then she was gone.

Riley stood in the doorway for a long time. He couldn't seem to process what had happened, as if his last few days had been too full to take in any more. The shadows grew longer on the beige carpet. He was in shock. His feet were hurting, but he felt too weak with hunger to make it to the bed, and he found he didn't care. He sat down on the carpet and stared at the bathroom linoleum.

He thought of the girl again, and a faint blue glow responded. The cord at his chest had appeared, a blue light moving along its length towards him, like water flowing down a river. He watched it, hypnotized, until realization snapped him back to reality. The girl was coming towards him. She was coming back.

He pushed himself to his feet, hope returning in a rush. If he met the girl soon, the creature might never know about it. But it could also wake up. He needed to plan for all possibilities.

Riley rifled through the drawers of the dresser, then the nightstand. In the nightstand's top drawer were a notepad and pen. He would write her a note, now, while the creature was down, then he could give it to her folded up if it was watching. He held the pen at the ready, but no words came to him that could cover what had happened to him, or what he hoped she could do about it.

He decided to start with the warning, so he jotted that down at the bottom of the page and tore it out of the notepad before the creature could see. Then common sense told him a warning wouldn't be enough. He couldn't just show up at her door and tell her to stay away. That would defeat the whole purpose. He flipped it over and scribbled his phone number.

There was a knock on his door. A brief flare of fear and annoyance sparked enough to get the shadow stirring. Riley couldn't afford a noise complaint, much as he deserved one. He squeezed the unfinished note in one hand and hurried to open it.

He took a sharp breath as the warmth of the hallway wafted into the room. It was the girl, looking as healthy as when he had visited her on the bus. Beside her stood a black-haired girl Riley had never seen before. He couldn't let the shadow know the first girl was special, so he fixed his eyes on the second. He took a chance that they could trust her and held out the note. Her eyebrows rose in surprise as she took it.

"Hi," the girl from the mirror started. "I'm—"

Riley slammed the door before the shadow could take in any more. With the door between them, Riley cringed. He'd be lucky if she gave him the time of day after such a rude meeting.

"What the hell?" he heard from the hallway.

He listened with an ear pressed to the door. The two girls didn't speak again, but he heard their footsteps retreating. He leaned against the door, chewing the inside of his cheek. He still needed to convince the creature that everything was fine, so Riley strolled over to the bed and turned on the TV.

His eyes had jumped to the bedside clock every few minutes for the next hour. By the time 7:00pm approached, the shadow had settled back down. Trying to keep his nerves under control, Riley forced himself to pay attention to the TV. He checked his phone to make sure it was working for the thousandth time. There were no messages apart from his mom's. He had blown his chance.

Then Riley went to the bathroom. As he flicked on the light, the girl suddenly pushed through his reflection, like his was nothing more solid than a ghost. He jumped in shock. Her skin was green again. Still, if this was as close as she was willing to get to communicate, he would take it.

Breathless, Riley raised an awkward hand as he said, "Hi."

She pointed at her ear and mouthed, "I can't hear you."

Her hand was trailing shadow again. He forced himself to ignore it. He begged with his hands for her to stay and ran to get his notepad.

Now the room was tidy again, and Riley was wiping his sweating palms on his shorts and pacing by the door. The knock came at last. Riley jerked the door open before the knock was even finished.

"Hi," he said.

The pale, black-haired girl was there at Hazel's shoulder. There was also a black girl with rows of thick braids and a tan, purple-haired girl holding a phone aloft with two more faces on its screen.

"Are you recording ...," he asked.

"No, no," Hazel reassured him. "These are my friends. They all know about shadows and want to help."

Riley stared at them for too long, stunned. He didn't know whether to shut the door or cry with relief.

"Can we come in?" Hazel took pity on him.

He nodded and stepped back. The group of girls trooped in. As they passed, Riley noticed they were all taller than him. In fact, he was probably the youngest in the room. They each found themselves a spot to stand around the double bed and turned to face him. Riley's cheeks grew hot.

When he still didn't speak, Hazel took the initiative and introduced everyone. Riley nodded at every introduction until he felt like a bobble head. When she finished, they all looked at him expectantly.

"I–I don't know where to start," he stammered.

"You said you have a shadow," Hazel said.

Riley swallowed. "It came from this well in the forest behind my house."

The girls exchanged looks.

"It came from a well?" the purple-haired girl, Jen, repeated.

"Yeah," Riley said. "It attacked me."

By the disturbed looks on their faces, Riley could tell this was not typical. "Is that so weird? I mean, I know it's weird but ... ?"

Hazel answered. "My Shadow initially attached itself to my grandmother. She never said anything about being attacked. I don't think she knew at all." She threw him a sharp look. "Can you see ghosts?"

He blinked, caught off guard. "Y-yeah," he admitted.

"Me too," she said.

They locked eyes, and it was like a bolt of shared loneliness and understanding passed between them. Riley had never met anyone like him before.

"Alright, well don't fall in love," Jen said, crossing her arms.

Hazel chuckled and nudged Jen with her elbow. Riley cracked an embarrassed smile and wished his cheeks would stop going red.

"Well," Hazel said, "this changes things. This means your shadow didn't latch onto you to wait for someone better to come along. My Shadow wanted me because I can see ghosts."

Riley nodded. "I can see why."

That gave Hazel pause. "What do you mean?"

He rubbed his arm. "Any time a ghost gets near me, the thing—the shadow—sort of grabs them with a-a sort of rope and reels them in. I don't know what happens after that. I don't see them again. But they ..." He cleared his throat. "They don't seem to like it."

He couldn't make eye contact. He was sure they were as revolted by him as he felt.

"So it doesn't need any corrupt," Riva said. "It's just going straight for ghosts."

"What's corrupt?" Kate, the black-haired girl, asked. It appeared Riley wasn't the only one learning about Hazel's Shadow today.

"The Shadow we know," Hazel explained, "killed my grand-mother and turned her into ... well, a zombie. A corrupted body. Anyway, her body killed more people and brought their souls—

their ghosts—back to it. But it wanted me because ghosts find me."

Kate's eyes were round and awed. Riley felt light-headed.

"It's going to turn me into a zombie?"

"No, no," Hazel reassured him. He must have looked pale because she got up and grabbed his elbow. "Are you alright?"

When he shrugged, she led him to the bed, where he sat and put his head between his knees. The girls shifted in the room around him, and then one pressed a glass of water into his hand.

"Thanks," he said. He drank it all at once. "I'm not weak," he assured them. "I'm just really hungry."

"We have food," Jen said.

"When's the last time you ate?" Riva asked.

The concern in her voice calmed Riley. "Yesterday."

"I'll take care of it," Jen said, more to Hazel than anyone else. She handed her phone to Kate and left the room.

"So," Riley went on, struggling to connect all the dots, "why won't it change me into a zombie?"

"Because of your ability. It can get ghosts straight from you, as you are. It doesn't need corrupt."

"So ..."

"So now we have to figure out what to do about it. The part I'm getting stuck on," Hazel said, leaning against the wall in front of him, "is what kind of possession this is. Is it possessing you, or are you possessing it? Because the way it attacked you isn't something I've heard of."

The girls were all nodding their heads in agreement.

"Tell us more about this well."

Riley, keeping all emotion out of his voice, explained about his dad's death and how the creature had lured him over to the well. When he looked up, the girls' faces registered various shades of horror and repulsion.

"But it lured you, and you went," Hazel pointed out.

Riley opened his mouth to justify himself, feeling stupid for falling for the trick, but Jen returned then. She held out a brownie on a napkin for Riley.

"This should bring your sugar level back up," she told him.

Riley's mouth watered as he bit into the rich chocolate. It was the best brownie he had ever eaten, and it was gone too fast. Then Jen handed him a takeout box.

"Dessert," she joked. "It's leftovers, but it's something."

He thanked her between mouthfuls.

"You know," Jen said when he had finished, "it's probably harder to control this thing when you're this hungry."

Riley swallowed. "I hadn't thought of that. You really think I can control it, though?"

"That's what I was getting to," Hazel said. "It sounds like it possessed you. But my Shadow ... It tormented me, but it never possessed me until I let it. I figured that was a sort of rule it had to live by." She paused. "What exactly did yours say to you?"

Riley wanted to ask what on earth she meant by 'let it' possess her. If he had a choice, he would have run the other way, and so would any sane person. He answered her question first, though the words stuck in his throat.

"It called my name. It sounded a lot like my dad. He asked me why I left him. And he said, 'Come back.' "

"Hmm," Hazel said. "So maybe when your shadow tricked you into thinking it needed you in the well, you going counted."

Hazel looked around at the others for input. Jen and Kate nodded, Riva shrugged, and Morgan said, "I guess."

"But it sounded like your dad?" Di asked. "How did it do that?"

It was Riley's turn to shrug.

"Do you think …," Di started, then stopped.

"What?" Hazel pressed.

Di grimaced on the screen. "Do you think it was your dad? Maybe what happened to him was so traumatic …"

There was a disturbed silence. Riley's immediate reaction was to reject the idea. His dad would never torment him the way this creature had. Yet, his dad had also never shown up as a ghost. If he had thought the bastards who murdered his dad were low before, the idea of their actions twisting Liam beyond recognition made Riley's stomach burn with rage.

He gasped in alarm. The shadow was waking. He couldn't let it see the girls. Riley did the only thing he could think of: he stuck his fingers in his ears, shut his eyes, and buried his face in his lap.

There was silence around him. He knew he must look ridiculous, deranged even, but he prayed they wouldn't speak. He tried to focus all his attention on the sound of his own blood pumping in his ears, but there were no muffled voices around him. No one asked what he was doing. A drip of sweat ran down his forehead. He could feel his own breath warming his face. Long minutes passed, and still he stayed there with his forehead pressed to his knees.

12

Hazel: Run

Hazel watched Riley's expression change. The idea of his dad becoming a shadow sent grief, anger, and rage flickering across his face in quick succession. When he buried his face in his lap, he did it so suddenly that Hazel jumped a little.

By the looks of consternation on the other girls' faces, she knew they were about to ask questions. Hazel waylaid them by waving her hands in a downward, hushing gesture. She knew an episode when she saw one. She mimed for Jen to hang up the phone on Di before she could ask why they were so quiet. They could apologize over text later.

They stood frozen for several minutes, communicating only with raised eyebrows and creeped-out looks. When this had gone on long enough, they crept to the other side of the bed and sat down without making a sound. Kate, Riva, and Jen's phones made their way into their hands, though their eyes kept darting back to Riley.

Hazel kept her eyes fixed on him. His breathing was shallow, and his hands were shaking. When, at long last, Riley breathed a sigh of relief and let his arms fall, Hazel was there to meet his eye. What with the anxiety in his expression and the bruise under his eye, he looked like he had been through a zombie apocalypse himself. Hazel waited for him to speak.

"I'm sorry," he said, and although his voice came out low and weak, Jen shrieked, having not noticed his return.

Her reaction made Riva and Kate jump, which made Hazel chuckle. Riley wasn't laughing. He stood up and paced before the bed, his shoulders slumped like he was carrying more than his own weight.

"What happened?" Hazel asked.

"I could feel it waking up," Riley said, "and I couldn't let it see you."

Hazel nodded. "I figured."

The other girls set their phones back down and leaned forward. Jen video-called Di and Morgan and lifted the phone into the air again.

Riva hesitantly raised the question that had halted them. "So, Di, you think what happened to Riley's dad ... resulted in the shadow's birth?"

"Maybe," Di said. "We know shadows feed on fear, and Riley's dad must have been ... scared."

Riley frowned. "My dad could speak though," he said, with the air of someone struggling to make sense of the incomprehensible. "I-I feel like this thing is learning to speak. At least, at first it was. It speaks okay now. ..."

"Is it learning from you?" Morgan asked. "Does it read your mind?"

Riley explained the conversation he had engaged in with the shadow in an orchard. He explained how he had tested the shadow to see if it knew where he was headed. It hadn't.

"Well," Morgan said, "at least we know your thoughts are

safe."

"But," Riley went on before she could get too excited, "I think it's learning from the ghosts. I think they make it smarter. And they give it enough power to mess with me."

"Mess with you how?" Morgan asked, eyes narrowing.

He told them about having visions this afternoon, visions that goaded him into almost attacking his neighbour.

"I don't understand," Hazel said. She had stood up without realizing it and was now pressing her back against the cool wall. The room was warming up with so many people inside. "It tried to make you angry? It didn't try to scare you?"

"Well, I mean, it was scary," Riley said. "But it always shows up when I'm mad, yeah."

Hazel looked around at the other girls, all of them dumb-struck.

"An anger-shadow," Di whispered.

Morgan recovered first. "Well, it's different. But ultimately, can't he starve it of anger the way you starve yours of fear, Hazel?"

They all looked at her.

"I don't know," Hazel said. "Some of it was luck. The Shadow had used up a lot of its power when I took it, and that might have given me an advantage."

"But his shadow was in a well," Riva said with a glance at Riley for support. "What can it feed on in a well? It had to be weak too."

Riley shifted and didn't meet her eyes. "My mom went there sometimes ... When she was angry about it all. She kicked in the front of the well once."

Riva made a face. "Okay, that sounds bad, but it didn't latch onto her, so maybe that doesn't mean anything."

"Or maybe she helped make it," Riley said. He swallowed. "It's just … my dad would have been scared when i-it happened. Not angry. But my mom …" He cleared his throat, but his voice still sounded constricted when he continued. "The shadow said, 'Don't leave me,' and, 'Come back,' when it called me. It had to learn that from her."

A profound silence followed. Hazel's heart ached for both Riley and his mother.

Di broke the silence. "I'm so sorry for your loss, Riley."

He nodded and stared at the floor.

Riva didn't disguise the sadness in her voice when she said, "Maybe it's a violent death and a violent emotion that creates them."

"That's all very interesting," said Morgan, then, almost as an afterthought she added, "and awful. But let's give him some practical tools here. Let's just say what works for Hazel will work for him. What does he need to know, Hazel?"

***

Hazel sat on the bed facing Riley for close to an hour. He asked questions about her Shadow, and she told him all about her favourite strategies to stay calm. The question they struggled to answer was how to keep his shadow from making meals of ghosts. In the end, they decided to sleep on that one. Riley gave Hazel his spare room-card in case of emergency, then they parted for the night.

"The thing is," Hazel said as she set the keycard down on her own dresser and prepared for bed, "my Shadow has never gone after ghosts like his. Am I stopping it somehow? I mean, Kelly said I protected her from it."

"Maybe it's part of your abilities," Riva said. She was already lying in the bed she was sharing with Kate. "But if that's the case, maybe you can protect ghosts from Riley's shadow just by being around."

Hazel climbed into her own bed. "So ... should I stay here with him?"

Riva was quiet. Hazel knew her house was too full to come home with a runaway. She settled into her blankets.

When Jen joined her after brushing her teeth, Hazel said, "I think we need to stay another night."

Riva and Jen exchanged a look.

"We didn't budget for that."

"I'll get it," Hazel offered.

It was only fair after they had covered tonight for Hazel. Hazel had inherited a small amount of money after her mom's death that she could dip into. She usually avoided spending it so she could ease the cost of university, but this seemed like a good exception.

"I'll chip in," Kate said. "I'd like to stay too. If that's okay?"

Riva, Kate, and Jen discussed rearranging their schedules so they could stay longer. Hazel closed her eyes, relieved to avoid the memorials for another day.

"Have you considered," Kate asked with a yawn, "just warning ghosts to stay away?"

Hazel was about to laugh, but then she frowned. "I actually haven't seen any ghosts since last night."

Kate sat upright, amazed. "Do you usually see so many?"

"Well, yeah," Hazel smiled. "People die all the time."

Kate thumped back onto her pillows, wide-eyed. Jen slipped her hand into Hazel's, smiling too. It was too hot to get any closer, but Hazel relished feeling those slender fingers wrapped around her own. The girls fell asleep one by one, but Hazel continued to stare at the ceiling for hours.

When 2:00am came and went, Hazel grabbed her phone. Burrowing under her blanket to shield the others from the light, she checked to see if she had received a text from Riley. There was nothing, but that didn't ease her worries. The heat under the cover grew with her indecision until Hazel had to throw off the blankets. She crept to the bathroom to check on him through the mirror. If nothing else, she always seemed to feel better after mirror-travel. Maybe it would help her sleep.

Her hesitations long gone, Hazel pushed into Riley's mirror. His bathroom was dark, but the lights were on in the main room beyond. There was a flicker of movement in the hall. Riley passed the bathroom on his way to the front door, staring at his phone, then returned, pacing up and down. He was still dressed apart from his bare feet. He slipped the phone into this pocket, but the agitated pacing didn't stop.

On his fifth pass, Riley saw her wave at him. His unfocused eyes bulged, and a spasm passed over his face. Hazel recoiled. Then a shadow seemed to burst from him, engulfing his whole body. The face was twisted in a mute scream of rage. Hazel screamed too, but the shadow jerked back into Riley then, like it had reached the end of a tether. Riley charged the mirror with a snarl. Hazel wrenched back as his fingers scrabbled the glass.

She fell to the floor in her own bathroom, gasping. She pushed through the usual dizziness and leapt to her feet. Riley was losing his battle against his shadow. Panic rose in Hazel's chest. She had offered him all the advice she could, and it had not lasted more than a few hours.

She shook Jen awake.

"Mmm?" Jen groaned.

"Something's wrong with Riley," Hazel said.   She

didn't bother to keep her voice down. "The shadow—his shadow—it's getting to him. We have to help him."

Jen sat up, rubbing her face with both hands. "What? Help who?"

Hazel pulled her out of bed and rushed her to the door. "Hurry!"

She grabbed Riley's room key, jammed her feet into her shoes, and threw open the door, leaving Jen to scramble after her. She bolted down the hallway and stopped outside Riley's room, where she pressed her ear to the door. Just as Jen arrived beside her, there was the sound of glass smashing inside. She and Jen exchanged a frightened look and Hazel stuffed the keycard into the lock.

She opened the door a crack. There was a scream of frustration from the bathroom. Hazel looked at Jen again. Her face had gone pale and Hazel cursed herself for not going alone. It was too late now. She tiptoed into the room with Jen at her heels.

Keeping out of sight, Hazel peered around the bathroom door. The floor, counter, and sink all sparkled with broken glass. Riley was kneeling in the shards, his breath ragged and his hands streaming blood.

She swallowed and stepped forward. In a low voice, she said, "It's okay, Riley. Keep breath—"

Riley whipped around and was on his feet in a split second, howling and brandishing a large chunk of broken mirror. Hazel tripped over Jen in her haste to back away. Jen dragged her into the motel hallway, narrowly missing his vicious swipes. Hazel yanked the door shut, catching Riley's arm so that he dropped the glass. He shoved the door aside.

"Run," Jen said.

They bolted down the hallway, their footsteps loud enough to wake anyone who hadn't already heard the glass shatter.

"He's going to kill us!" Jen cried.

Hazel chanced a glance over her shoulder to see Riley pick up the glass and charge after them.

Ahead, Riva and Kate's heads were popping out of their room. Hazel waved at them to get back inside. Soon, more guests would come out into the hall to see what was going on. Hazel had to get Riley out of here.

As they reached the room, Hazel shoved Jen inside and said, "Bring the car around."

She ran straight past, leaving Jen no time to argue. Riley stayed on Hazel's trail, so close his next swipe with the shard of glass narrowly missed.

Hazel took a corner and slammed open the upper door to the pool courtyard. Riley just managed to slip through the door before it closed, but Hazel was already racing down the metal steps. The night air threw Hazel's hair back as the stairs rattled under her. She leapt down the last few. Riley copied her.

Hazel ran around the outside of the pool, which glowed green in the moonlight. She could hear Riley's bare feet slapping the ground, but his grunting breath was more alarming. He tore across the courtyard after her, still clutching a shard of glass, which stabbed at the air with each pump of his arms.

Ahead there was an open tunnel through the motel that led to an outside gate, and Hazel steered that way. Her adrenaline spiked as her eyes adjusted to the dark tunnel and she saw the dead end. A gate was blocking her exit.

She was still holding Riley's keycard. As she shoved the card into the slot, Riley's swinging glass nicked the back of her right arm. Pained seared across her skin, but a light on the top of the lock flashed green. She shoved through the heavy black gate and swung it shut behind her as hard as she could. Already halfway through the gate, Riley cried out in pain.

Hazel didn't stop. She swerved around cars in the parking lot, trying to put something between them, but he was too fast. She made for the deserted road, leaping over a tidy row of bushes that separated the motel parking lot from the main road. Hazel turned in the opposite direction of the little town. She had to keep him away from other people.

Out of the lamp-lit parking lot, it was dark. The road blended into shadows and Hazel didn't know if she was about to roll her ankles in potholes or meet a flat surface. Yet she was on an open road, and a touch of confidence came back to her. She used to love running. Her lungs might already be burning, and her calves were protesting, but a tiny part of Hazel calmed. Riley was falling behind, just a little, in his bare feet.

A short distance down the road, a forest started on their left. Hazel kept running straight, willing Jen to drive by with the car. At last she heard the squeal of tires in the distance, then the roar of acceleration as the SUV came flying after them. She threw a glance over her shoulder and realized Riley was squarely between the headlamps. She gasped.

Hazel darted into the trees, and Riley plunged after her. She didn't know how to stop him, but hitting him with a car couldn't be the answer. If she could just get the glass out of his hand, Hazel was sure she could rely on her wrestling skills to do the rest.

The forest floor was a tangle of brambles and twigs that grabbed her shoelaces as she ran. Behind her, Riley roared with frustration. She led him into a thicket that scratched at her legs, then heard a whistling sound. Something zinged past her ear. Riley had whipped the glass at her. Immediately, Hazel turned around, ready to face him.

He lunged, teeth bared like he meant to bite her, but Hazel ducked under his arm. She stumbled over the trampled blackberry bushes. Riley lunged again and Hazel backed towards the trees, where the ground was clearer. A crashing sound in the distance told her someone was struggling through the forest after them.

She braced herself with one leg forward as Riley lunged a third time. Seizing one of his bloody wrists, she yanked it past her body and down. She had pulled him off balance, and he tumbled face first into the dirt and pine needles. He snarled, flipped around, and snatched at her legs, forcing Hazel to abandon the idea of pinning him. She skipped out of reach but took a second too long to calculate her next move. He was back on his feet.

She cleared her head. This wasn't a high school match, where they might take a second to study each other before acting. A clawed hand swiped at her face, and Hazel knocked it aside, relying on muscle memory and instinct. She closed the gap between them and grabbed both his shoulders. His hands naturally sprang up to grab her arms in return, but Riley grabbed with his nails, and Hazel cried out as he scraped her bare skin.

His snarling face was far too close. She ducked under his left arm, crouching at his ankle. It caught him off-guard. He clawed at her back with his left hand. In the same swift move, Hazel seized his ankle and stood up, slamming her shoulder into his chest. The shove pushed him back enough that he was off balance, the end of his leg firmly in Hazel's arms. As fast as she could, Hazel hooked her own foot around Riley's standing leg and swept it out from under him. His back slammed to the dirt floor.

Hazel heard the air leave his lungs. At the same time, Jen arrived with Riva and Kate, all still wearing their pajamas. She heard Kate's impressed swear but didn't have time to acknowledge it. She needed to pin Riley on his stomach to stop him tearing at her. It was time to break the rules.

She dragged Riley by the ankle she still gripped in her arms. He twisted over in an attempt to get up, planting his forearms on the ground. Hazel flattened him then, weaving her arms through the gap under his armpits and locking her hands against the back of his neck. The air left him again as she splayed her elbows, taking out his arms so that his chest hit the ground, holding him in an illegal full nelson.

His legs scrambled for purchase, but Hazel wound her own legs around one of them, locking her ankles. He squirmed against her, his free leg flailing to no avail. He was trapped. Hazel held firm, even with her muscles burning. If she was breathing hard, Riley was struggling to breathe at all, and Hazel wondered if it would be for the best if he passed out.

"What can we do?" Jen asked, twigs crackling under her feet as she danced closer.

"Just wait," Hazel grunted.

She pressed a little harder against Riley's chest, careful not to add pressure to his neck. The last of his breath hissed out like a deflating tire, and his waving leg slowed to a feeble wriggle. Hazel immediately backed off. Riley slumped against the dirt. She put a hand under his nose to make sure he hadn't stopped breathing altogether. She wiped her brow with relief when a puff of warm air met her hand.

Hazel pushed herself into a sitting position and brushed pine needles from her knees. She accidentally smeared them in blood.

"I think we should tie him," she panted.

"I'll check the car," Kate said, and she ran back the way they had come.

"Are you alright?" Jen and Riva asked together.

Hazel nodded and looked down at her hands. "This is his," she said. His hands were in rough shape. Then she remembered Riley had sliced her arm. "How bad is this?"

She raised her arm for them to inspect and saw the little rivers of blood Riley's fingernails had made on the sides.

Riva moved closer to see in the dark. "Not great, but not deep. It all needs cleaning."

Hazel nodded, still catching her breath.

"I think there's an emergency kit in the car," Jen said. She called for Kate to please bring it with her.

Her voice echoed through the trees, and Hazel cringed. They couldn't afford to get caught in the woods with an unconscious teenager. Then Jen knelt in front of Hazel and squeezed her hand. Hazel tried to reassure her with an exhausted smile.

Riva made to turn Riley over, but Hazel stopped her. "He's easier to subdue if he's like that."

"He was really scary," Jen said, her voice low, as if Riley might hear. "He's going to end up in jail, or locked in a psych ward."

"He wasn't himself," Hazel reminded her.

"I know," Jen said, "but if we can't help him, that's his future."

Hazel watched Riley's ribs expand and contract with his breaths. He had come to her for help, but she didn't know how to help him.

They waited in silence as the distant car door slammed and Kate hurried back through the woods.

"I found this," she panted, holding up a soft blanket. "What do you think? Is it okay to cut it for ties?"

Riva shrugged. Kate tossed Jen the canvas emergency kit. She and Riva used a tiny pair of medical scissors to start tears in the blanket. Jen found little packets of wet napkins soaked in rubbing alcohol and used these to clean Hazel's cut and scratches. Hazel scrunched up her face at each sting.

"Cut one for his mouth too," Hazel said as they bound Riley's hands, feet, and thighs, while Jen applied bandages to the worst of Hazel's wounds. "He tried to bite me earlier."

She felt Jen's hands fumble and remembered how the corrupt had bit Jen in their mad dash from the high school.

"This is different," Hazel whispered.

Jen didn't reply until she had finished cleaning up Hazel. Then she said, "We better clean him up too."

Riley's fingers were sliced so bad Hazel worried they wouldn't heal without a trip to the hospital. His hands required the rest of the alcohol wipes, and Jen resorted to wiping down his feet with the extra pieces of blanket. When she stood back, all four of them looked down at Riley, at a loss for what to do next.

"I don't think we can go back to the motel," Jen said. "I'm sure someone called the police. I bet they think Riley abandoned the room."

"We have to get our stuff and check out though," Riva said. "Two of us can stay with him in the car."

"We can't do that in the middle of the night," Hazel said.

"We can't go back in broad daylight, when more people are around to see this maniac," Riva returned.

When no one offered any more suggestions, Kate said, "So ... are we camping tonight?"

In the end, they decided to sleep in the car. Jen and Kate carried Riley to the road, Jen at his head and Kate at his feet. Hazel and Riva tried to shield his body in case of other cars. The awkward way Jen and Kate were shuffling along was a dead giveaway that something was off.

Riva opened the back hatch and they lifted Riley into the trunk. Then they stood there and stared at him for a long time. No one wanted to shut the door on him. Hazel shivered. She couldn't help feeling like a criminal.

Eventually, Riva hid Riley under her other blanket, and Hazel shut the trunk.

"I don't know if I can sleep with him back there," Jen said as she and Hazel climbed into the back seat. Only the bench separated them from Riley.

Hazel saw Kate's eyes dart to the rearview mirror and away. Kate was unlikely to sleep tonight too. Hazel, on the other hand, remembered last year. She had learned to seize sleep whenever she could. But one thing was better than last year.

"Come here," she said to Jen, holding out her arms.

Jen tipped into Hazel's embrace, pulling her feet up onto the seat. Hazel tucked Jen's hair behind her ear and felt her breathing even out. She watched her eyelids flutter for a few minutes until they finally closed. Hazel leaned against the leather headrest. After a while her head nodded, and she fell asleep too.

13

Hazel: The River

The sky was turning a watery blue, and a gold tinge hovered behind the mountains encircling the town. Riva slipped around the side of the motel to the pool entrance. In the front seat of the car, Kate's head was nodding as she snoozed on and off, unable to keep her eyes open for more than a few minutes at a time. Hazel hadn't slept much either. Jen's warmth had been the only saving grace. Of the four girls, Jen had fared the best, and she was now watching Riva disappear with semi-alert eyes.

Hazel shifted around in her seat to check that Riley was still covered by the blanket. When they had checked on him first thing this morning, his face had been so pale that Hazel worried he had bled out. Checking the bandages on his hands, they had discovered that they were indeed red with blood, but agreed it was not life threatening. In any case, he wasn't going to walk into the motel on his own for a while.

Hazel ran a hand over her face. Riva was making sure the coast was clear and booking another night. Hazel couldn't wait for Riley to wake up so she could go up to bed, but she dreaded finding out who he would be when he did. She dozed off for another fifteen minutes and awoke when the driver's door opened and Riva climbed back in. She had changed out of her pajamas and now wore jean shorts, a t-shirt, and a zip-up sweater.

"How'd it go?" Jen asked before the door had even closed.

"I got us another night," Riva told her. "And I asked if they ever figured out what that noise was last night—"

Jen gasped. "You asked about it?"

"Relax. They apologized for disturbing me. Said someone broke a mirror and ran off so they wouldn't have to pay for it."

Jen breathed a sigh of relief and slumped back against her seat. "That's good."

"I don't think that was the whole story, though," Riva went on, twisting around in the driver's seat so she could see them. "Riley left all his stuff in there. That's suspicious. I'm sure the motel got the police involved, and they'll search his ID. They'll find out he ran away."

"Plus, there was blood on the floor," Hazel chipped in.

It occurred to her that Riley's mother would hear this detail, and she felt a surge of pity for the woman. Then her stomach lurched. She couldn't think about mothers today.

"I threw some of your clothes in here," Riva said, hefting a backpack onto the middle seat. "I didn't think we should draw attention to ourselves."

It was a struggle to maintain privacy and dress within the confines of the car, but they managed it with a few bumped heads and elbows.

"What should we do now?" Hazel asked, panting a little from the effort.

Riva had an answer for that too. "Find a private spot by the river. Somewhere we can keep the car close for when he wakes up. Then we can wash the blood off that blanket."

Before the river, they dropped Jen off at a breakfast place while Riva circled the block. They thought it was best to keep the car moving so no one noticed Riley. Then they started down the winding road beside the river. They were on the road for forty minutes before they discovered a single-lane dirt road through the trees. It led straight towards the rocky riverbed.

As they left the main road behind, the sun streamed through the birch branches in the early morning light. The car shook and rattled over the dips and rocks. There was a groan from the trunk. Hazel whipped around and craned to see over the seat. The blanket had fallen off Riley's face, and though his eyes were still shut, he was frowning. She and Jen exchanged a look but didn't speak.

When the car came to a stop within walking distance of the river, Kate and Riva unbuckled their seatbelts and grabbed their coffees.

"What's the matter?" Kate asked when she realized Jen and Hazel weren't moving.

Hazel put a finger to her lips. Both girls froze when Hazel pointed over the rear seat. There, Riley was opening bleary eyes and staring around the trunk, a frown creasing his brow. His confusion convinced Hazel.

"Good morning," she said with a subdued smile.

Riley squinted up at her through his good eye, the other one closed against the light. A strip of blanket still covered his mouth to stop him from biting anyone.

"Hazel?" he croaked through it.

She reached out to pull the cloth down, repressing the fear that he might bite her. By the wary look in his eyes, he clearly thought she might do the same.

"How are you feeling?" she asked.

Riley shifted as if checking but didn't answer. He looked up at her with that same guarded expression. "Why are my hands tied?"

Two and two came together. Riley didn't remember last night. Hazel hastened to explain why he had woken tied up in the trunk of a car. Horror and guilt crossed his face, and he looked so pitiful huddled in the trunk of the car that Hazel climbed out to go open the trunk.

"Promise you won't attack me?" she asked through the window.

Riley nodded, but Jen, who had followed, whispered, "Are you sure that's a good idea?"

Hazel hesitated with her hand on the latch, then said, "We won't leave him alone. We can keep an eye out for signs of the shadow and help this time. It's what we should have done last night."

She untied Riley's feet, and he shifted around so she could free his hands. When he saw the state of his fingers, his jaw dropped.

"You smashed your bathroom mirror," Hazel said sympathetically.

He looked up at her as if seeing her from a distance and said, "You were in the mirror."

Hazel nodded. Jen looked sideways at her, and Riva and Kate said, "You were?"

"I told you something was wrong over there," she replied, trying to shrug off Jen's accusing glare.

Riley was still holding his hands out as if they were bombs about to go off.

"I saw you," he said, and Hazel didn't like how his voice had gone down to a whisper.

"I know. You attacked me."

Riley shook his head. He wet his lips and started over, "My shadow … saw your Shadow."

Hazel frowned.

"I saw it before too. But this time my shadow was there."

"You saw my Shadow?"

Riley nodded. "Around your hand. And you looked dead."

Hazel stared at him, disturbed by this new detail. "I looked dead?"

Riley nodded again. Jen smacked Hazel's arm in a wordless 'I-told-you-so.'

"But last night it wasn't just on your hand, it was all over you," Riley said, his eyes still unfocused with the memory. "I could see it because … my shadow was awake this time. I-it was furious. It wanted to murder you."

"It had a good try," Hazel said with a wry smile.

"I'm so sorry," Riley said.

The sincerity in his eyes made Hazel's insides twist with guilt for joking.

"I'm fine, I promise," she assured him, setting the last of the blanket strips down in the trunk. Then the smile was back. "There's a lot you don't know about me."

Riva passed Riley some breakfast then, and the girls explained the problem with the motel while he ate. Riley thought going back to the motel for another night was dangerous but didn't care too much about the loss of his dying phone. He had other things to worry about, like his mom thinking he was in some kind of trouble.

After crumpling up the wrapper of his breakfast sandwich, they decided to sit down by the water while they thought everything over. Riley winced with each step over the rocks. He was wearing a borrowed pair of flip-flops Riva had tossed into the backpack for him. By the time they settled at the river's edge, he was out of breath.

"Hazel?" Jen asked, staring over the fast-moving water. "Weren't you scared last night?"

Hazel raised an eyebrow. "Yes. Of course I was. It was a nasty little trip down memory lane."

"But then your Shadow must be stronger today," Jen pointed out.

Hazel watched the water curl around a rock in the middle of the river and didn't answer. She felt like she had swallowed a rock herself, and it was stuck in her throat. She was disappointed. She had allowed herself to hope the Shadow was dead, but now she knew for sure. It seemed likely to be with her for life. She rubbed her eyes. One year had been exhausting enough.

"Is that what we saw in the bathroom?" Kate asked now.

They all looked at her.

"All those shadows flashing around when you came out of the mirror," Kate elaborated. "Was that your Shadow?"

Hazel opened her mouth to speak, but no words came out. She had seen shadows darting around when she came out of the mirror too, but she had attributed it to mirror-travel making her dizzy.

"I didn't see anything," Riva said, and Jen shook her head in agreement.

"Huh," Kate said. She looked at Hazel.

Hazel nodded once. "I saw that too."

Jen and Riva looked back at Kate in astonishment.

To their surprise, Kate gave a happy sigh. "I always knew I

could see something."

No one knew quite what to say to that, so they stared at the flecks of sunlight flashing on the river. Hazel marveled over how much she didn't know about the supernatural.

Riley broke the silence. "I think I have to die."

All four heads turned to him, but he continued watching the water. He was sitting with his knees up, his wounded hands resting on them, palms up.

"We have to kill it before it hurts someone."

"Killing it *would* hurt someone," Hazel countered.

Riley's brow furrowed, not to be deterred. "What if I almost die? Like, if I die for a minute?"

Hazel kicked a pebble into the water with her toe as she thought it over.

"Could that work?" Kate asked.

"Maybe," Hazel said. "But what if it just ate your ghost while you were dead and then it had full control of your body?"

She glanced up to see all four of them staring at her with repulsed expressions. She laughed out loud. The sound carried across the water.

"That would be bad," Hazel agreed. "But it probably can't possess a dead body anyway, or the shadows wouldn't have bothered with us. They'd have just gone to a graveyard. I'm pretty sure if you died, your shadow would be free to go find someone else."

Hazel met Riley's eye and was sure he was thinking what she was: if they died for a minute, the shadows might leave and go be someone else's problem. They both looked down in shame.

"Hazel," Jen said, "by that logic ... when you die—of old age, say—this Shadow will eat you."

Hazel didn't want to think about it. She shrugged an 'I

suppose.'

Jen wasn't going to let it go. "You'll never see Kelly again."

Hazel's stomach clenched. She cleared her throat. "There's no guarantee I'd see her anyway."

"But there's a chance," Jen argued. "We know the Shadow didn't get her. She must have gone somewhere else! You can't just keep your Shadow in your body until you die. It–it's giving up on Kelly!"

With a sinking feeling, Hazel knew this was true. It was going the way of her grandmother and mom. It was accepting nonexistence, no possible afterlife. To be fair, she didn't know if Kelly was in some kind of afterlife anyway. The thought made her feel cold despite the full morning sun. She was surely feeding her Shadow just thinking about it.

She pictured herself as an old woman, dying, and the Shadow victorious at last. The blackness. Hazel rejected it. Besides missing her sister, Hazel was a medium; if anyone deserved to know what came after death, it was her. The question had plagued her all her life. Pursuing the answer was in her core, in her bones.

"I have to kill it," she agreed. "One day, I need to know what happens next, even if it's nothing."

"But about last night," Riley said, not to be distracted. "People could have gotten hurt. There is still a chance that if I die, or if you die, the shadow dies." He turned to Hazel. "If things get really bad ..."

Hazel nodded. "The last resort."

Riva, Jen, and Kate all protested, but Hazel and Riley knew it was already agreed between them. Morbid though it was, Hazel smiled as the warm wind lifted her hair. She felt her burden grow a little lighter, and the cord between her and Riley grew warm.

"The more important question," Riva was saying, "is how do we kill these things?"

"Weakening them is good," Jen put in, "but apparently not enough."

"And lavender doesn't work."

"Wait ...," Riley said.

"What?" Riva and Kate asked, both sitting up straighter.

"Well ...," he said, "I visited Hazel before, and the shadow-thing didn't know. I sort of left my body for a while. Maybe there's something there. Maybe we can do something to it while I'm ... away."

"How *did* you do that?" Hazel asked.

"I used the cord. The cord you sent a message down."

Hazel opened and closed her mouth. "I did what?"

"You know the blue cord?" he asked, indicating the invisible bond between them. Hazel nodded. "One day I heard you ask who I was ... Or I felt it, anyway. I didn't know how to answer, but later, when I was thinking about the cord, it showed up again and I sort of ... pulled myself along it. I was gone so long I'm pretty sure I almost died."

"That's how you were like a ghost, but not quite," Hazel breathed, pleased that they had gotten to the bottom of another mystery.

"So if you killed me," Riley went on, turning to face them in his excitement, "and my soul was out of the way, the thing couldn't get me."

"But once it's free of your body, it can go get someone else," Riva reminded him. "Maybe one of us."

"And by the way, I don't really want to kill someone," Jen interjected. "It could go wrong, you know. If you actually died we would have to live with it, not to mention go to jail for manslaughter."

"We're not there yet," Hazel said. "It's an interesting idea, but Riva makes a good point; we can't do anything until we know how to kill the shadows."

"To kill a human," Kate said, dipping her toes in the lapping waves, "you have to destroy their body, right? But that doesn't destroy the human's ghost. Only a shadow can do that."

"Or the ghost can 'go on,' " Hazel confirmed with a nod.

"So maybe we can't kill a shadow, but what if other shadows can?"

"You want to pit them against each other?" Riley asked, raising a skeptical eyebrow. "I don't know, my shadow seemed furious with Hazel for locking up its buddy."

"Or was it furious because it saw a threat and wanted to kill it?" Kate suggested.

"Either way," Hazel said with a shiver, "if the killer shadow absorbs the loser, it might end up stronger than ever."

"One shadow is better than two?" Kate said, though even she didn't sound convinced.

Hazel chewed the rim of her coffee cup. "I don't know how we'd get them to go after each other anyway."

"Well, they definitely know each other exist," Riley said.

That gave Hazel an idea. "So they should be connected. Hang on."

She closed her eyes. Her own Shadow's cords had disappeared a long time ago, when she had possessed it. The cords had been hideous chains with lethal hooks on the ends that the Shadow attached to its victims. She remembered well the feeling of having a hook in her own back, the dark niggling sensation always tugging at her. She searched for that now.

And she found something. There was a cord, but it was off-centre, like it was catching someone just past her shoulder. It passed through her and reached out to Riley, green and slimy, like it had been rotting at the bottom of a pond. Somehow, it was also sticky. Tentatively, Hazel tugged at it in her mind.

Her Shadow roared to life. Its presence dropped onto her shoulders like a yoke over her back. It hadn't been this alert since the beginning. Hazel tensed with fear, and the Shadow lapped it up. She opened her eyes and looked at Riley, whose face reflected her terror. She had woken both shadows.

Riley jumped to his feet, even as the anger flashed into his eyes, taking over. Hazel sensed her Shadow pulling at the cord, hand over hand, drawing Riley closer. She could feel its triumphant grin.

14

Hazel: Tug-of-war

"Everyone get back!" she cried, terrified for the girls separating her from Riley.

"What's happening?" Jen demanded as she scrambled out of the way with the others.

Hazel fought to keep her fear down, and she could see by the pained expression on Riley's face that he was trying to control his anger.

"Breathe!" she implored.

With her mind's eye on the rotting rope, Hazel's concern for Riley lit up his cord. Hazel gasped. It was tangled up with the slimy, sticky rope. Her Shadow was going to take both Riley and his shadow.

Riley lunged. His bandaged hand seized the front of Hazel's shirt as she backed away, stumbling over the rocks. She twisted away from him, and her shirt slipped out of his grasp. Riva and Jen tried to grab his arms, but he elbowed Jen in the face, and she fell back, clutching her eye.

He wrenched his other arm out of Riva's grip and dove at Hazel, grabbing her around the knees. Hazel cried out as she fell backwards and hit the ground, half-submerged in cold, shallow water. Riva mimicked him and dove for his legs too, but it didn't stop him from crawling after Hazel on his stomach. Kate splashed into the water and aimed a kick at his side, but even that didn't slow him.

Hazel scrambled to her feet, but the rocky riverbed offered little purchase, and she had to throw out her arms for balance. Riley fought through the shallows in an army crawl and lunged for her knees again, slipping from Riva's grasp. When she fell, Hazel's whole face went underwater this time. Riley crawled up her body using her clothes for leverage, pushing her to the bottom of the river. His hands found her neck.

Under the water, Hazel lost the advantage wrestling had given her last night. She felt her panic rising in the blur of water and dirt. Then Riley tipped towards the shore like someone had seized him by the hair. She managed one gulp of air before he fell on top of her again. The rushing water dragged them from the shore.

At the same time, Hazel could feel an internal battle burning. Both shadows clawed at each other, breathed each other in like black air under the swirling water. Hazel's own voice was screaming at her to stop panicking, to stop feeding the Shadow, but she couldn't focus on it. Self-preservation instincts were kicking in. Forget anything else, she needed air.

She managed to roll over so that her arms were free, her hands brushing against the rocks along the bottom. Riley's hands tightened around her neck, his weight on her back pushing her under. She couldn't get anywhere with him clinging to her like that, so Hazel wrenched down and backwards. Her head slipped through his arms.

She pushed to stay at the bottom despite the call of air above.

Riley's knee collided with her mouth as he swept over her. The water was lighter without him above her, but the black shadows still swirled. Hazel swam up when he was clear. Her head broke the surface and she gasped in the warm summer air.

Voices screamed her name, but she could barely hear them over Riley's frantic strokes as he fought to get back to her. The water swept Hazel towards him. She dove for the shore, her arms cutting through the current as fast as she could go. Riley clutched at her kicking feet. Her shoes were slowing her down. Hazel screwed up her whole face with effort, focusing on making it to a patch of overhanging tree roots by the shore.

Concentration blocked out the fear. She squinted to see the roots through the haze of swirling black shadow and splashing water. A little farther. The current tossed her into the roots, and Hazel strained to catch a sturdy enough strand before it was too late. Dirt and stones rained down on her as pieces came away from the natural embankment, but her left hand finally clutched a thick root. Her body swung against the wall of dirt below.

Riley flew past her, but Hazel threw out her foot for him to grab. Whether it was her own death sentence, or saving his life, she didn't know. The water was strong enough that it buffeted him against the wall, and Hazel trusted that hanging on would take all his focus. She adjusted her grip on the roots so she could use two hands.

The roots strained under the weight of two people. By a weariness that didn't match Hazel's frantic heart, she knew the shadows were tiring. Then she felt a tug at the blue cord, not the green rope, and her horror intensified. The shadows had discovered Riley's soul tangled in the line between them.

Hazel gasped and choked on the river. She shoved down her

fear and screamed an internal "no!" down the cord. It lit up like a beacon.

Smoky hands and swirling black shadows dove at the cord, picking at the tangled lines. They darted back as if burned, then attacked again. Hazel's internal cry burst out of her until she was screaming "no!" down the line, hardly breathing in her effort. She clung to Riley's soul as he clung to her foot, his nails gouging at her ankle. The smoky hands kept tackling the cord, but Hazel could feel the frustration and fatigue rising in her Shadow.

Unbidden, the image of Kelly rose in Hazel's head. Somehow, Hazel had protected her from the Shadow. She had protected her for years before the Shadow had found a way to kill her. They were not going to get Riley, not today of all days. Not on the anniversary. She clenched her teeth so tight her jaw ached. Grief and rage burst down the cord in a streak of light so bright it stung Hazel's eyes. Tears trailed down her cheeks, mingling with the river water.

The river tugged at them relentlessly, and Hazel's arms shook with fatigue. The shadows seemed to be fading as they depleted their energy, but their desperation only increased. The tearing at the rope, the tug-of-war, grew more frenzied. She only had to maintain her resistance a second longer than the shadows.

The grip on her ankle changed. Riley slipped down to her foot. Glancing at him, Hazel recognized the humanity and pain in his eyes as blood trickled into the water from his hands. His shadow was almost burnt out.

Never letting go of the cord in her mind, Hazel yelled encouragement down at him. "Do not let go!"

Her own hands slipped down the roots. Hazel gasped,

clinging to the ends. Riley was almost dislodged. She felt him struggling for a better grip around the ball of her foot, choking in the water. His shadow faded from the fray.

"You are not getting him!" Hazel screamed at her own Shadow.

The black hands paused over the rope. The Shadow didn't fade away like Riley's had but reversed, pulled back into Hazel as if retreating. It was wrong, somehow, but Hazel wasn't about to argue a victory. She released her hold on the blue cord at last, and the world around her went fuzzy as mental exhaustion swept over her. Her arms were burning, begging her to let go as well.

"Can you grab anything?" she asked Riley.

His hands had managed to creep up to her ankle again. One of them disappeared, and she watched as Riley grasped at roots along the embankment. He gripped a handful of short roots against the wall.

His hand didn't leave her foot, but she felt the drag lighten as he let the roots take his weight. Hazel readjusted, this time wrapping her wrists in the roots like Riley's tangled cord. Just as she settled, Riley suddenly plunged underwater as his handful of roots gave way. He came up spluttering, still clinging to her foot.

"Climb higher!" she called.

Riley wrapped his left arm around her leg and began pulling himself up. Hazel's lower half sunk deeper into the water. When he had made it to her waist, Riley stopped, resting his forehead against her ribcage, exhausted.

Hazel raked the riverbanks with her eyes. Nowhere could she see a beach or even people to help them.

"I don't know how to get out of this," Hazel admitted, and

panic seeped out of her voice.

Riley filled his lungs and shouted, "Help!"

Hazel started at the loud sound. He managed a few more cries for help before he ran out of steam. There were crashes somewhere in the woods over their heads.

"We're here!" she shouted, but it came out weak.

The snapping sounds turned to voices, and at last, some branches along the shore just ahead of them parted.

"Hazel!"

"Here," Hazel called.

"They're here!" whoever it was echoed. To Hazel she called, "We're coming! We'll be right there!"

The embankment over their heads must have been thick with trees and brambles because it took an eternity for the girls to arrive. They dragged Riley over the short cliff first, showering Hazel in dirt. She waited, feeling weightless without him. Then Jen was there, hanging over the edge by the waist and securing Hazel in a tight embrace. Hazel fought her way up the crumbling wall with energy she didn't know she had left. The others hauled Jen up by the legs, and they landed in a heap on the flattened raspberry bushes.

The second Hazel was safe, Kate turned to Riley and began binding his wrists with her sweater. Hazel caught Riley's eye. He didn't resist, but she had the impression he had been fighting to keep his eyes open to make sure Hazel was okay. She slipped her hand past Kate and squeezed his hand gently with her own. Then they both closed their eyes.

15

Riley: Recover

Riley tripped through woods, Kate marching him along by the upper arm. Her grip was to make sure he didn't murder anyone but also to keep him from falling over the rocks in his bare feet. He had already done this several times, earning new scratches on both his knees. All Riley wanted to do was lie down and sleep until the seasons changed, probably longer.

The last time he remembered feeling fatigue like this was when he was four years old and his dad had taken him to a fireworks show. He had been looking forward to the fireworks for days, but it was well past Riley's bedtime when the time came. No matter how bad he wanted to stay awake, his eyes kept closing.

Liam had wrapped him in a blanket and lain back in the grass, Riley's head in the crook of Liam's arm. He narrated the fireworks for Riley, describing the colours and shapes until Riley thought he could see them even with his eyes shut. He had listened to Liam's low voice until the world disappeared, feeling like he hadn't missed a thing.

Riley nodded off while walking.

"Woah!" Kate cried, tightening her grip as his legs gave way.

Riley couldn't even muster the energy to apologize. He had good reason to be tired, but he had never fallen asleep walking before. With his feet back under him, they trudged on. When they reached the end of the tree line and emerged back onto the rocky riverbed, he discovered the terrain was much worse here. He could see the car in the distance, but every step on the smooth rocks sent his ankles rolling. The sun had reached its peak and beat down on their heads.

Behind them, Jen and Riva led Hazel over the rocks, their arms wrapped around her back like they were posing for a picture. Hazel wasn't faring much better than Riley was, but her friends kept up an endless stream of encouragement.

At last, Riley hoisted himself into the hot vehicle on shaking legs. Kate buckled him in, replaced her sweater with the blanket pieces from last night, and retied his legs. Jen went to the bank to collect their coffee cups and returned with water. Hazel had already passed out on her side of the bench, but Riley gulped down the water that had almost drowned him and thought, "Take that, you stupid river." He might have said it out loud because he heard a reluctant laugh.

He followed Hazel into oblivion and woke up to glorious air conditioning. They were still in the car, but now they were facing the motel. Kate was prodding him awake.

"We can't leave the car running all day," she said. "We have to go in. If I untie you for a few minutes, can you handle your shadow and not kill us?"

"I'll try," Riley said. He couldn't feel his shadow at all, but he didn't dare hope it was dead.

Kate shook her head as if she was doing this against her better judgement. She put a ball cap on his head and pulled it lower to hide his face, then untied him. He got out of the car like his body had turned to stone. Kate tucked an arm around his waist like a girlfriend. Riley had never done this with a girl before. He woke up just a little more.

"This is our cover," Kate said. "Don't kill me."

She pinned one of Riley's bandaged hands between their bodies, then indicated he should pocket the other. She fixed a bright smile onto her face, then led Riley around the car to the others. Jen was holding Hazel up in much the same way. Hazel was putting on a pair of sunglasses to hide how miserable she looked. The sunglasses didn't cover a swollen lip, but it was the best she could do. Hazel leaned on her knees for a second.

"This is worse than a hangover," she moaned.

Riva was busy giving the parking lot a shifty once-over. "Okay, let's go."

They followed her out of the car's shade, and the pavement scalded Riley's feet. In a burst of energy, he dragged Kate across the parking lot and collapsed in the shade of the motel.

"Are you okay?" she asked with a grimace. She didn't wait for an answer. "Get up, quick. You're drawing attention."

She hauled him to his feet, and they reorganized themselves while Riva opened the gate to the swimming pool. As they passed through the tunnel, the shouts and splashes of kids playing in the water made Riley want to throw himself in. The metal stairs up ahead were sure to melt his feet, but Kate was on it this time.

"We'll just go as far as the pool, and you can quickly dip your feet in," she said. "Just keep your head down so no one recognizes you."

They dashed across the hot courtyard, Riley cursing under his breath. He swung down to sit at the edge and plunged his feet into the water. A hiss of pain slipped through his clenched teeth. The chlorine burned his cuts.

"Calm down," Kate whispered.

He flashed her an annoyed look and saw a spark of fear cross her face. He realized her nervous gaze was no longer sweeping the guests but fixed on him. Ashamed, he looked down at the water. It was amazing that something as simple as pain could make someone angry. His shadow had better be dead, or he had no chance.

Kate slipped off her sandals and offered them to Riley. He offered her a small, apologetic smile, hoping to put her at ease. Behind her, the other girls had already made it up the stairs.

"Okay," he said. He slipped his feet into her sandals, his heels crushing the back straps. Then he looked at her bare feet. "You better go on ahead. I'll meet you at the top."

By the time Riley reached the top, his thighs were burning and he was panting like he had climbed a mountain. The journey was so slow that when they arrived in Kate's motel room, Hazel was already passed out on one of the beds, her face turned away. Kate let Riley drop onto the other.

"Is she okay?" he asked, craning his neck on the sheets to see her, his feet still dangling.

No one answered. Jen and Kate tied him back up again, taking no chances this time. Riley didn't argue, but he didn't help them either.

"We were hoping you could tell us more," Riva said as she adjusted the air conditioning across the room. She kept her voice low so as not to bother Hazel. Riley suspected it wouldn't make a difference. "What happened out there?"

Like last night, Riley had blacked out when the shadow took over. He had come to in the coursing river, clinging to Hazel's feet while something black swirled across his vision. The last thing he remembered before that was Hazel trying to see if the shadows had a cord like they did.

"She pulled on their cord," he said at last, frowning. "It woke them up. I don't think they knew about it before. They ... used it to attack each other."

"And?" Jen asked, forgetting the strip of blanket she was double knotting around Riley's hands. "Did they get each other? Did they finish each other off?"

Jen and Kate were leaning towards him now, hope in their eyes, while Riva stood frozen in anticipation by the window.

Riley shook his head. "I don't know."

They sagged as one. Jen asked, "How can you not know?"

"Do you want me to go poke at it and find out?" he grumbled.

She went back to tying his hands. "Maybe later."

He didn't like the sound of that but said nothing. Riva walked out to pick up some food. Jen and Kate settled on either side of Hazel to watch TV. Riley didn't wait for Riva to return. He dragged his feet onto the bed, slumped back on the pillow, and was asleep the second he closed his eyes.

***

When he woke up, the room was black and the girls were in their pajamas. He had slept through the entire day. He still felt groggy.

Jen looked up from her phone at the sound of his stirring and said, "Welcome back. Eat some food before you go back to sleep. Here."

She unwrapped a sub sandwich for him as he sat up against the headboard, then placed it in his bound hands. He had fresh bandages on now, but a few of his worse cuts had already bled through. Riley ignored them and demolished the sandwich.

It was a bit soggy from sitting out, but his head felt clearer afterwards. Jen opened a bottle of water for him then, and Riley demolished that too.

"Has Hazel woken up yet?" he asked as he passed it back to Jen.

Jen shook her head and looked down at Hazel, chewing her lip. Riley felt a sting of guilt. He shouldn't have gotten Hazel involved at all. It hadn't accomplished anything and had nearly killed them both. He turned his gaze to the TV but didn't take anything in.

Maybe it was time to tell his mom. She knew about the ghosts, after all. She might not think he was crazy. Then Riley remembered holding the shovel as Charlie barked at him. He couldn't risk endangering them. He shouldn't be endangering Hazel and her friends either.

"Do you think I should go?" he asked aloud.

"Go where?" Jen asked.

Riva leaned around Jen to see Riley better. Kate, who had pulled an armchair up to the TV, looked over the back of it.

"Like ... into the woods. Where there's no one to hurt. There's endless mountains out there," he said, remembering Sophie's book.

Riva said, "No," but the other two looked thoughtful.

"There are lots of other things you'd have to worry about," Riva explained. "Exposure, food, dangerous animals, injury ... "

"Yeah, but that's just me, just one person," Riley argued. "Think of all the people who'd be safe from me."

"You matter, too," Riva countered, crossing her arms.

"But think about it," he persisted. "Think about the numbers."

Jen shook her head. "I agree with Riva. And if the shadow got strong again, I bet it would make you find people. It's a temporary fix, at best."

"This is a temporary fix," he argued, waving his bound hands at the room.

"You're better off with us," Kate said, "especially Hazel."

Riley didn't agree, but he couldn't find the words to articulate his point.

"Let's talk about it more tomorrow," Jen said. "Give yourself a minute to recover."

Riley frowned but, outnumbered, lapsed into silence. In time, they each turned back to the TV, one by one.

16

Hazel: Spiders

Hazel woke late at night with her head pounding. The digital clock on the nightstand told her it was a quarter past one. In its green glow, there was a water bottle. She snatched at it in her haste and it rolled to the floor. The plastic thumped on the carpet but not loud enough to wake the others. For a second Hazel debated leaving it there, but her tongue was glued to the roof of her mouth. She slung her aching legs out of bed. They felt like cement, stiff and heavy.

She retrieved the bottle and downed it all while staring at the clock. She supposed in some twisted way she had gotten her wish; she had made it through the anniversary. Hazel felt a sinking, disappointed feeling. She didn't want to examine it.

Jen was fast asleep beside her, while Kate and Riva were sleeping in the bed next to them. With a start, she realized Riley was watching her from the small armchair. He waggled his fingers in greeting, which was the most he could move. The girls had tied him to the chair with a rope Hazel had never seen before. She cocked her head questioningly at him, and he raised one shoulder in a shrug.

She wanted to talk about what happened. Moving like a stiff corpse from zombie movies of old, Hazel shuffled over to him and pulled him free of the ropes that strapped him to the armchair. She motioned to the bathroom and helped him shuffle inside.

Only when she had eased the door shut behind her did Hazel turn on the overhead light.

"Any sign of your shadow?" she whispered.

Riley shook his head. "I've been afraid to try too hard. Yours?"

"Pretty sure it's still around."

Riley didn't look surprised.

She switched topics. "Did you see them? In the river?"

"All the black stuff?"

Hazel nodded. "They were fighting."

"Do you think we should try again?" Riley asked. "But with me tied down?"

Hazel mulled it over. Riley didn't know how close he had come to getting ripped apart by the shadows.

"No," she said at last. "It almost killed us."

Riley's shoulders slumped. "What do we do then?"

Hazel spotted her swollen lip in the mirror. She did a double take at the mirror itself.

"Hey," she said, "can you do mirror-travel?"

"I–I dunno," Riley said, taken aback. "I've never tried it. Why?"

"You said you could see my Shadow. So if you can do it, I could confirm if yours is still here!"

Riley stared at the mirror, his expression conflicted. "Do you really think it would work for me?"

"I don't see why not."

Riley still hesitated. "But you looked all … messed up."

Hazel had forgotten that part. She shrugged it off. "Probably from possessing a Shadow all year."

Riley inched closer to the mirror. "How do you do it?"

"All I did was touch my forehead to the glass. The first time I was thinking about the Shadow. But after that, I was thinking about you."

He turned back to her. "Should you be in front of another mirror?"

Hazel gave a curt nod. There was one just outside, where the armchair was supposed to be. She squeezed out the door, trying to contain the light, and took her place in front of the main room's mirror. For a while, she listened to the breath of the girls behind her. Her legs were so tired she had to lean against the dresser.

"Come on, Riley," Hazel encouraged under her breath. A blue cord lit up then, reaching not from the bathroom but from the mirror to her chest.

Hazel touched her heart in surprise. Then Riley's reflection in the mirror pushed through her own. She could see the expression of wonder on his face and grinned. He only looked as bad as he did in person, and certainly not dead. He grinned, raised his bound wrists, and slid his hands across the glass like a mime stuck in a box. Hazel clapped a hand to her mouth to stop herself from laughing.

As Riley's hands waved, a trail of black followed his fingers. It was like Hazel had been staring at a bright screen too long, only the image stuck to her eyes was dark instead of light. The smile slipped off her face. His shadow was still around. Riley cocked his head to the side, then took hold of the cord. Hazel watched as he pulled himself along it and emerged from the mirror right in front of her, his lower half flickering into existence before her eyes.

He grinned and mouthed, 'It worked!'

Hazel's mouth had dropped open. She waved at him to go back, her smile back in place. She had to try this. A realm of possibilities burst before Hazel. She thought of Derrick. If this worked, she could follow his cord and check in on him right now. Riley disappeared and Hazel stepped up to the glass, pressing against the cool surface.

She opened her eyes in the bathroom, and they immediately started to freeze over. Before she could pull herself along the cord, she spotted the growing terror on Riley's face as he looked over her shoulder. Hazel whipped around to see what he was looking at but achieved only the sucking sensation that yanked her out of the mirror. She clung to the dresser as her senses realigned. A strip of light spilled out of the bathroom, and Riley waved her inside, panic on his face.

"Your Shadow," he breathed, his voice cracking as she joined him. "It was behind you!"

"I thought you said that was normal?" Hazel whispered back.

"Not like this! It wasn't attached to you, it was standing behind you grinning at me like-like a maniac!"

Hazel remembered that grin well. A shiver ran up and down her spine.

"But it doesn't mean anything, right?" she pleaded.

Her mouth had gone dry. Even as Hazel asked it, she pictured that grin, the corrupt, and the death they had caused. The Shadow could not be free again. Not when there was only herself to blame.

"Don't try the mirror again," Riley warned, as if Hazel was about to touch the glass.

She shook her head. She didn't dare follow the cord now, no matter how much she yearned to try.

Her breath hitched as an idea struck her. She sifted through her cords again but not to follow them. There was the one for Riley and the one for Jen. But there, embedded deep in her spine, Hazel found what she was looking for. The rusty, blackened hook. It was back. She clutched the counter for support.

Riley whispered, "This is bad, isn't it?"

Hazel could only nod. Her breath shook. She had to control herself. Or maybe not. If the Shadow was gone, Hazel could go ahead and fall to pieces if she wanted. She was free. Selfish relief gushed through her veins, where it mingled with her terror. The combination was heady, dizzying.

Riley was studying her face. "What happens now?"

"Depends how much power it has," Hazel answered, her own voice lacking. "If it has enough—" She remembered her panic as she almost drowned. "—it can start creating fear."

"How does it do that?"

"It's creative," Hazel said, and the shadow of her past trauma darkened her eyes.

Riley ran nervous hands over his face.

"It's going to want me dead," Hazel added.

Riley paused his fingertips over his lips. "Should we wake the others?"

Hazel's stomach turned over with dread, but as she glanced at the mirror she realized with a jolt there was one thing they should have already done to protect themselves.

"We have to cover these!" she gasped. "Quick, grab a blanket or something!"

She dashed from the room and seized a fleece blanket that

rested, unused, on the end of Riva and Kate's bed. It was just long enough to cover the mirror in the main room.

"Check the closet!" she whispered as Riley stared around, empty-handed.

He pulled open the door with his bound hands. It creaked and clattered on its hinges, loud enough to wake Riva, who was closest.

"What are you doing?" she croaked. When she saw Hazel affixing the blanket to the mirror, she sat bolt upright. "What's going on?"

Hazel's jaw tightened. She couldn't admit what she'd done, but Riley had rushed back into the bathroom, and now the other girls were waking up too. She steeled herself with a sinking heart.

"We think the Shadow's free again."

There was a gasp from Jen's direction.

"What makes you say that?" Riva demanded.

"Where's Riley?" Kate interrupted, throwing off her blankets in alarm.

"He's fine, he's covering the mirror in the bathroom," Hazel said.

Kate threw her an angry look. It was the first time Hazel had ever received one from Kate, and it stung.

"We could have been murdered in our sleep!" Kate accused as she hurried to the bathroom.

Before Hazel could answer, something dark moved on the carpet, racing towards her.

She shrieked and leapt onto Riva's bed in one bound.

"Ow!" Riva cried. "My foot!"

It was a spider big enough to see in the dark. It followed Hazel, scrambling up the blankets that trailed to the floor and emerging over the peak for Riva to see. Riva screamed too. Shadow forgotten, both girls fled to the other bed, dogpiling Jen in their haste.

The spider scuttled across the nightstand that bridged the beds, and Jen's eyes bulged at the sight of it. She fell off the opposite side of the bed in a tangle of sheets.

"What's happening?" Kate cried, re-emerging into the chaos with Riley in tow.

Hazel leapt off the end of the bed, but Riva was too slow. The spider ran up her bare leg. Riva collapsed the moment it touched her skin, her head twitching from side to side as she screamed into the bedsheets.

"Riva!" Hazel cried.

Riva went on screaming and screaming. Hazel stood frozen, unable to think. Then Kate dove at the bed with a shoe, which she swung at the spider, flinging both it and the shoe into the curtains of the window.

Jen's screams erupted from the floor. Hazel could just see Jen's face over the bed. Her eyes had gone blank and she was staring in horror into the distance. Kate launched back into action, crawling over Riva to snatch up the shoe. This time she crushed the spider as it ran up Jen's arm. Kate knocked the mangled body off her and went on slamming the shoe against it until she was sure it was dead.

"Jen?" Hazel asked, her throat constricted. She helped a shaking Riva sit up. "Are you alright?"

"No," Jen answered. Tears sprang to her eyes. A terrible understanding seemed to pass between her and Riva.

"It was like before," Jen stammered as she tripped out of the tangled blankets.

"Terror-visions," Riva finished, breathless.

Hazel's eyes found the crumpled spider on the floor.

"Are you saying," Hazel asked, trying to assemble her sluggish thoughts, "that this is a corrupt spider?"

A scream pierced through the quiet motel. The sound cut through Hazel's heart like a shard of glass. Everyone's heads turned towards the door, as if they could see through it to the source of the noise. Then came another scream from another direction. Then another. All at once, Hazel was transported back to school, to the screams of her classmates over the PA system. An unknown one of those screams had been her sister's. Someone else's family was suffering now.

In the moonlight, Riley's face went paler than ever. He turned questioning eyes to Hazel, but she couldn't speak.

"It can't have an army already," Riva said in a hoarse voice. "Right?"

Hazel looked down at the spider, but it was gone. She shrieked and pointed, causing Jen and Kate to leap onto the bed. The corrupt last year had been indestructible too. Riley turned on the light, and Hazel braved a quick check under the bed, but she couldn't see anything. Just like the first time she and Riva had seen the spider, it had vanished through some invisible crack. Hazel had no doubt that it would be back.

"What do we do?" Jen asked, clutching Kate for balance. "Run?"

There were nods of agreement all around, but Hazel felt the rusting hook in her back. No matter where she went, the Shadow would know.

Riva jumped off the bed and ran to stuff her feet in her sandals, eyes darting around the floor. Jen followed while Kate untied Riley's feet. New voices kept adding to the screams.

Out in the hallway, a nervous-looking man emerged from

the motel room next to theirs. He opened his mouth as if to ask them something, but then a high-pitched scream erupted in his room.

He was gone so fast Hazel had to dart forward to catch his door before it shut behind him. Inside, a ten-year-old girl was writhing on the floor, her hands clutching her face in terror. Her hands muffled the screams, but their volume was ear-splitting.

"Ellie, what's wrong?" the man cried, throwing himself down at her side. "What's wrong?"

He pried her arms away from her face. Fixated on the terror in the girl's expression, the man didn't see what Hazel did. She pushed him aside and kicked the spider off the girl's ankle, where it was resting like the ugly gem of an anklet.

It was not the same spider from Hazel's room. This one was black and round-bodied. She dragged her foot against the ground, hard enough to smear the spider across the carpet. Surely it couldn't survive that. To Hazel's alarm, the girl didn't stop screaming. Looking closer, she saw two red bites on her ankle.

"What's wrong with her?" the man asked, his voice shaking with fear and his eyes shining as he turned to Hazel. "Was it poisonous?"

Hazel didn't know how else to answer. She nodded. "Call an ambulance."

He fumbled out his phone and began dialing. Over her shoulder, Hazel saw the others in the doorway. She slipped back to them.

"What if she turns?" Jen whispered.

"It didn't work like that last year," Hazel said.

"When the corrupt killed someone, they did turn," Jen

disagreed. She lowered her voice even further, "And if this girl dies from the bite while they're at the hospital ..."

Hazel felt the blood slip from her face. If the girl died at the hospital and turned into a zombie, she would be just like Gran, starting the same horror over again. New screams burst from a distant room. Hazel's heart fluttered in panic.

The man scooped up the writhing girl while they whispered. Hazel ducked aside as he ran past, his phone tucked to his ear. She glanced back at the smeared spider one more time. It had disappeared.

Jen noticed too. "With the corrupt, we had to take out their eyes," she reminded Hazel, "because we couldn't kill them."

"What, now we have to carry tiny thumb tacks and take out eight tiny eyes?" Riva asked.

Jen rolled her eyes and grabbed Hazel's arm, trying to hurry her up. "I'm sure crushing its head did the trick—"

A woman in pajama shorts bolted past them in the opposite direction, jostling Jen. More guests were peering out into the hallway as the little girl's screams faded into the distance.

Riva was urging them to run, but Hazel heard her as if from the bottom of a well. The screams, the dim lights, the people running by—it all felt surreal. Hazel remembered Riva's face peeking out of their classroom door to usher her inside. Here, there was no safe place, no help to be had. Here, Hazel had brought hell down on innocent strangers.

There was no denying it anymore. The Shadow had been slipping away ever since Hazel first used the mirror. It might have even attached to the spider because Hazel feared them. She stopped walking and pressed her hands to her temples. Her breath was coming in short bursts, far too short. This was all her fault.

Jen tightened her grip on Hazel's arm. "Come on Hazel, we have to go!"

But Hazel was frozen.

17

Riley: Shadow

A long, drawn-out scream rang out from the room opposite of theirs. Riley, at the edge of the group, glanced back to where Jen and Hazel were having an urgent conversation he couldn't hear. He didn't know what the holdup was, but he too was now rooted in place. Riley stared at the door, his breath caught somewhere in his core. Someone needed help. With his hands tied, he felt both useless and vulnerable at the same time.

"Hey," Riley croaked to the group. No one heard him.

He stared at the brass number, goosebumps rising with continued screams, until he couldn't stand it a second longer. He exhaled three rapid breaths through his nose, then kicked hard near the handle. The sudden boom made Kate scream. The door rattled in its frame. He kicked again, his face screwed up with the effort. Kate backed away. Riley didn't care if he looked angry. He kicked again, and this time the door smashed open.

Hazel was at his side in an instant, whatever spell over her broken. She nodded to him like they were a pair of police officers about to clear a room. Her eyes betrayed no fear, only palpable relief. Riley didn't understand it, but he nodded back.

He followed her across the threshold. Sprawled in front of the TV was a middle-aged woman with vacant eyes who was screaming up at the ceiling. Her head rocked from side to side, unaware of the intruders. Beyond her and past the bed, a man lay curled against the wall. His head was rocking as well, banging against the baseboard. On the floor between the couple was a heavy book, its pages splayed as if one of them had thrown it.

"There are two red bumps on her knee," Hazel called over all the noise, stooping to check on the woman while Riley scanned the floor. "No spider."

Riley cast a suspicious look at where the bedsheets met the floor. He moved to lift the sheets as Hazel crept towards the man, and just as she passed the bed, a small brown body came tearing out.

"Look out!" Riley cried.

Hazel shrieked and her feet lifted off the ground. She stomped in a chaotic dance, trying to kill the spider as it dodged and pressed towards her. She raised herself up onto the dresser. The TV rocked and toppled, crashing to the ground.

Riley seized the abandoned book with his tied hands and slammed it down on the spider as it careened out of the TV's way.

"Pass me that glass!" he said, stepping on the book for good measure.

Hazel handed him a short glass from the courtesy tray, and Riley flipped the book over with his foot. In a flash he swapped the book for the cup, then leaned down to get a good look at it. The spider was smaller than he expected. It was only the size of a quarter now that it was all curled up. This one was different than the first one they'd seen. It was furry, a wolf spider.

Hazel slid off the dresser. "Is it dead?"

"I think so." Dead or not, Riley had no intention of lifting the glass.

He and Hazel hurried over to the man, whose screaming made Riley want to clap a hand over his mouth. He gritted his teeth. The tiny red bumps were all over the man's legs.

"What do we do, drag them out of here?" Riley asked.

"Yes," Hazel said with a glance at the hallway. Kate, Riva, and Jen were all hovering in the doorway, looking eager to leave. "We can get them outside. Closer to help."

Riva opened her mouth to argue, but Hazel cut her off.

"We have to help!"

"You did help," Jen said, skirting the spider in the glass so Hazel could hear her better. "You killed the spider for them. But you saw our neighbour calling an ambulance. Help will be here any second. Let the paramedics do their job and let's get out before we end up like this!"

"But there are people screaming everywhere!" Hazel argued, making a sweeping gesture that took in the whole motel.

"You plan to go to every room hunting spiders?" Jen asked, aghast.

Hazel glanced at Riley.

"Yes," Riley said.

Relief broke across her face again and she smiled at him.

"Hazel," Jen said, laying a hand on Hazel's shoulder, "you could get bitten." She looked down at the man and woman to illustrate her point.

Hazel nodded. "And I'd want someone to help me if I did."

They locked eyes.

"Can you untie me?" Riley asked. "I can help much better

if—"

"Absolutely not," Jen said. She gave Hazel a stern look, as if she were the one who asked. "Absolutely not. Look, I'll help if that's the crazy thing we're doing here, but no, he doesn't get untied again."

Riley bristled. "How am I supposed to help then?"

Riva had ventured closer. Despite looking queasy, she said, "Maybe you should leave it to us, Riley."

Riley shook his head. There was a strange echo in his ears, his dad's unanswered screams for help. He set his jaw, rose to his feet, and went straight to the woman, sliding his arms under her back to raise her to a sitting position. Her twitching limbs tipped the spider cup. Riley's heart jumped into his throat, but the cup rocked back into place. Kate hurried to steady the woman.

"You obviously can't lift anybody," she said. She called to the others, "Why don't Jen, Riva, and I carry people out, while you two start trapping spiders."

"No," Hazel said, and everyone looked at her. "I mean, we need someone to cover the mirrors."

All faces turned to the mirror on the wall. It reflected the room and nothing more. Regardless, they all burst into action. Jen wrenched a sheet off the bed and Hazel helped her throw it over the mirror. Kate and Riva carried the woman out by her feet and armpits. Riley held the door for them.

"We'll go by the pool, it's fastest from here," Riva said to Kate as they disappeared down the hall.

Hazel slid a garbage bin along the floor to Riley, and he used it to prop the door open so Riva and Kate could still collect the man. Then they wasted no time following the screams to the next victim. Their eyes swept over the floor and walls for spiders, paying close attention to the cracks under doors as they headed deeper into the motel.

Jen nodded with her chin to a room up ahead. "I think someone's in trouble there."

She and Hazel moved as a seamless team and kicked the door open in sync. Riley's eyebrows lifted of their own accord. It was like they had kicked down doors together before.

Inside, the screams issued from the closed bathroom. Jen pushed it open and a black spider came hurtling out. It beelined straight for Riley, who backed into the closet door opposite with a cry of alarm. The spider was on his bare feet in seconds. Riley lost the room.

Hazel's Shadow had him by the upper arms, forcing him to look at Liam on the forest floor. Riley could feel rocks pressing into his knees. The attackers were beating Liam to death as he begged them to stop.

Shocked, Riley tried to look away, but the Shadow gripped his head and twisted it back. He struggled, but this was no insubstantial Shadow. Its grip was firm, and its laughing breath was hot on the back of Riley's neck. He closed his eyes, but the vision was just as clear behind his lids, just as real.

"Stop!" he begged as a bloodied fist hit his dad's mess of a face. "I don't want to see it! Please!"

Liam stopped fighting back, his last breath barely an exhale at all. One of the attackers drew an arm across their forehead and Riley recognized Hazel. She motioned to someone Riley hadn't noticed before, and a man dragged a resisting Charlie forward by the collar.

"No!" Riley cried.

Charlie was whimpering. Somewhere behind the well, Elisabeth was sobbing, and Riley knew he was about to watch the slaughtering of his whole family.

Then he was staring at the bathroom door again. The hell was over. Jen and Hazel were stomping and slamming a garbage bin, trying to smash the spider to death. Riley sunk down the closet doors, his cheeks wet with tears. The image of that fist striking his dad wouldn't leave him.

"Got it!" Jen cried, her foot planted in front of her.

Hazel swiped a new glass off this room's courtesy tray, and Jen swapped her foot out for the glass. Hazel turned to Riley, who stared through her.

"Did it bite you?" she asked.

Riley looked down at his foot. There were no marks. The spider must have only been on him for a few seconds. He shook his head and his eyes roved over the bathroom, where a grey-haired woman was screaming and jerking around on the floor. If contact with a spider was this bad, he couldn't imagine being bitten.

"Kate and Riva will get her," Hazel reassured him. "Come on, next room."

She took him by the arm to lead him out, but Riley tensed, seeing Charlie dragged forward at her command. Hazel released him immediately. She looked hurt for a split second, then composed herself.

"The terror-visions are bad," she said, a knowing expression on her face. "Kelly once told me the Shadow tried to pit her against me. It gave her visions of me killing her. It was something like that, wasn't it?"

Riley had not regained his voice yet. He gave a jerk of his head, but the tension in his shoulders eased. She propped the door open with a tight smile and moved on to the next room. Riley got to his feet and followed, still shaking.

They met Kate and Riva in the hall. Both were panting.

"Police have arrived," Kate said, leaning on her knees as she tried to catch her breath. "They're trying to keep everyone calm outside. I bet they'll be in to do the evacuating themselves in a minute. They'll kick us out."

"But they don't know what they're really up against," Riva finished for her.

Hazel nodded. "Let's keep going. The less time they have to spend in here, the safer they'll be."

"Can we switch?" Kate asked, clutching a stitch in her side. "Unconscious people are heavy."

Jen nodded. "I can take over for you. Riva, why don't you—"

"No thanks," Riva interrupted, stretching out her own stitch. "I'd rather lug unconscious people than get attacked by spiders, if that's alright."

Hazel grinned. "I deserve that for making you deal with the spider in our first room."

Riva chuckled and then got back to work.

Jen squeezed Hazel's hand before following her. "Be careful."

Riley led the way to the source of the next scream. Hazel tried the lock, then kicked. Kate stood behind with Riley, rolling her aching shoulders.

"How can there be so many spiders?" she asked.

"I read somewhere," Riley said, surprised to hear his own voice was back, "that BC has more species of spiders than anywhere else in the world."

Kate made a little *tsk* of disgust. The door gave way. Riley made to go inside, but Hazel wrenched him back by his shirt.

"What?" he choked.

She pointed, her expression grim. At first, Riley didn't see anything. Then he realized she was pointing at the air between the doorframes. Tiny red spiders were drifting from invisible threads. The door had burst through their web and they were falling like hundreds of dust motes.

Hazel yanked the door shut again, pulled off her shoe, and began slapping the spiders still on this side of the door with it. Kate and Riley inspected the door and pointed out any she had missed. The screaming went on inside.

"We can't go in there," Kate said at last. "But the people ..."

"Someone's going to have to fumigate the room," Riley said.

"They can't do that with people in there," Hazel pointed out, her brow creased with concern.

A piercing scream cut across their conversation, different than any they had heard so far. Hazel and Riley whipped around to look down the dim hallway.

"Help me!" a woman cried.

She came tearing around the corner, stumbling into the wall, her blonde hair flying. She clawed at the wallpaper as if something was dragging her backwards. Riley couldn't make sense of what he was seeing. She seemed to be fighting against an invisible force. He had already started running towards her when a massive form rounded the corner. An enormous black leg filling the hallway before seven more followed.

Riley couldn't slow down fast enough. He skidded to a halt on the threadbare carpet. The spider's legs were bent at steep angles just to fit in the hallway, several of its feet resting directly on the wall. Its colour kept shifting. One moment Riley thought it was black, and the next, grey. The two colours swirled up and down its legs and body, like dark ink poured into water. With its two front legs, the spider began reeling the woman in, and Riley realized what the invisible force was.

The woman's hand stretched out towards Riley as she screamed. He met her pleading eye as the spider dragged her away. The ability to move had left him now, and all he could do was stare, helpless, knowing that look would haunt him for the rest of his life. In seconds she was under the spider. Its head darted down as if to bite, but instead it opened its mouth wide and sucked at the air over her face, like it was stealing the breath from her lungs. She screamed into its mouth. Then her whole body flickered and vanished.

A hand landed on Riley's shoulder. Kate was speaking to him, but he couldn't take in a word. As the woman vanished, the spider blackened, and Kate shrieked like she'd only just noticed it. Riley turned his head, and the movement was so slow it was like he had turned to stone. Hazel's mouth was wide in a silent scream of her own. As if in slow motion, he grabbed both girls by the arms and turned them around. Then adrenaline kicked in and they were running.

The spider came tearing after them. It treated the hallway like a tunnel, pushing off the walls in its race to hunt them down. Doors flashed past them on either side, the brass numbers winking in the dim light. Windows ahead showed the starry sky over the pool, but Riley took an abrupt right, pulling Hazel and Kate with him. He took the next left, hoping the spider wasn't quick enough to see where they'd gone. A sick thumping sound told him it was still on their tail.

Towards the end of the hall there was an open door on the left. Hazel was pulling ahead, but Riley's lungs were burning so bad he couldn't call out to her. He prayed she would notice it. At the same time, he and Kate grabbed for each other, both desperate not to get left behind. She caught hold of Riley's t-shirt sleeve, and he clutched her elbow, and they pulled each other along as the spider loomed over them.

They were a breath away from the open door. Hazel darted inside, but just as Kate dragged Riley across the hall after her, he felt a tug at his back. He was ripped from Kate's grasp, wrenched backwards onto the floor. Riley looked up to the hellish view of an upside-down spider bearing down on him, smoky black fangs shining with saliva. A strand of sticky, greenish web extending from the point of its abdomen to Riley's back, like the rotting rope from a well.

Riley crawled backwards, stomping on the rope as he tried to get away, hoping to tear the connection. His bare foot slipped along the slimy web, and then the fangs descended over him. He looked up into the gaping black hole behind the fangs. Disembodied screams echoed from inside.

Hazel's arms wrapped around his chest, her grip firm and defiant.

"I said you can't have him!" she roared up at the spider.

The dual voice that answered set Riley to trembling.

"Watch me ...," it said.

18

Hazel: Shatter

Hazel stared up at her old enemy, clutching Riley to her chest. In her mind's eye she clung to Riley's cord as well. She could feel it reaching her heart, spanning such a short distance that their bodies contained it. She remembered all too well the moment Kelly's cord disappeared forever.

"What are you going to do to me?" she demanded of the spider towering above her. "What can you *actually* do?"

Riley gasped, his hands tensing on Hazel's arm. It was a gamble. Hazel thought she was right in guessing that the Shadow's spiders had not succeeded in killing anyone yet. The Shadow was using up energy maintaining its form, but she didn't know how much fear it was reaping from the fleeing motel guests and victims.

The cavernous hole of a mouth stayed open, watching them like a ninth eye. Tiny obsidian teeth pierced the black gums in innumerable shark-like rows. Beyond the teeth, saliva stretched in ropes across the dark, wet hole.

A warm, repulsive breath washed across her face. At first it smelled of rotting eggs and the kind of sludge that collects at the bottom of a compost bin. Then Hazel caught a whiff of perfume that reminded her of Gran's arms wrapped around her after a nightmare. On its heels was the clinical scent of rubber gloves and hand sanitizer her mom always wafted into the house after a shift at the hospital.

Hazel's hands clenched tighter around Riley, and he let out a tiny exhale of pain. The faint screams coming from the spider's gullet escalated until they drowned out those of the motel guests. Hazel couldn't stop herself straining to hear someone familiar, someone she suddenly hoped was dead and gone, lost to oblivion. Oblivion seemed a small price to escape the Shadow's internal hell. As Hazel watched, she saw a flicker of movement deep down the spider's throat. Fingertips. Then someone was shaking her.

"Get up!" Kate screamed. "get up!"

In a burst of strength, she hauled Hazel and Riley to their feet. Dragging them both by the upper arm into the motel room, Kate slammed the door on the spider. It watched them go, revolving on its eight legs, as if curious to see what they would do next.

"The door won't stop it," Hazel said. She felt dazed, like she had just woken up.

"Then what do we do?" Kate screamed, still at top volume.

"C-cover the mirror," she stammered, taking a step back in surrender.

Kate ripped a blanket off the end of a bed and threw it over the mirror in the main room. Hazel slammed the bathroom door, but not before noticing there was no Shadow in it. Riley's eyes were wide and unblinking as he stared at the crack under the main door. His mouth was moving, but no words were coming out.

"Come here," Hazel said, and she snagged the rope on his wrists to lead him into the main room. She shoved a glass into his hand, hoping to snap him out of it. "You're on small spider watch."

"So it *was* a big spider?" Kate demanded. Her voice was shrill. "I thought it might be a trick of the light. ..."

Hazel rushed to the window on the opposite side of the room. It was a sliding patio door. She sagged, wondering how on earth they could fortify so much glass. Then she shook herself. This wasn't like last time. It wasn't about corrupt bodies breaking in after them. Spiders could get in any tiny crack. The Shadow had doomed them far better than before.

She stood on her toes to see what was down below and saw the pool glowing in the dark. The tunnel leading to the outside gate was somewhere below and to the left, but Hazel couldn't see Jen or Riva returning. With any luck, the police had held them back and they were safe for now.

"Hazel," came Kate's urgent voice.

Hazel turned so fast the room spun. Kate was peering into Riley's face. He was muttering something under his breath, eyes fixed on a spot on the floor as if afraid to look left or right. His fingers were white on the glass in his hands. Something had changed since Hazel passed him that glass. He clenched his jaw even as he spoke. Kate reached a hand out to touch him, but Hazel grabbed her wrist.

"What's he saying?" she whispered.

They both inched closer.

"Useless," Kate said. "He's just repeating 'useless.' "

Hazel and Kate shared a frightened look. They both knew what danger they would be in if Riley had an anger episode now.

"Riley?" Hazel said, sliding in front of him. He didn't look up. She swallowed. "Riley, you are not useless. Whatever this thing is saying, don't listen. We need you here."

Riley tilted his head like he was hearing her voice from a distance. She took his bound hands and traced a finger across his knuckles.

"Breathe in across all four," she instructed. "Then breathe out for four on the way back."

Riley's breath followed the pattern of her finger, and Hazel was encouraged. She let her own breath fall into sync with her finger.

"Hazel," Kate whispered. She was shifting from foot to foot, too nervous to stay still. "We don't have time for this. It could burst in at any second, couldn't it?"

"It wants fear," Hazel explained, keeping her voice low and calm. "The longer it makes us wait, the more anticipation builds up. It was always smart like that."

Riley's breath hitched.

"Riley, stay with me," Hazel said.

His face spasmed. The air rushed from his lungs in a gush. She pressed the pad of her finger down harder, trying to draw his attention back to its progress. His forehead slammed into her face. She gasped and fell backwards to the floor, her eyes rolling in their sockets.

"Hazel!" Kate cried.

Hazel lay stunned on the threadbare carpet, a ringing sound loud in her ears. A scuffle was happening near her feet, but as the ringing receded, pain blossomed around her eye and Hazel couldn't focus on anything else. The dim, silvery moonlight left streaks across her vision. Then something scratched her calf, and Hazel felt Riley's weight land on her legs as he soldier-crawled his way towards her throat.

She locked her legs around his, knocked his bound arms out of balance, and jerked to the side. The move sent him slamming into the dresser. The TV wobbled on top.

She pinned Riley's chest under her elbow, but his hands still clawed at her neck, drawing blood. Hazel's head throbbed with her heartbeat, and her vision blackened. She fought to stay conscious, the darkness draining away in tiny, rain-like pinpricks.

The claws turned into fists and Hazel's teeth clacked together as Riley struck her chin from below. She dropped her full weight onto him. Immobilized, he bared his teeth, but Kate dropped beside his head just in time. She pressed his forehead down with both palms so he couldn't bite Hazel.

Kate had a bloody lip that smeared across her cheek, but there was a determined set to her jaw.

"Kill me. ...," Riley wheezed.

Hazel met his eye and saw the Riley she knew, even as he strained against her.

"Please," he choked. "Get rid of it."

Kate gave a horrified gasp that turned into a scream. Hazel's head snapped up to see what she was looking at. The blanket over the mirror was bulging and shifting over their heads. Long, slender legs slipped out from underneath it and tore the blanket aside. The Shadow-spider was halfway into the room, its body squeezing through the mirror.

Icy blood pulsed through Hazel's veins, a shiver following its path down her arms. The Shadow's front legs began reeling in a rotting cord that led to Riley. Hazel realized with a fresh burst of horror that it had learned that trick from her. Less than an hour ago she had set it free trying to follow Riley's cord through a mirror.

Everything in Hazel told her to run, that she had lost, that she should leave Riley to his death as requested. Across from her, Kate had fallen back and was staring up at the spider, propped up by her hands. Hazel's forearm moved to Riley's throat, keeping him secure. She and Kate could leave. They could slam the door behind them and leave the Shadow to the next person. Maybe it would let them go, glad to see the back of Hazel.

Then Hazel remembered the fingers down the spider's throat, and she concentrated with all her might on Riley's cord. It lit up with a blinding light that brought tears to her eyes. Shame burned in Hazel's stomach at how she had flipped between saving Riley and abandoning him.

Hazel clamped her hands down on Riley's throat and squeezed.

"What are you doing?" Kate cried.

"What he asked."

"You're going to kill him!"

"I know."

She saw Kate's aghast expression in her peripheral vision. The Shadow was pulling too hard on the rope to respond. If she could just get them down to one shadow, they might stand a chance.

"Run, Kate," Hazel said through gritted teeth.

Kate didn't move. Riley's struggling grew more frantic as he ran out of air, his shadow refusing to let him go. He almost knocked Hazel off balance, but she leaned harder against his chest.

The Shadow's hair-raising voice spoke again, mocking. "I'll take care of him, Hazel."

Riley's eyes rolled up into his head. Hazel didn't stop

squeezing. This wasn't like last time, when all she wanted was to make him pass out. Kate made a sudden movement, and a resounding crash rent the air. Hazel flinched as the cup and mirror smashed, then shattered glass rained over her. She hunched over Riley, shielding their faces as the TV fell and bounced across the floor, missing them by inches.

The Shadow let out a shrieking roar of pain and rage. Kate had sliced it in two, half its body in their world and half in the dismantled mirror. An eruption of black blood burst over Hazel like tar as the torso of the Shadow-spider writhed on the dresser. The screech was so loud and terrible that Hazel almost released Riley to cover her ears.

Then the blood withdrew as if sucked back to the Shadow. It engulfed the severed torso in a whirling blob, while the legs thrashed against the dresser. The Shadow settled into a grotesque spider-human form and let out a shrieking hiss into Hazel's face.

The blood in her cheeks drained away as she stared into eight empty eye sockets on a human head, each covered by a thin layer of skin. The mouth and fangs belonged to a spider. At the ends of its spider legs were long, skeletal hands, the skin swirling between black and grey.

The hands seized Riley's cord and began pulling fast.

"No!" Hazel gasped, caught off-guard by the sudden return.

She redoubled her grip on Riley's cord. Her hands were still at his throat, her whole body tensing with the effort. At last, he went limp.

"Hazel, what can I do?" Kate cried, now on her feet. Then she screamed.

Hazel saw movement out of the corner of her eye. The floor was twitching as an army of spiders descended upon them.

They raced towards Kate, who backed towards the dresser, towards the spider.

The cord between Hazel and Riley pulsed, and she knew he had left his body and hovered somewhere before her. At the same time, the rope that stretched to the spider pulsed too. Riley's shadow was out of his body. It hovered before the spider. Begging inwardly that the Shadow would take this as a fair trade, Hazel seized Riley in a fierce embrace and hauled him to his feet. The spiders descended on them.

"Kate!" Hazel cried.

She dragged Riley to the balcony, stomping on spiders along the way as Kate raced after her. The Shadow-spider lunged after them on its long-fingered legs. There was something sloppy about its movement in this new form, like it was injured. Kate threw open the sliding door for her.

Hazel dashed out onto the balcony, and Kate slid it shut behind them, stamping on the spiders who managed to bolt through the crack. The Shadow lurched towards the door, and Hazel knew glass wouldn't stop it. She shoved Riley into Kate's arms and climbed over the railing.

Riley's soul slipped from Hazel's mental grasp, and the cord and rotting rope sprang together again in a jumbled twist. The line felt taut as his soul slipped towards the Shadow.

"What are you doing?" Kate cried, even as she helped Hazel pull Riley over the ledge.

Facing outward, Hazel clung to the cold railing with one hand. Teeth gritted against the physical effort, she wrenched Riley's soul all the way down his cord and into her own chest. She didn't wait another moment. Just as the spider burst through the glass, looming over Kate, Hazel pushed off against the balcony as hard as she could.

The wind blasted her hair back as Hazel and Riley plunged towards the pool. The slimy rope that contained Riley's shadow snapped, stretched beyond its capacity between Hazel, Riley's body, and Hazel's Shadow. It tore into tiny wisps of smoke that drifted in the night air.

Hazel and Riley hit the pool, missing the side by inches. The crash of water cut out the dying scream of Riley's shadow as it echoed over the empty courtyard.

19

Hazel: Reinforcements

Hazel hit the bottom of the pool. Her left leg crumpled beneath her as Riley's weight pushed her down. Inky black swirls clouded her vision, like in the river, but they were feeble and fading away. She released Riley's body and pushed off the bottom for a gulp of air. Still clinging to his soul, she caught a brief glimpse of the balcony and saw it was empty. She dove back under.

He was drifting near the bottom, lifeless, his hands still bound. As Hazel swam, a figure appeared beside her and she gasped in some water. Then she recognized the dark hair. Kate grabbed one of Riley's arms, and Hazel grabbed the other. Together, they pulled him to the surface and pushed him over the ledge.

"Are you okay?" Hazel choked, clinging to the ledge and looking up at Kate, who had climbed out.

Kate nodded. She was kneeling beside Riley, pool water streaming from her hair. She began CPR without another word. Hazel released her hold on Riley's soul at last. To Hazel's alarm, he materialized beside his body, not in it. She cut to the nearest ladder, envying how easy it had been for Kate to haul herself out of the pool, then raced to her side.

"Don't stop me," Kate warned as she pressed down on Riley's chest.

"Of course not," Hazel said in surprise.

She bent to untie Riley's hands, hoping Kate would see she was trying to help, and not finish him off. She looked over her shoulder at Riley's ghost as she worked out the wet knots. There was something brittle in his expression as he looked down at his own corpse.

"You're going to be okay," Hazel said.

"Am I?" he asked. Worry creased his brow.

Hazel tried to calculate how long Riley had been dead as Kate administered mouth-to-mouth. Everything had happened in a heartbeat. Surely it couldn't have been more than a minute or two. She willed Kate to bring him back.

Then Hazel's heart clenched as a whole host of new problems presented themselves to her. If Riley died, his blood would be on Hazel's hands. It would be obvious she had strangled him—then thrown him in a pool as if to cover it up. She could go to jail.

Hazel shoved all her terrible thoughts into a corner of her mind as the knot gave and Riley's limp hands fell to his sides.

"I'm going for help," she told them both. "Keep an eye out for the Shadow. I'll be back as fast as I can."

She ran for the tunnel that led out of the courtyard, her wet shoes squelching. The walls lit up red and blue from the flashing lights in the parking lot. She didn't want to think about what spiders went unseen over her head, so she raced through to the gate, which was wide open. On the other side, the parking lot was full of emergency vehicles arriving and departing. Frightened guests stared up at the motel or gathered around the backdoors of ambulances.

"Help!" Hazel called into the crowd. "My friend isn't breathing!"

Everyone in the vicinity turned her way. Hazel heard her name, but two paramedics were already running towards her, a man and a woman, so she wasted no time in leading them back the way she came.

At the pool, they dropped to Riley's side and Kate scurried out of the way. They slid a mask over Riley's mouth and nose, continuing chest compressions. Kate let out a small sob. It was this sound that finally sent Hazel's panic over the edge. She turned to Riley's ghost.

"Get back in there," she whispered. Her fists opened and closed, desperate for something to do. She wanted to grab him and push him to his body but couldn't.

"How?" Riley asked, staring between his body and Hazel.

"I don't know," Hazel answered. There was a tremor in her voice that she couldn't suppress.

Riley looked frightened at the sound of it, but, determined to try, he nodded. He drifted around the paramedics and knelt at the head of his body. Raising a hesitant hand, he looked at Hazel for reassurance. She nodded her encouragement and held her breath. Riley touched his forehead. He disappeared.

One of the paramedics pressed a defibrillator to Riley's chest. They had already cut through his shirt. Hazel heard the power surge through it and into Riley. His body jolted.

"He's breathing," the woman said at last.

Hazel felt her knees go weak. Kate clutched her arm in relief.

"Is he going to be okay?" Kate called to the paramedics. Her voice shook worse than Hazel's.

"How long was he underwater?" the man asked as he unfolded a stretcher.

Kate and Hazel exchanged a glance.

"Just a few minutes," Hazel said. If he couldn't tell Riley had been strangled, she wasn't going to enlighten him.

"Are you family?"

"He's my brother," Hazel said without pausing to think.

She stifled a cringe when the words were out. She had already called him a friend a minute ago, but she felt so responsible for Riley she couldn't help it. She cast a nervous glance at Riley. His skin was darker than hers, but the pool concealed that his hair was a sandy colour, whereas hers was brown. If their features were alike, Hazel couldn't see it. Their likeness wasn't visible to anyone but them. She would have to claim he was her half-brother if anyone prodded further.

The paramedics lifted Riley onto the stretcher and carried him out of the courtyard with Hazel and Kate on their heels. Hazel watched Riley for signs of life, but he remained still, his lips tinged with blue. Nausea rose in her stomach. What if she had sent him back to a body that no longer functioned?

The second Hazel stepped into the parking lot, a crowd of girls engulfed her.

"What happened?"

"Is he okay?"

"Are you okay? Why are you wet?"

"We're fine," Hazel said. She was about to explain what happened with Riley as she followed the paramedics, but then she registered the white hair of one of the girls. Di and Morgan were among the crowd surrounding her.

Flabbergasted, she stopped in her tracks and stuttered, "What—How did you?—"

Morgan half-smiled. "Jen told us all about the river incident earlier today. We decided we had to come help."

Di nodded in agreement. "We were going to wait 'til tomorrow, but ..." She shivered. "Well, neither of us could sleep anyway."

"Yeah, and good thing," Morgan added. She nudged Hazel towards the ambulance. "Look what we arrived to."

"But," Hazel said, letting Morgan guide her to where Kate was hovering next to Riley, "what about school?"

Di was in grade 11. She had exams coming up.

"We have the week off for the memorial, and to study," Di said, hurrying after them on Jen's arm. "Exams aren't 'til next week. I'll be fine."

Hazel hadn't realized Jen had been updating the girls all day, but then again, she had been unconscious for most of it. The fact that they had driven all night touched Hazel. A painful surge of love made her press her lips together, unable to speak.

The paramedics were securing Riley in the ambulance. Hazel stood on her toes to check on him. He was still unconscious.

A gentle hand landed on her shoulder. "What happened?" Riva asked.

Hazel took a deep breath and faced the girls. They were a year older, and a year more scared than when they had first faced the Shadow together. They had rebuilt their lives in spite of everything. Hazel wished she could tell them nothing had happened. A freak accident, maybe. She looked to Kate for support, but Kate looked like she had lockjaw as she stared at Riley. Hazel felt a surge of guilt for bringing another innocent person into all this. Everyone here was in danger because of their connection to her.

"The Shadow is free again," Hazel said, confirming the

worst.

The way Di's eyebrows inclined in the middle of her forehead made Hazel sick at heart. Morgan's gaze was so intense it almost burned.

"I think we're in more trouble than last time," she went on. "If the Shadow has—" she lowered her voice "—corrupt spiders this time ... I mean, how do we even fight that?"

"None of them have come out here," Riva said. "Maybe they have a limit—"

Hazel interrupted with a shake of her head. "We wounded the Shadow. I don't think it has the strength to send them out here right now. Besides ... I wasn't out here."

Everyone immediately checked the dark pavement. To Hazel's relief, it was clear.

A police officer called out to the paramedics, and the girls ducked out of the way as they jumped down to assist a screaming man.

Keeping her voice quiet, Hazel asked, "Any luck keeping the victims here?"

Jen shook her head, but before she could explain more, Morgan interrupted.

"Did you say you wounded the Shadow?"

"Yes," Hazel said. "And we killed Riley's shadow."

Jen and Riva both gasped, and Hazel started. Jen grabbed Hazel's forearm with both hands, her eyes shining with hope.

"How did you do it?" she demanded. "Can we do it to the other one?"

Hazel gave a grim smile. She gestured towards the ambulance. "You saw Riley ..."

She exchanged a worried look with Kate, who hadn't said a word since leaving the courtyard. She had the look of a lost child, and Hazel wanted to give her a hug. Unlike the others, Kate had no experience with shadows.

"Kate was amazing," Hazel said, giving her the kudos she deserved. "The Shadow started coming out of a mirror and Kate smashed the glass. She split the Shadow in half."

The corner of Kate's mouth twitched. "Y-you're the one who …" She raised her chin to point at Riley. "You had the guts to …"

She fell silent. The others waited.

"To kill him," Hazel finished for her.

The following silence was only broken by the commotion surrounding them. Hazel stared at the pavement, feeling like she was on trial and awaiting a verdict.

"So his idea worked?" Jen asked at last. "Drowning him killed his shadow?"

"I didn't drown him," Hazel corrected. She flexed her fingers with distaste so they would get the message but realized she had to say it aloud for Di. "I–I choked him. And no, it didn't quite work like he thought. Killing Riley did sort of … evict him and his shadow. But since my Shadow was using its hooks to get at them, I had to hang onto Riley's cord and shield him to keep him out of it. All the pressure ripped his shadow to pieces. But if he never wakes up …" She trailed off.

"Technically it worked even if he doesn't wake up, as long as his shadow is dead," Morgan said with her usual lack of delicacy.

Riva smacked her arm.

"What? Obviously I hope—"

"So the other Shadow," Jen interjected, "did it absorb Riley's shadow? Do you think that would balance out getting chopped in half?"

Hazel could only shrug.

"One down is excellent news," Morgan said, "but we're back at square one, aren't we? I don't know about you, but I don't want to go find a scarier shadow to come battle this one. So how do we kill the freaking thing?"

"Keeping the Shadow weak bought us some time," Riva said. Her eyes were on the paramedics as they tried to tranquilize the writhing man on the ground. "We know we can keep it down. So what we need to know is …," she heaved a sigh and met Hazel's eye, "Is Hazel willing to take on that burden again?"

Hazel ran her hands through her wet hair to give herself time to think. "The problem is, I doubt the Shadow wants anything to do with me. It wants me dead."

"Riley," Kate said. "It's going to want Riley."

They all turned to look at Kate. The truth sunk in. Riley had only just shaken his last shadow. Hazel hated the idea of asking him to take on another. What was worse, the Shadow might already be after him.

"We have to get him out of here," Hazel said.

"But," Di said, "he might be the only one who can—"

"Yes," Hazel agreed, "but the Shadow might be hunting him as we speak, and who knows what it can do to him like this," she gestured to Riley's motionless form. "We have to get him somewhere safe. It has to be his choice."

"I'm not sure he should take it on at all," Riva added. "Riley barely managed to keep his own shadow down, remember?"

"But this one lives on fear, not anger," Jen said. "He might be able to cope with that better."

"I don't know," Hazel said. "I'm beginning to think fear and anger are like siblings. Wherever one is, the other's not far behind."

There was a pause.

"If he says no," Morgan said, "where does that leave all these bite victims? What do we do then?"

Hazel raised both hands in a gesture of helplessness. She felt like a traitor for the small part of herself that wanted to pass the baton to Riley.

Her eyes stung as she looked in at the unconscious figure in the ambulance. "Let's hope he says yes."

20

Riley: A Decision

Helpless. The word finally came to Riley. Ever since his dad had died, his predominant feeling had been helplessness. Even Hazel's Shadow had put a finger on it before he had, sending him a vision of Hazel killing his family while Riley watched.

Riley could still feel Hazel's hands around his neck. He could feel the shadow struggling to throw her off even as he, himself, surrendered. Standing over him shouting abuse were Aaron, Sophie, his mom, and even Jordan, the guy who had let him hitchhike. Riley could barely remember the things they had screamed at him in their panic. The hardest struggle had been fighting his own urge to live.

The Shadow endured a taste of helplessness itself as its kin bore down on them in spider form. Riley smiled. Who was useless now?

He opened his eyes to the metal interior of an ambulance. Sound came back to him then. He lifted his head to see a crowd of people at the open doors, where a man was twitching and screaming.

"Hey," he croaked, trying to raise a hand. His arm was

strapped down to the gurney. He raised his voice, but it still came out hoarse. "Hey!"

"Riley!" Kate cried, grabbing the end of the stretcher in relief.

One of the paramedics glanced his way.

"You can let me go," Riley said. The strap across his chest was making him feel claustrophobic, and it was hard to conceal how desperate he was to be free. "Take my spot."

Then Hazel was there, vouching for him. "We'll take him to the hospital," she promised.

The paramedic didn't answer right away. He left his partner with the police officer and climbed up to do a brief assessment of Riley. He shined a light in his eyes and checked his blood pressure.

"Okay," he said at last. "Take it slow. Go easy on your voice." To Hazel he added, "Make sure he gets to the hospital."

The man undid the straps. Riley had had enough of being tied down. He breathed more freely as soon as he could sit up, even if it made his head spin. The man took his arm and passed him off to Hazel, who helped him climb down. As soon as they were out of the way, the paramedics brought the man on board. As they passed, Riley saw a red welt on his face.

Hazel pulled Riley out of earshot. Then she looked him up and down with tears in her eyes. Riley's stomach contracted with guilt. He had asked her to do the unspeakable.

"You look like—" She stopped herself short and tried again. "Well, you look really pale."

"I'm fine," he said in his hoarse, tired voice. He didn't know if it was true.

She threw her wet arms around him. Riley's startled hands rose automatically to return the hug, but no sooner had they touched her back than she released him. He swayed, all the sudden movements throwing off his balance.

"Sorry," Hazel said, brushing a tear from her cheek. "Here, let's go sit down."

She took his elbow and led him to Riva's car, leaving the others in their wake. As they passed Jen, Riley saw hurt in her downcast eyes.

"Wait," Di called. "Check for spiders!"

It was only then Riley registered she and Morgan were there. As Jen and Morgan set to work pushing back the seats to inspect the floors and cracks, Riley supposed he shouldn't be surprised. Hazel seemed to have so many devoted friends. A wave of exhaustion rolled over him.

He looked up at the motel, whose windows looked blank and foreboding. The air wasn't cold, but Riley began to shiver in his wet clothes.

"What happened to your Shadow?" he asked Hazel.

She shifted in place. "It's hurt. We think."

Riley smiled, but Hazel avoided his eye. When they finally climbed into the car and all the doors closed, there was a long silence. Riley closed his eyes. His limbs felt heavy and comfortable on the leather seats. Riva started the car and eased out of the busy parking lot, heading in what Riley assumed was the direction of the hospital.

"Can I borrow someone's phone?" he asked, his heart a strange lurch that was both relief and nerves. "I need to call my mom."

The quiet that followed was unsettling.

"What?"

"Riley ...," Morgan began from the middle seat beside him. She sighed and went on like it pained her, "Don't call your mom just yet."

"Why not?" he asked, his teeth chattering.

Jen passed a blanket forward from where she and Kate were sitting in the trunk.

"We need you to consider something," Jen said.

"I'm not going to like it, am I?" Riley asked, starting to feel nervous as he wrapped the blanket around his shoulders.

"No, probably not," she agreed.

Riva sighed as she turned a corner. "It's all these people with spider bites ... If they die, we think they'll turn into corrupt. Into zombies. And they'll kill a lot people."

"But I'm sure they'll be cured," Riley said. "The doctors will take the venom out or give them a shot or something."

"I don't think there's a shot for this," Hazel finally chipped in from the other side of the bench. She kept her eyes on the scenery outside the dark window.

"Didn't they cure anyone last time?"

"The corrupt weren't able to bite someone to turn them last time," Hazel said. "It all depended on contact. I think the Shadow got lucky using a creature with venom this time."

"So it has to be stopped," Morgan explained. "But we only know one way."

"And it's only temporary," Di said over her shoulder. She was sitting in the passenger seat. "But it gives us a chance."

"Possession," Riley guessed.

"Exactly."

"And there's only two people here it might want," Morgan said.

With a sinking feeling, Riley looked at Hazel. She grimaced and looked down at her clasped hands.

"We don't think the Shadow wants Hazel anymore," Jen said

over the back seat.

Riley's mouth went dry. So that was it. "You want me to—to choose to—?"

He looked around at each of them, but now Hazel was the only one able to meet his eye. Her expression was pitying.

"I just got rid of a shadow!" he said, addressing her. "You want me to willingly—?"

Hazel cringed but nodded. "You can say no. But—"

"But I'd be the bad guy," Riley finished for her angrily. He was outnumbered, cornered.

"That's not what I was going to say."

"No, you were going to say I can save people's lives, but the truth is they might not need saving, and it's probably at the expense of my own life!"

"We just want you to think about it," Hazel pleaded, sounding miserable.

"But think quick," Morgan added.

Hazel frowned at her. Riley turned his back on them as best he could and glared at his reflection.

"We could go to the hospital," Di suggested after a moment. "Try to check on those first bite victims."

Riley seized on that. "Yes! Let's see if they even need my help."

Riva made a small noise from the front seat.

"What is it?" Hazel asked.

"It's just ...," Riva said. "Even if the victims can be cured, the Shadow is still going to find someone else to latch onto."

Riley had no retort for that. She was right. He didn't want to be possessed, but he didn't want people to suffer either. Resentment and fear bubbled in his stomach. He hadn't had a chance to breathe, and now they were asking him to go back in.

There was no guarantee that he could do what Hazel had. By agreeing, he could be signing up for his own death.

Riley put a hand to his chest, where there was an ache. Hazel didn't miss the motion.

"They used a defibrillator on you," she said. "Does it hurt?"

Riley shrugged one shoulder. He watched the headlights illuminate the forest as Riva drove in aimless circles.

"Let's go to the hospital," he said finally. "I want to see for myself."

***

Seeing as so many of them were dripping wet, they waited in the car while Morgan went into the little hospital's ER. She was gone fifteen minutes, but Riley spent the whole time with his thoughts running in unpleasant circles. He was so relieved that his shadow was gone, but guilt overwhelmed him about not wanting to tackle a new one. When Morgan returned, he sat up straighter, eager to hear her news.

She settled back onto the middle seat, the car rocking as Hazel shut the door.

"I ran into the guy whose daughter got bit," Morgan said, shaking her head in pity. "He is a complete mess. I asked how she was, and he said they threw him out of her room. Sounds like she attacked a nurse and they had to lock her up. She's just a kid. The guy started yelling about how they should have let him try to soothe her. ..."

"So she turned?" Jen asked, her knuckles whitening as she squeezed the seat behind Morgan. "She was our neighbour."

"It could be something else," Riley said without much hope.

"Like what?"

He had no real answer, but it was too awful to accept that the little girl was dead.

"Well," Morgan went on, "there was a lot of running around in there. I couldn't read the nurses' faces, but they were definitely rushing."

Hazel put one hand on the door handle.

"Hazel," Jen said, restraining her with a firm hand on the shoulder. "If the staff isn't running for the door, they probably have it under control."

"They might have one under control," Hazel said, "but what about when the others turn?"

The car locks all clicked, making everyone jump.

Riva pressed her lips together like she was stifling a smile. Then she said, "The best way to stop anything at the hospital is to stop the Shadow itself. We don't need to put ourselves in any more danger."

Riley's thoughts were now circling around the little girl. He could feel her dad's grief like his own just months ago. There would be more families ripped apart if he did nothing. Then he felt a pang for his own mother. This very hour he had harboured hopes of reaching out to her.

"Let's just say I went ahead with this," Riley said, "what would I have to do?"

Everyone turned to Hazel.

"All I did was let it in," she said. "But it wanted me for a long time. If it knows what you can do, it should be easy."

She paused there, and Riley knew why. The Shadow would be wary of possessing someone after what Hazel had done. Riley would have to convince it he was a safe choice.

"I don't think you should come," he said to Hazel, his heart sinking. Hazel looked like she was about to argue, but he went on, "It won't trust me if you're around."

"Does that mean you'll do it?" Morgan asked.

Riley let out a deep sigh before answering. "I have a condition. Promise me we'll kill it. You can't all just go home and go back to your lives. You have to stay and help me."

Now there was hesitation on their end. There were families to think about, and jobs, and school. Riley allowed himself a moment of grim satisfaction. Now they had a taste of what they were asking him to do.

Hazel was the first to nod. "I'll figure something out."

As he stared around at the others, he caught a flicker of hurt in Jen's eyes again. Nevertheless, she was the second to speak up.

"Whatever it takes."

Kate nodded, her brow furrowed with worry.

Riva looked apologetic. "I can't stay indefinitely." Riley glared at her, ready to fight, but Riva hurried to explain, "But you'll need other kinds of support! If I go back to work, I can chip in for your stay. And I can come back on my days off."

"Riva's right," Morgan said. "It wouldn't be practical for all of us to stay. But we can all promise to help and to make it our priority. Above everything else."

"I can agree to that," Di said.

They waited for Riley's response. He half wished they hadn't been so reasonable. His heart beat faster as he thought of the Shadow waiting for him in the motel, the Shadow who would be all too thrilled with this fear.

At last, he said, "Okay."

Hazel reached across Morgan and gripped his hand so tight it hurt.

21

Hazel: The Hospital

Hazel watched the SUV pull out of the hospital parking lot and thought of Gran, her mom, and Kelly, all moving further and further away from her day by day. The brake lights came on at the corner, then the car disappeared into darkness. Hazel's stomach knotted with worry. She had an intense urge to chase after the car and tell Riley to run and never stop.

"Nothing better happen to that car," Riva said beside her, arms folded.

Hazel let out a shaky laugh in spite of herself. "With Ms. Responsible driving? I'm sure it'll be fine."

Jen was looking up at the hospital, her face bathed in the dim fluorescent light that spilled out of the entryway.

Hazel sighed and joined her. "I can't let this happen again ... not at a hospital."

She steeled herself for an argument, but then Jen said, "Maybe we'll be pleasantly surprised and it'll all be under control."

The corner of Riva's mouth turned up in a doubtful smile. "And Hazel will just put her feet up for a change."

"Fat chance," Hazel returned with a grin.

Riva's smile spread at the old joke. Jen looked askance at them.

"It sort of means 'proud to be us,' " Hazel explained, though she wasn't sure she was doing it justice.

Jen's lips pursed in approval. "I like it."

Hazel raised her eyebrows. Jen was always telling her to relax and let someone else take charge.

Jen smiled. "You just let Riley take on the Shadow without you. I'll grant you saving a few people here. Now come on, let's see if we're needed."

She led the way through the sliding front doors. On the left, a security guard leaned over a high information counter manned by a grey-haired woman. They both looked up when the girls entered, but Hazel looked down at her clothes. Her shirt was no longer dripping, but it was still wet. Riva and Jen appeared just as conspicuous in their summer pajamas.

Trying to look like she knew where she was going, Hazel directed Jen and Riva to the right. They strode down a wide hall with windows viewing the parking lot. The hall was full of tiny tables where weary people sat drinking coffee from paper cups.

Hazel ran through options in her mind. One thing was certain from their clothes alone; there was no faking authority here. She was certain someone would kick them out of the hospital if they drew too much attention to themselves.

"We need to find out who's in charge of the victims," Riva said, thinking out loud.

"We should start with our neighbour," Jen said, pointing with her chin to the man from the motel. "He can probably tell us who his daughter's doctor is."

He was sitting near the emergency room doors at the far end of the hall, his elbows on his bouncing knees. He kept running his palms over his buzzed hair. He was a wiry sort of man, and Hazel would have pegged him for a long-distance runner. She wove her way through the tables towards him. With his attention fixed on the ER door, he didn't notice Hazel until her shadow reached his feet.

"Sorry to bother you," she said. She gestured towards Jen and Riva to remind him of who they were. "We were in the room next to yours. Your daughter … Is she okay?"

He raised his hands palms up while taking in the state of Hazel's clothes.

"My brother was also bitten," Hazel went on. "But we're not allowed to see him."

Anger hardened his expression. "Dr. Carvahlo?"

"That's the guy."

"Woman," he corrected.

To cover her blunder, Hazel ran a hand over her face and said, "I'm exhausted."

He bought it. Sitting up a little, he asked, "Where are your parents?"

"Dead," Hazel said. Well, it was partially true. "I'm going to see if I can find out more. Are they still in there?"

He took her cavalier attitude in stride and nodded to the ER. "I got kicked out, but good luck. If you find anything out, I'd appreciate it."

Hazel's nerves grew as she pushed open one of the double doors. It was just as busy as Morgan described. Families were crowding around the nurses, demanding information. The benches were full of more people waiting their turn. Several of them looked grey, whether sick or worried, Hazel couldn't tell. Paramedics were rushing still more patients in through the sliding doors that opened to an ambulance bay.

Hazel made her way to the inner wall, where two women sat at computers behind a glass divider. They both looked grumpy and frazzled.

"Excuse me," Hazel said, "I need to speak to Dr. Carvahlo, please. It's urgent."

"What's your card number?" one of them asked, pausing with her hands hovering over her keyboard.

"No, I'm not hurt," Hazel corrected her. "I-it's about the spider bite victims."

"Are you looking for a family member?"

"No," Hazel said again. "I have ... information that will help."

The woman took in her wet clothes with a surreptitious eye. "You're a spider expert or something?"

Hazel stood straighter. "Yes, actually. The spiders ... were mine."

Both women at the desk stared, forgetting their other tasks.

"We were here for a conference," Hazel lied. "But they got out of their cage." She tried to inject some urgency into her voice. "Listen, they're poisonous and I can tell Dr. Carvahlo how to treat their bites. But we have to be fast."

The women exchanged a glance.

"Please," Hazel begged. She clasped her hands in front of her chest. "You have to let me fix this."

After another quick glance at each other, the first woman raised a finger to tell Hazel to wait while she grabbed her phone. Hazel hardly dared to breathe. From the corner of her eye, she could see Riva rubbing her triumphant mouth to hide her smile. Hazel kept her gaze straight-on.

The woman covered the mouthpiece and said, "Dr. Carvahlo will meet you at the doors as soon as she can." She indicated to a set of double doors at the end of the counter. To Jen and Riva, she pointed to the chairs in the waiting area and said, "You two can wait over there."

Hazel didn't want to press their luck, so she thanked the woman and left the others with a nod. Five minutes passed. Then ten. Hazel had to duck aside as paramedics wheeled in a moaning woman on a stretcher. Hazel was jumpy. There was no way to know who was close to turning and who wasn't. Impatience made Hazel want to slip through the doors after the paramedics. The longer she waited, the dryer her eyes became and the sorer her feet felt.

Finally, Dr. Carvahlo emerged.

"Are you the spider expert?" Dr. Carvahlo asked without preamble. She was a tall woman with warm brown skin. Her black hair was pulled back into a braided twist, and there was a sheen of sweat on her forehead.

"Yes," Hazel said, trying to inject some confidence into her voice. "How many have turned?"

Dr. Carvahlo looked taken aback. "What do you mean 'turned'?"

"I mean gone from screaming to attacking."

The doctor opened and closed her mouth. "I'm not at liberty to say."

"Then please, tell me this," Hazel said, "are they secured? Are they locked in a room they can't get out of? All of them? Even the ones that haven't turned yet?"

The doctor's eyes narrowed. "We administered the usual medication for spider bites. Is there something else I need to know?"

Hazel pressed on. "Did the medication help? Were you able to give it to someone before they turned?"

Dr. Carvahlo crossed her arms and gave Hazel a shrewd look. "You think it's too late if they've already 'turned.' "

"They're a danger to anyone who touches them," Hazel confirmed. She remembered what the news speculated last year as the attack began and twisted it to fit. "Once the venom reaches the brain, it corrupts the amygdala. They go into a fight response. Anyone who has a bite is a serious threat."

"We're trained to handle violent patients," Dr. Carvahlo said shortly. "I was under the impression you came to give me information about treatments."

Hazel hesitated. "I-I did. It's just ...," she lowered her voice, "nothing has ever worked before. Once they turn, it's permanent. Please tell me your treatment got to someone in time. If anyone has recovered," she paused to let out a shaky breath, "it would be incredible news."

Dr. Carvahlo unfolded her arms, her stern expression cracking just a touch. "We're closely monitoring all the bitten patients. We'll know before long if it worked. Is there anything else I should know?"

"Just, don't let anyone near them," Hazel said, feeling deflated by how little she was helping. "Even if they seem fine. They can change so fast. ..."

The doctor gave a curt nod. "Thank you for your input." She turned to leave, then paused. "It might be helpful to leave your name and number with reception."

Hazel promised she would, and then Dr. Carvahlo left. Hazel stood on her toes to see over the doctor's shoulder into the next room. Through the hurrying staff, she caught a glimpse of a nurse picking up small medical instruments from all over the floor. Then the door shut.

Caught somewhere between disappointment and relief, Hazel gave her name and Riva's number to the women at the counter, then returned to Jen and Riva near the ER entrance. She was about to suggest they wait next door, but she didn't get a chance. The room shattered in an explosion of glass and noise.

All three girls grouped together on instinct, hands covering their ears. On the far side of the room, people were screaming. An ambulance had driven straight through the glass doors and smashed into the inner wall beside the reception desk. The woman at the counter threw herself out of the way, toppling her chair. Her desk mate hurried to help her up. Likewise, people in the waiting area rushed forward to help fallen family members.

Stunned, Hazel's eyes locked on the ambulance. The hood was crumpled against the concrete wall, and the siren-less lights were painting them all in a blue-and-red glow. The bearded driver was screaming in agony and terror, trapped by his seatbelt as his partner's teeth tore into his neck. For a moment Hazel stood frozen, seeing the ambulance as if from one end of a long, black tunnel. Then the driver pushed the door open with a weak hand, and Hazel snapped out of it.

She sprinted for the door as the corrupt paramedic crawled across his dying partner towards the exit. He was halfway out. Hazel leapt over broken glass and slammed into the door, pinning him in the ambulance. His clawing hand snaked around the door and raked her arm. Hazel cried out in pain as a new trail of claw marks joined the ones Riley had already left on her arm.

Then the hospital was gone as a terror-vision hijacked

her mind. The world was shadow-black and the Shadow itself was looming over her in its old, long-limbed form. Its gaping, elongated mouth was larger than Hazel, wide enough to swallow her whole. She could see the reaching hands down its throat as its mouth plunged towards her.

Then she was back, gasping on the hospital's laminate floor. Riva shoved at the door, but it was too late. The corrupt was out. Jen hauled Hazel to her feet, both of them backing away as Riva shielded them. All the patients and guests in the waiting room stared at the blood dripping from the paramedic's face and the wound at his own neck. Hazel frantically scanned the room for weapons as the corrupt locked eyes on Riva, but there was nothing to defend her with.

He lunged. Riva tripped backwards, but Jen had darted to the side and ripped a clipboard out of a patient's hand. She caught up the attached pen and skid in front of Riva. With two swift jabs, Jen punctured both of the corrupt's eyes, dancing out of reach of the swiping arms. Bystanders screamed at this fresh act of violence.

The corrupt itself screamed in agony, but the girls had no time to explain. The bearded driver had climbed out of the ambulance, growling like a hell hound. He shoved his screaming partner aside and advanced on the girls as they backed deeper into the room.

The security guard arrived, panting from his race down the hall.

"Stop right there!" he yelled at the paramedics.

They both turned to him. At least ten innocent people stood between them.

"No!" Hazel cried as the corrupt advanced on the guard.

At the same time, Dr. Carvahlo arrived behind her, flooding

the room with more doctors and nurses. Hazel panicked. There were too many people.

"Get tranquilizers," Dr. Carvahlo ordered her staff.

"You can't stop them!" Hazel yelled to her, clapping her hands to win back the corrupts' attention. "You can't touch them without a terror-vision!"

They locked eyes over her shoulder, and in that one glance, Hazel knew the doctor had already experienced one.

The corrupt made their decision. With a growl that raised the hair on Hazel's arms, they spun towards the girls and broke into a sprint.

"Here!" Riva cried, racing to a door opposite Dr. Carvahlo's and leading them away from the doctor. All three girls crashed up against it. The door wouldn't budge.

The blind paramedic reached them first, clawing at Riva, who dodged into the corner.

"Here!" Dr. Carvahlo cried. She pulled a card from her pocket and tossed it to Hazel.

It flew wildly and ricocheted off the wall, landing on the floor behind the two corrupt. Hazel dove for it, but the second paramedic twisted as if to dive after her. Jen, still clinging to the pen, winged the attached clipboard at his head. To Hazel's horror, a spider fell from his collar. It landed next to Hazel's outstretched arm.

Then Dr. Carvahlo was there, flat on her stomach with her arm extended, crushing the spider under a small notebook. They locked eyes again. Hazel snatched up the card and slammed it against the keypad, almost snapping it. All the while, Jen beat the bearded corrupt about the head with the clipboard.

Riva had been clapping her hands to lead the blind corrupt

back into the main room and away from Hazel and Jen. When a tiny light on the keypad flashed green, Riva darted past it and shoved the door open with her shoulder.

"This way!" she called to the zombies as Jen tossed the other door open wide.

"The on-call room!" Dr. Carvahlo shouted after them.

Hazel didn't have time to acknowledge or question her. She clapped her hands as she ran, feeling like she was calling a dog to her, not a blood-soaked zombie. An announcement blared over their heads, something about a 'code white.'

There was a flurry of movement at the far end of the narrow, bleach-scented hall as staff responded to the code. Then they were alone in the nightmare.

The former paramedics were running full tilt as the doors to the ER clanged shut behind them. All three girls were barely keeping their feet as the bloody hands swiped at their hair. The growls and racing footsteps echoed off the walls. Hazel clenched her teeth as she strained to run faster.

The end of the hallway was too far away. Hazel knew it with a sinking certainty that made her stomach clench. This moment—the fluorescent lights, the hallway, the footsteps—it all stretched on for an eternity like time itself knew there would be nothing after.

Then Riva fell. She dropped faster than a rock. The zombie behind her tripped over her body, grabbing Hazel for purchase. The Shadow flashed before her eyes again, its gaping mouth closing over her. Then she was on the cold floor in a tangle of limbs and a mess of screaming.

The hallway ahead was clear. Hazel had tumbled farther than the others. The clipboard skidded out of Jen's hands, coming to a halt across from Hazel. She dove for it, freeing her legs, and turned back with it raised over her head like a weapon, terrified of what she might see.

The zombies separated Hazel from Riva, but Jen was buried under them. Her scream sliced through Hazel's ears, and she felt as though her soul was knocked from her body. One of the zombies tore into Jen's thigh with its teeth, and the other wrenched a chunk off her neck. In seconds there was blood everywhere. Then Hazel was hitting every inch of the zombies she could reach, snapping the clipboard in two and screaming with who knew what air. That feeling came over her again, that this was the end-all moment, and that it would go on forever because there was no possible living afterwards.

The zombies turned on her. Their mouths drew Hazel's fixed attention. That was Jen's blood, so red and thick.

"Run, Hazel!" Riva screamed.

Hazel tripped backwards but kept to her feet. The long moment was still going, her life was still ending.

"go!" Riva screamed again, and Hazel realized Riva's arms were wrapped around Jen's chest.

She was hauling Jen back the way they had come. She was going for help. The time-warp snapped. The zombies lunged at her, and Hazel turned on her heel and fled, close enough for them to follow, far enough to avoid their hands. She had to give Riva time.

At last, she rounded the corner of the interminable hallway. She couldn't keep her thoughts on survival, but she couldn't stand where they were landing either. Her brain whiplashed between Jen bleeding out and her own imminent death.

All the doors off the new hallway were shut. But Dr. Carvahlo had shouted something about an on-call room. Hazel's eyes swept the hall ahead. There were numbers above most of the doors, but some had little plaques. She strained to read the tiny writing but couldn't get more than the first two letters before they were out of sight.

As her eyes swept to the next door, she realized it was ajar. She thought the plaque above might start with an o, but she didn't pause to find out. She swung into the room at a reckless speed, almost crashing into a set of metal bunk beds. There were four sets in the dark room but no windows or doors, and the beds were covered with plastic sheets. A collection of tools and pipes was off to one side.

Hazel had thrown the zombies off with her sudden turn, but now they forced their way into the room, grappling with each other. Hazel leapt onto the small desk at the opposite end of the room and hauled herself up onto one of the bunk beds. She rolled onto the mattress, whipping her foot over the edge just before they could grab it. The plastic crinkled as she rolled to her knees.

Their hands reached over the edge. The bed was narrow. Hazel stood and had to hunch under the ceiling with her back to the cold wall. From this height, she could see the pipes on the floor and wished she'd had time to grab one. The bearded paramedic climbed the desk as the blind one stepped onto the lower bunk. Their hands grabbed the plastic sheet for leverage, pulling Hazel's feet a little closer. Panicked, Hazel kicked the sheet out from under her until she was standing on the spongey mattress. The blind zombie fell back, but the bearded one made it onto the bed. Jen's blood glistened in his scruffy beard as he crawled towards her.

22

Riley: A Deal

Exterminators in hazmat suits had joined the emergency response team surrounding the motel. Morgan pulled into the still teeming parking lot and slipped into a spot at the back. Some of the motel guests had retreated to their cars to sleep. Lines of caution tape strung between the police car mirrors separated the remaining crowd from the motel.

"Do you think bug spray will do the job?" Kate asked, eyeing the exterminators.

"No," Morgan answered. She put the car in park and pulled the e-brake, which ticked into place. "They're already dead."

"Poor spiders," Di said with a sigh.

Riley and Kate both spluttered, "What?"

"You can't be serious," Morgan said.

Di shrugged. "We felt bad for all the corrupt last year. They died. Why should I feel different about the spiders?"

"Because they're spiders," Morgan said, but there was a hint of a smile on her face. She unbuckled her seatbelt. "Come on, animal woman."

Riley saw the woman from the front desk sitting on a bumper

with a blanket wrapped around her shoulders. Avoiding her by keeping to the edge of the crowd, they crept to the back corner of the building.

"One, two, three, four ..." Kate did a head count under her breath. There were no onlookers behind the motel, but there were several exterminators. "Five, six, seven ..."

Riley eyed up the short hill that separated the back of the motel from the parking lot of an industrial building next door. The grassy slope was littered with drifting plastic bags and take-out cups. He could see why there was no need for caution tape here. The whole space was derelict and dark.

There was only one officer at the edge of the motel parking lot, and right now his eyes were on the ambulance. Morgan took Di's arm and nodded towards the industrial office building. She wanted to approach the motel from down below, where there were no officers to slip past.

"Eyes out for spiders," Kate muttered.

"Yes, please," Di replied.

The dry grass crackled underfoot, and Riley worried it would draw the officer's attention. It was so dark that he had to keep his eyes trained on the ground just to see where he was stepping. As soon as their feet hit the next parking lot, they sped to the shadows of the building. Pressing their backs against the wall, they looked up at the motel, panting. The officer was still facing away from them.

Morgan pointed to the corner opposite him. "Look, they're gathering over there."

Riley squinted and saw the last few exterminators leaving a door in the middle of the motel and trotting over to join a group. Their shadows grew and shrunk as they crossed dim triangles of light cast by wall-mounted outdoor bulbs.

Kate pointed to the door. "Doubt we'll get a better chance," she said, but she didn't move.

"Nah," Riley said. "They're way too close. They'll hear us."

Morgan shook her head. "They're trying to organize. They won't even notice us. Let's go, Di."

With that, she took Di's elbow again and started up the slope. Riley and Kate were left with their mouths hanging open. Together, they scurried after her.

"What do we say if they catch us?" Riley hissed at Morgan's back.

"Shhh," she replied.

Heart pounding, Riley tripped up the hill, staying as low as he could. Their feet touched the sliver of pavement at the base of the motel. Just across the path was the door. Riley's head was on a swivel. The police officer was talking to someone in the parking lot, but the exterminators were wrapping up their conversation. Morgan grabbed the back of his shirt and thrust him across the pavement.

The girls shielded him from either side as if they had planned it. Riley grabbed the cold door handle, and with one smooth twist he was inside, Kate at his heels.

Di had one foot over the threshold when a voice shouted, "Hey!"

Riley and Kate froze in the darkness of the hallway, locking eyes with Morgan, who was still on the outside.

"Go!" she whispered through her teeth.

Riley and Kate slipped farther into the shadows, ducking behind a mop bucket.

"You can't go in there!" the voice shouted.

"I'm sorry," Di called, turning her blind eyes to the distant speaker. "I'm looking for a bathroom."

"You're off limits, Di!" Morgan said. She managed to sound out of breath, like she had just caught up. "You should have asked me. Here, take my hand."

Di gave Morgan a covert grin as the exterminator's hurried footsteps closed in.

Under her breath she said, "Using my eyes against the Shadow. That's beautiful." The smile slipped away as she whispered in Riley's direction, "Take it down, Riley."

The footsteps came to a halt, but some of the anger drained from the exterminator's voice as he looked at Di. "It's very dangerous here. You want to get yourselves killed?"

Riley and Kate slunk off down the hallway, leaving Kate and Di to be escorted back to the parking lot.

"Let's go," Kate said when they were far enough from the door.

They broke into a run, their feet pattering on the laminate floor. They were in the staff-only part of the motel, but no matter how many corners they took, it remained deserted. The silence was unnerving. Riley's eyes swept the walls and floor for spiders but saw only empty cobwebs. At last, they emerged onto the green carpet that marked the guests' halls, and their footsteps were finally muffled.

"Where do you think it is?" Kate asked, looking back over her shoulder.

Riley made a face to show he had no idea. Spiders liked the dark. It would follow if shadows did too, but everywhere seemed dark to him.

"Maybe we should try the room we left it in," he suggested.

"We could try," Kate agreed, as they jogged down the next hall, "but I smashed the mirror in there. I bet wherever it is, there'll be mirrors."

Riley slowed to a stop. He had once followed Hazel's cord through a mirror. Maybe he could find the Shadow the same way.

He closed his eyes. "Watch for spiders."

Blue cords sprang to his vision. He sifted through them, apprehension and hope constricting his chest. Then one twanged like a taut guitar string, a low sound that filled Riley with dread. This was not the rope of Riley's shadow. It was a combination of dripping chains and sticky spider webs. The chain links extended from his chest and rose up through the ceiling. The Shadow was somewhere above them. When he opened his eyes, Kate was looking up at where the chain disappeared.

He cocked his head at her.

"It's upstairs," she said, looking frightened.

Riley nodded. "Could you see it?"

Kate put a hand to her heart, still staring at the ceiling. Her voice was faint when she answered, "I could feel it."

A hissing sound and voices made them jump. The exterminators were making their way through the halls with their bug spray. Kate grabbed Riley's hand and pulled him to the nearest stairwell. Like the one in the lobby, it was narrow and made an unbelievable amount of noise. They took it two steps at a time.

They arrived near the wall of windows overlooking the pool. Riley crouched to pass the windows unnoticed, following the cord by the light of the moon. They rounded a corner. He knew where the Shadow would be before they arrived. They had abandoned their belongings in their old room, and the Shadow knew they would be back for them eventually. Riley shivered. It really did want Hazel dead.

Kate pointed at the bottom of the door with a shaking hand.

Tiny shadows twitched and scurried under the crack. Riley watched them for a long moment. There was no way he could open the door without disturbing them.

At last, he looked up at Kate and mouthed with a silent laugh, "Do I knock?"

She clapped a hand over her mouth to stop a shocked laugh. "That's not funny. What is wrong with you?"

They had a mimed fight over who should open the door to their potential deaths, both shaking with fear and inappropriate laughter. Riley's whole body was so tense that his teeth chattered.

Kate took a steadying breath. Riley copied her. There would be no more delaying. She grabbed his hand in hers and they faced the door. Their palms were equally icy.

Riley cleared his throat and called, "Shadow?"

His voice cracked, but this time Kate didn't laugh. The myriad of legs at the bottom of the door all froze and he cleared his throat again, plunging on before they could attack.

"Let us in, and I'll let you in."

The door blasted open, banging off the inner wall, and Riley was wrenched into the room. He landed hard on his stomach, dragged by the chain. The spiders cleared a path for him like water parting at the bow of a boat, only this water was brown, black, and living.

Thousands of spiders covered every surface, their bodies like a thick lace blanket over the beds. They painted the walls black, hung from the corners of the room, and watched him from under the dresser.

Riley craned his neck up to see the Shadow menacing over him, half-human, half-spider. Then Kate was beside him, jerked forward by a hook of her own. Riley stared up at the human skull that Kate could only sense. Thin layers of skin stretched over the eight empty eye sockets, but he was pinned by their impossible glare. Grey hands on the end of the legs held their chains fast. The fingers on the remaining legs tapped on the ground like additional spiders, impatient for orders.

The fangs parted. "Take her," the Shadow said.

"No!" Riley cried.

Kate rolled towards Riley and he hauled her onto his back in one seamless motion. The spiders descended, rearing at them with their front legs. Riley forced himself to his feet, but the spiders came no closer, unwilling to attack him. Kate wrapped her legs around him, repositioning into a piggyback.

"If you want to hear my deal, you have to leave her out of this!" Riley yelled into the Shadow's face. They were alarmingly close, but Riley didn't dare back away.

The Shadow gave him the chilling smile he had seen in the mirror, and it turned its gaze to the ceiling. Spiders were sliding down strands over their heads. Kate's arms tensed around Riley's throat.

"Stop!" Riley cried. "Listen to me!"

The spiders slipped ever lower.

"You know what I can do!" Riley said, speaking as fast as he could. "I can help you! You'll have the living and the dead at your mercy! But I want to be a part of it!"

The bald skull tilted to the side, and the spiders finally slowed to a stop, twisting like acrobats on a line.

"I don't want to trap you, like Hazel did," Riley said. "I want—I want to rule with you."

Silence stretched between them as the spiders' legs made ticking sounds on the walls. Riley wet his lips. He had to make this convincing.

"My dad is dead," he said. "His killers are alive, but he is dead. They took him away from me, even though he did nothing to them—*I* did nothing to them! I didn't deserve to lose him." Real tears sprang to Riley's eyes, and he was glad. "There's nothing I can do to change the fact that he's gone. But I can make them pay."

Riley said the last through clenched teeth, and his hands gripped Kate's thighs so tight that she gave a little gasp of pain. He couldn't seem to let go.

"The other shadow," he went on, his voice shaking, "tried to control me. But I'm sick of being powerless. I want to destroy those murdering bastards. And I need you to do that."

He didn't break eye contact with the sightless Shadow as he trembled with rage. For a moment he saw what was possible: with the Shadow, he could rip his dad's killers limb from limb. Even if Riley stopped short of killing them, the Shadow could make them see things. It could make the murderers see things that would haunt them to their dying days. It was only fair. It was justice, and they deserved it. And when it was done, Riley could take control back from the Shadow.

Riley realized he wanted it bad. He could twist this terrible deal to his favour. He could do right by his father. All it would take was the guts to make it happen.

"And after ...," the Shadow pressed, both of its voices low.

"After," Riley echoed. He had to blink to refocus. "After ... I'll lead you to as many ghosts as you want. And we'll make the living fear you."

Saliva dripped from the Shadow's fangs at the talk of fear.

"Threats to me ...," it said, a hint of delight in the high, witch-like voice, "will be harvested."

Riley nodded.

"Hazel," the Shadow clarified with relish.

Riley swallowed, and nodded again. "But not Kate."

The Shadow gave that wicked smile again, and without a word or even so much as a nod, the spiders retreated back up their webs. Kate slipped off Riley's back but stayed close enough that their arms pressed together.

"Yes," the Shadow agreed, but as its smile widened, Riley didn't need Kate's sudden grip on his arm to know it was a lie.

The Shadow pounced, its jaws unhinging as wide as a Riley. It inhaled with enough force to pull him forward. He slipped from Kate's grasp. She forced herself between them instead, shielding herself with one arm. The Shadow and Riley came to the realization at the same time. Kate, who couldn't see the Shadow, had sensed what it was about to do.

The Shadow changed targets. Throwing herself in front of Riley was all the permission it needed.

"No!" Riley cried.

The jaws angled towards Kate. The sucking inhale intensified until it was like wind moaning through a mountain pass. It pulled at the strands of Kate's hair. She screamed, but the hoarse inhale was deafening, and it snatched her voice unnaturally from the air. Her feet slid towards the gaping mouth.

Riley threw his arms around Kate and tried to wrench her away, but it was like prying apart enormous, powerful magnets.

"Riley!" Kate cried.

She slipped out of his grasp until all he had left were her hands. Her fingers were freezing. To Riley's alarm, Kate's next breath drew in ribbons of the Shadow, its body stretching like the tendrils of Kate's hair. Shadow and hair mingled together in the air until they seeped down each other's throats. Riley clenched his teeth and managed to wrap his left arm around Kate. He forced his other hand between her and the Shadow in a last defense, sweat pouring down his forehead. The black strands engulfed him.

His hand touched something in the air. He closed his fist, clinging to anything he might physically resist with. It was the chain that connected him to the Shadow.

Riley seized it with both hands and swung away from Kate with all his might. The torso of the giant spider twisted with him as if on a leash, but the face stayed locked in on Kate. Riley wrenched at it so hard that he fell back against the bed.

"Leave her!" he shouted, and with an enormous yank, he looped a chunk of the chain around his elbow.

The Shadow's body jerked towards him, its legs skittering on the carpet. For a fraction of a second, its face turned towards Riley, breaking contact with Kate. Riley acted on instinct. He imitated its intake of breath, both pulling the chain and sucking the Shadow into his lungs at the same time.

One of the legs soared towards his mouth, the grey hand stretching until it was long and slim. It slid into Riley's mouth as smoke. He gagged at the somehow fur-like texture. The Shadow was resisting, trying to return to Kate, but Riley inhaled through his nose, calling it towards him. More and more Shadow sank into his lungs. The room was a swirl of competing black air currents that tossed his hair from side to side.

He managed another loop of the chain around his elbow. Spiders raced up his legs and poured over the mattress onto his shoulders. They covered him in such a thick blanket that he appeared to be melting into the floor. They sunk their teeth into every inch of him, but no terror-vision took hold. The

Shadow in his lungs had made Riley immune.

Across the room, Kate had sensed her own chain and was straining to pull the Shadow from Riley. She slipped, and the spiders swept over her too. Her grip on the chain stayed firm even as her face contorted with pain and she breathed in more Shadow.

Without planning it, Riley called up Hazel's cord. He didn't have to sift through the others to find it. It rose to his mind as if waiting, glowing a brilliant blue. In desperation, he screamed her name down it.

23

Hazel: Chains

Hazel braced herself for a terror-vision and kicked the bearded zombie in the forehead as hard as she could. Her contact was brief, but in that split second she saw the Shadow's cavernous mouth again, about to close on her forever. At the same time, she heard a scream.

"Hazel!"

Riley. Her attacker recovered, snarling, as the blind zombie moved to climb the desk behind him. The open end of the bunk bed was left unmanned.

Hazel hurled herself off. Pain ripped up her heels as she landed on the hard floor like an uncoordinated superhero. The bearded zombie threw himself after her. She tore over to the collection of pipes near the first bunk bed, picked up a brass pipe as long as her arm, and turned around swinging. The open end of the pipe scratched across his face.

As a smattering of blood flew through the air, she heard Riley's voice again.

"Hazel! The chains!"

His voice couldn't be from a terror-vision. Hazel hadn't

touched the zombie. Confusion battled against her survival instinct. The zombie grabbed at the pipe and Hazel jabbed it towards his stomach. It was a mistake. He seized the pipe and yanked her closer. She released it and stooped to grab a new one, the pipes and tools on the floor rattling as her heels jostled them.

The zombie threw aside the old pipe and dove at her just as she raised the new one. The pipe stabbed into his abdomen and met ribs. Hazel gasped, staring up at him as blood ran down the pipe. He let out a roar of pain that echoed throughout the box of a room and chilled Hazel's heart. He freed himself with a backwards jerk and a slight *squelch*.

"Hazel! Please!" the voice cried.

"I'm busy!" Hazel cried aloud, swinging the pipe frantically to keep the enraged zombie at bay.

The blind paramedic had found her again, and now they both bared down on her. She faked darting deeper into the room, and when the bearded zombie went to follow, she swiveled, ducking under his outstretched arm. Using the pipe to keep him at a distance, Hazel sprinted for the door. Hope swelled in her chest as she reached it.

She burst into the hallway, threw the pipe aside with an echoing clang, and pulled the door shut. The slam reverberated up her wrists as she held it fast. Her head was full of yelling, but it wasn't coming from the corrupt.

The door almost slid out of her grasp as the corrupt fought to open it from the other side. Hazel's hands were slick with blood. The door jerked open a fraction and shut again. She braced her feet on either side of the door frame and leaned back, seeing a brief memory of Alexis in this same position a year ago.

Then a shadow appeared beside Hazel and she screamed. The figure seemed to shudder and contort, but then Hazel realized she was seeing spiders clambering all over a body.

"Riley!" she gasped, horrified.

Riley was on his knees, the blue chord stretching between them. He had traveled to see her again. Something black seeped into his nostrils as he, like Hazel, strained against something.

"What's happening?" Hazel screamed as the door rattled and shook her entire upper body.

Just like the last time he traveled to see her, Riley's mouth moved but no sound came out. The chains, he had said. Hazel squeezed her eyes shut and felt for the hook in her back. Its direction had changed, and it now emerged, hideous as ever, from her chest. It was pointing towards the motel.

Using all her concentration, she willed her body not to waver and, for the first time, followed the chain. Her mind flew towards an enormous spider. Ribbons of black shadows were peeling off of it and whirling around her like a living tornado. On the floor, in the midst of the tornado, Kate was screaming and straining against another hook. This was all wrong. The Shadow was supposed to possess Riley, not Kate. Kate was not like them.

Panic rising, Hazel glanced around the room and saw Riley kneeling on the ground. His eyes were glassy and his body stiff, as if his essence wasn't really there. He had looped one of the Shadow's chains around his arm. Spiders crawled across his face, across the beds, across the ceiling. Then Riley gave a great, shuddering gasp, and his eyes lit back up.

Hazel opened her own eyes back in the hospital hallway, struggling to make sense of it all. It seemed as if the Shadow was trying to take them both.

Just then, one of the zombies got his hand through the crack in the door. Hazel slammed the door on the fingers three times, and the zombie howled in agony. Its other hand slid through the crack, gripping the door's edge and forcing it open farther as blood ran down its fingertips.

She was going to lose. *The Shadow*, Hazel thought. If she could finish the Shadow, the zombies would die. Riley had wanted her to notice the hooks. He had wrapped the chain around his arm. Hazel gasped as realization struck her. They weren't trying to free themselves as the Shadow reeled them in. They were reeling the Shadow in.

Her hands were not available to grab the chains, but Hazel seized them in her mind's eye. She had never dared to grasp them before. She imagined the metal in her hands instead of the door handle and she pulled with all her might. Her teeth clenched together so hard she heard a crack.

Strands of swirling black shadow surrounded her right there in the hallway, like a cocoon of darkness. The fluorescent lights appeared to flicker as the fragments flew past. Hazel's hair swirled around her face, sticking to blood she didn't know she had smeared there.

"You can't have Kate!" Hazel shouted through her teeth, sending the message down the line to the Shadow.

I can, came the booming response in Hazel's head, and she nearly lost her grip.

"You—" she grunted, "belong with—me!"

No one came running to her aid at the sound of Hazel's voice. There was no hint of a door opening or footsteps approaching. The hospital was following lockdown procedure. Hazel was on her own.

"You would starve me," the Shadow accused. "And the boy

would use me!"

Hazel was beginning to feel dizzy from the spiraling wind. She couldn't hold the door against two full-grown corrupt much longer.

"I have the body I need," the Shadow cackled.

The hair on Hazel's arms rose, as, for a moment, she saw Kate in the middle of the darkness. That's what they were to the Shadow: just bodies to be manipulated, souls to be shoved aside and subdued. She couldn't let that happen to Kate.

"Come back to me!" she demanded, bile rising in her throat. "Come home!"

A burst of rage shot down the chain and hit Hazel square in the chest, the force blasting her off her feet. She crashed into the opposite wall and crumpled to the floor. The collision knocked the breath out of her. Her lungs made a strange, ghoulish moan as she struggled to draw air.

Across the hall, the sudden release of the door had knocked the corrupt off their feet, but they were already getting back up. Hazel didn't lose another moment. She grabbed hold of the chains with her hands. They were as cold, as real, as she imagined. She pulled hand-over-hand. Her desperation to breathe and to protect Kate and Riley jumbled together until the thought of pulling in air and reeling in the chain became one.

The corrupt burst through the doorway. Tears spilled from Hazel's eyes as she watched them thunder across the hall through the whirl of black. She didn't run. She tried to inhale again, but all she achieved was that strange, inward wail that tore through her throat. Then she heard Kate's voice.

"Now!"

Hazel heaved against the cord, scrambling down the hall

with her feet as the corrupt threw themselves at her. Their pressure jolted life back into her lungs. Sparks appeared before her eyes, and the black shadows that muddied the air poured into Hazel's lungs.

The hallway vanished. She was in the motel room. On the ground in front of the Shadow, almost unrecognizable under all the spiders, was Kate. She was using her legs to push herself away, dragging the Shadow by the chain, an inch at a time. Riley was lying with one arm braced around the foot of the bed, the other wrapped up in his chain. Like Hazel, black shadows were pouring into their mouths and noses.

The Shadow towered over all three of them, screaming in both its voices. The hands on the ends of the Shadow's folded legs were opening and closing convulsively. Hazel cringed against its deafening screams. Even in the vision, Hazel clung to the chain. She stuck out her chin in defiance and gave an almighty wrench.

The Shadow roared in agony. Hazel saw the hands down its throat just before they exploded into thick, black tar. The Shadow's head and torso ripped apart from its body with a shredding sound and crashed at Kate's feet. The rest of the abdomen and several legs toppled onto Riley, while a tangle of the remaining legs crashed in Hazel's direction. Shreds of shadows burst into the air like the ashes of burnt paper.

The body melted like the hands inside it, flooding the floor with black sludge. The spiders fled, scuttling all over each other in their haste to escape. The shadows still in Hazel's lungs collapsed into tar, and she retched.

Hazel turned on her side to cough up the sludge and found the hospital floor. The tar merged with a pool of blood. She pushed a limp hand off her and crawled out from under the bodies of the corrupt, still heaving. She collapsed a short distance away.

The pool of blood was her own. Hazel's shoulder and ankle were gushing from half-moon-shaped wounds. She clapped a hand to her shoulder to stem the flow. When she'd brought up the last of the Shadow's poison, Hazel pressed her forehead to a clean patch of the cool floor and hugged herself tight.

The Shadow was dead. Relief washed over her so fast it made the hall shimmer and wobble. Her limbs felt like jelly. Then, unbidden, the memory of hands down the Shadow's throat sprang forward, and on the next breath, she was sobbing.

"M-Mom ...," she choked. "Gran ..."

She buried her mouth in the crook of her arm and let out a howl of misery. Some part of her, some childish part, had been clinging to hope. As long as she had the Shadow, maybe she had them with her. Maybe one day she could think of a way to free them. Now all she had left of them was tar. Hazel curled in on herself and sobbed and bled until the world went dark.

24

Riley: The Damage

"Hey!"

Morgan was waving with both hands from a table beside the hospital food court's dark windows. Di sat opposite her. Riley kept his head down to avoid the stares as he crossed through the tables. He and Kate were covered in ugly red bites.

"Is everything okay?" Di asked, offering some of her muffin with a wave of the hand.

"Thank you," Kate said, taking the spot beside Morgan and helping herself to a piece. "I need to wash away the taste of … it."

Riley took a piece too. His taste buds recoiled at the lemon flavour, but it was heaven compared to the taste of tar.

He answered Morgan. "They treated the bites but weren't able to find anything else wrong with us. The tar seems harmless."

"Good," she said, nodding with satisfaction. "Now what the hell happened?"

Kate and Riley had been wheeled out of the motel strapped to gurneys after the exterminators found them coughing up black tar. Morgan had only managed to grab Riley's hand in passing to say, "We'll meet you there."

At the little table, they explained how the spiders had attacked and the Shadow had ripped to pieces. Morgan and Di listened to the whole story with their mouths open in horror and awe.

"So it's gone now?" Di asked in a hushed voice.

"It's gone," Riley agreed. Saying it aloud made him feel light enough to float. He gave Kate a tired grin.

Morgan dusted off her palms. "Well that was easy," she joked.

Kate laughed. "So where're the others?"

There was an uneasy pause, and Di's face fell. "Well, it turns out there was an outbreak here after all. When I spoke to Riva, she said there are four dead that she knows of. And Jen ... Jen got bit. It was bad. She needed a blood transfusion."

Kate clapped a hand over her mouth.

"Is she going to be okay?" Riley asked, gripping the edge of the table.

"They think so."

Riley let out a shaky breath. "And Hazel and Riva?"

Di squirmed, uncomfortable with breaking all this bad news. "Riva is okay, but Hazel was bitten too. They were stitching her up when I spoke to Riva. She said Hazel was unconscious and covered in black stuff, like you two."

"When will we know more?" Kate asked.

"I'm waiting for Riva to call back."

There was a sober silence.

Morgan squeezed the bridge of her nose. "I need to take a walk or I'm going to fall asleep."

Kate stood up. "Same."

The two girls left Riley and Di at the table to do a loop of the hospital.

"So," Di said, shifting in her seat to face Riley, "will you go back home now?"

He looked down at his hands. "I guess so."

She heard the nerves in his voice. "You can tell your mom the truth now. That you left to protect her."

Riley swallowed. "But I'll have to tell her what I was protecting her from."

"You don't think she'll believe you?"

"It's not that." Riley stared at the muffin wrapper without really seeing it. "It's my dad."

"But the shadow wasn't really your dad," Di said.

Riley felt like something was stuck in his throat. "Even if it wasn't, now we know Dad isn't at peace somewhere. He's just gone." His voice went hoarse. "I don't want to tell her that."

Di held out her hand under the table. After a long moment, Riley took it.

"Being gone could be peaceful too," she said. "Like when you wake up with no memory of being unconscious. I think it must be like that. It's not good or bad. It just is."

Riley struggled to wrap his head around the idea of not existing. It was difficult to see past how scary it seemed to be wiped away forever. That, and he missed his dad so much that he didn't want to look too close.

"Do you remember before you were born?" Di asked, tilting her head to the side.

"No, of course not," he answered.

"And does it bother you?"

"I've never thought about it before."

"So no," Di said with a small smile. "I've thought about it a lot over the past year. The Shadow took so many ghosts." She shook her head. "But most people don't give a second thought to before they were born. If we didn't exist then, why does it bother us so much that one day we won't again?" She squeezed his hand. "It's a small comfort, maybe. But it helped me get through."

They didn't speak for a long time. Riley wanted to put his head down on the table and sleep. He thought again about how lucky Hazel was to be surrounded by friends like Di. He missed his old friend, Wyatt, he realized. He was tired of feeling so angry and lonely all the time. Maybe when he got home he would reach out to him again.

When he remembered he was still holding Di's hand, Riley released it and cast his thoughts around for something neutral to say.

"Thanks for getting us back into the motel."

Di gave a sly smile. "Happy to turn my curse into a gift. Thank you for giving the Shadow what it deserved."

"We got lucky," Riley said on an exhale.

When he didn't elaborate, Di nudged him with her shoulder and said, "You might have been lucky it worked, but luck isn't what made you try."

At last, Riley smiled.

25

Hazel: Reflection

The first thing Hazel wanted to know after opening her eyes to a hospital room was whether Jen and Riva were alright. She sat on the edge of her bed, tapping her good foot as the nurses assured her the girls were okay but that she could not go see for herself. Their concern and care pushed Hazel closer and closer to tears. She couldn't stand seeing her mother in the way they pushed water into her hands or suggested she lay back and rest. She wanted to run and heap care on someone else.

It was a relief when Dr. Carvahlo arrived and grilled Hazel on why she had tar in her lungs. Hazel admitted she wasn't a spider expert so much as a zombie expert. Dr. Carvahlo asked questions but kept her face impassive. She had seen the zombies for herself, and apart from the bites, Hazel was healthy. With no other reason for a healthy teen to cough up tar, she had to accept the story of the Shadow.

Even so, Hazel supposed her file might suggest she was delusional now. In truth, she was amazed to have lasted this long. She found she didn't really care anymore.

The second Dr. Carvahlo left, Riva flew into the room, almost knocking the doctor over on the way. Hazel sprang up, then gasped as the stitches on her ankle pulled.

"Are you okay?" Riva demanded, taking her elbow and making her sit back on the bed, side by side.

"Are you?" Hazel returned, her eyes filling with tears again.

"Oh, I'm fine," Riva said with a dismissive wave of the hand.

Hazel pulled Riva into a firm hug. She could only manage it one-handed with the stitches and bandages covering her shoulder.

Over Riva's shoulder Hazel said, "Thank you."

"For what?" Riva asked in surprise.

"For being the best friend I could have ever asked for."

Riva tried to pull away, but Hazel refused to let her go. She held on until she felt a slight hitch in Riva's breath. Then she knew she had gotten through.

When they drew apart, Hazel pulled some tissue from a box on the side table and shared them.

"How's Jen?" she asked. "Besides okay, which is all anyone will tell me."

"I haven't been able to visit her yet," Riva admitted. "They had to give her blood, but apparently it's going well. She was in the right place for this to happen."

"You saved her," Hazel said, the tears sparkling in her eyes.

"Team effort," Riva corrected. "And please don't start that again."

Hazel chuckled and dabbed at her eyes. Riva patted her leg.

"I need to talk to her," Hazel said when she had thrown the tissue away.

Riva studied her with unusually serious eyes. "To break up with her, or to tell her you love her?"

Hazel stopped breathing.

"You can't break up with someone right after they've been hospitalized," Riva warned.

"No, I—of course I'm—" Hazel spluttered.

Kate, Riley, Morgan, and Di came in at that moment, and the bites all over Kate and Riley's faces distracted her.

"Oh, wow," she gasped.

"Oh, very nice, Hazel," Morgan teased with a snort.

Hazel's face went red, but both Riley and Kate were grinning.

"Bad night?" Hazel joked in a small voice.

Laughing, the visitors perched on the bed or shared the one stiff chair, taking care to watch out for Hazel's bad ankle. When they were all situated, they got down to the business of rehashing the night in whispers until the nurses kicked them out.

***

By the faint pink of the clouds outside, Hazel gathered she had been sleeping for only a few hours when a nurse came to wake her.

"I'm sorry," she said, "but your friend is asking for you."

"Jen?" Hazel asked, throwing her blankets off and getting out of bed so fast she got a head rush.

She gripped the side table for balance, feeling sick with exhaustion. The nurse took her arm to escort her through the halls.

"She's just through there," she said at last.

Hazel already knew. The cord connecting her to Jen was glowing softly. She left the nurse at the door. Like Hazel, Jen had a shared room. All the other occupants were fast asleep. Although blue privacy curtains shielded the beds, Hazel headed straight for Jen's. She pulled the fabric aside.

"Hazel!" Jen gasped. She reached a hand out to pull Hazel

closer.

Hazel grasped her hand in both of hers, but stayed back. She took in the thick bandage covering the crook of Jen's neck and the pallor of her skin. Hazel had almost lost her last night. Riva's words replayed in Hazel's head: you can't break up with someone right after they've been hospitalized. She felt a twist of guilt deep in her stomach. If Riva didn't know how Hazel felt about Jen, then no one did. Not even Jen.

"I—" Hazel choked. "I never realized how bad it was for you."

"I'm going to be fine." Jen smiled. Her voice was weak. She caressed the bandage on Hazel's shoulder.

"No," Hazel said, and when she shook her head, a tear rolled down her cheek. "I mean how bad I was." The last word came out in a whisper.

Jen readjusted her position with a wince. "What are you talking about?"

Hazel took a big, trembling breath. "I've never told you I loved you." Jen's hand froze in Hazel's. Hazel stared down at the blankets. "I couldn't let myself feel it. I was so scared to lose you. I-I couldn't even argue with you."

Jen opened her mouth in confusion, so Hazel went on, "When you told Kate and the rest of your team that I can see ghosts, I was mad at you. But I stuffed it down because I was too scared to fight."

By the tilt of Jen's eyebrows, Hazel knew she was about to speak words of comfort, so she waylaid her, determined to say it all.

"And I knew how much it bothered you when I shared things with Riva and not you," Hazel went on, crying in earnest now, "but it's because I already loved Riva before ... everything happened. And I know it wasn't fair to you. You were so patient with me." Her voice pitched too high, and she had to take a breath to bring it back down. "But loving someone after felt …"

"Scary," Jen supplied, nodding with understanding.

"Terrifying," Hazel agreed.

They locked eyes. Tears were shimmering in Jen's eyes too, turning the rich brown glossy and beautiful.

"I feel so stupid," Hazel said, shaking with emotion. "Of all people, I should have known how important it is to tell someone how you feel about them. …" She broke off, wiping her nose on her sleeve as grief for her family poured over her.

Gentle but firm, Jen pulled Hazel closer. Hazel knelt at the edge of the bed and sobbed into the sheets while Jen stroked her hair.

When the sobs had abated, Jen said, "You aren't going to lose me, Hazel. And I'm glad you have Riva. You're the bravest person I've ever met. I knew if I just waited … you'd find a way through."

Hazel settled her chin on the mattress and looked up at Jen. Even with dark circles under her eyes from sleepless nights and losing blood, she was so beautiful. Hazel was certain that no words were strong enough to express how she felt right now, but she did her best anyway.

"I love you."

Jen wiped a tear from her own eye and said with a happy sigh, "I love you too."

Hazel rose from the floor, bent over Jen, and pressed a soft kiss to her lips. The cord that connected their hearts was warm and glowing. Their foreheads met and Hazel closed her eyes. If she could choose a moment to live in forever, this one would be it.

***

It was no surprise that dawn brought scorching heat to the parking lot outside the hospital. Hazel, Kate, and Riley were waiting on a bench in the shade. Jen was still inside with her mom and dad, waiting to be discharged. They had driven out this morning.

The others had gone in Riva's SUV to collect Morgan's car from the motel. A hot breeze blew through the trees next to them as the trio waited to go home. They were going to drop Riley off at the bus stop on the way. Hazel had overheard his conversation with his mom from the hospital phone.

Her relief had come out as shouting and crying. "Do you have any idea how worried I was about you?"

Hazel didn't envy Riley his reunion. Love could be so painful. Then again, maybe she did.

She pretended to watch the leaves swaying in the trees, but really she was watching Riley and Kate. No one had had a good night's sleep in days, but she suspected their silence was more than that.

"You know," she said at last, "it would be a shame for the three of us to lose touch."

Riley looked up from studying his plastic gift-shop sandals. Di had bought him the shoes because the motel had refused to let guests back in. Their belongings would only be shipped home when the motel was cleared for habitation again.

Riley lifted his palms. "I have no phone. But I can give you my email if you want?"

Hazel didn't have a phone either. She had left it in the motel when the screaming had first started. Kate had lost hers to the pool.

Hazel snorted. "Actually, I don't think we need any of that stuff, do we? We've got the cords."

Riley grinned. "Does that make us telepathic?"

"I guess," Hazel said with a smile and a shrug.

"I don't know," Kate said, running a finger over a bite on her chin. The dots of white ointment all over her and Riley's faces made them look like plague victims. "I know you heard my voice last night, but I'm not sure I can do it again." She sighed. "I wish my sight was stronger. I'm never going to trust a shadow again."

"You're better off," Riley said. He nodded towards the hospital to make his point. "The little girl is over there. The one from the room next to us."

Hazel's heart sunk. The ghost was sitting alone against the side of the ER, her arms wrapped around her knees, looking lost.

"Oh, no," Kate said in a sad, low moan, "that poor girl. What did she do to deserve this?"

"Nothing," Hazel answered, the breeze lifting her hair as she watched the girl. After a pause, she realized they were waiting for her to elaborate. She sighed.

"When my family died, I used to think it must be to teach me something. Because I knew they certainly didn't deserve it. But what kind of world kills someone to teach someone else something?" She shook her head and shrugged again. "It was dumb to think it was about me. So now I don't believe anyone deserves anything."

Riley looked alarmed. "So it's all just chaos?"

Hazel chuckled. "I think if you're good, good things are more likely to happen to you. And vice versa. But when bad things happen to good people ... No, they probably didn't deserve it.

It was bad luck. Terrible luck."

"A small comfort," Riley said with a nod, as if to himself.

"Exactly," Hazel agreed.

Riley stood up.

"Where are you going?" Kate asked.

"To turn this curse into a gift," he answered. "I'm going to go help the girl."

"Do you want company?" Hazel offered.

Riley smiled and shook his head. "Nah, I got this one."

Hazel watched him go and felt a weight ease from her shoulders, a weight she had been carrying since she was a little girl. She excused herself to the washroom.

Inside, Hazel caught sight of herself in the mirror over the sink and stopped. Her hair was still a wavy mess from air-drying after her leap into the pool. Her gift shop t-shirt didn't quite cover the bandages on her shoulder, and she was still wearing her pajama shorts. Hazel looked rough. But life had been rough for over a year.

She crossed her arms, studying her reflection. It wasn't just how she looked, though. For the first time, Hazel acknowledged how much she had contributed to her own sadness. She hadn't just blocked her heart towards Jen. She had stopped doing so much of what she loved.

Hazel lifted her chin in defiance. That was over now. When she healed, she would start running again. Maybe even wrestling. She missed Coach Tom, and she knew he would be glad to see her. She might even move out of Riva's busy household and ask Jen if she wanted to move in together. Hazel felt a thrill of excitement instead of fear. She grinned at her reflection. No one but herself smiled back.

About the Author

Nicole MacCarron is an accident-prone Canadian from BC's Fraser Valley. The accidents started at 8, when she rolled off the top bunk and broke her arm. In pursuit of her Education and English degrees, she nearly broke her neck and back. Nicole currently teaches kindergarten and dreams of returning to Ireland (where she once broke her cheekbone in two places). Nicole is a firm believer that any misadventure can be turned into a great story. As such, most physical pain depicted in her novels comes from a place of experience, and helped to make it all worthwhile.

Interested in supporting this Indie author? Please leave a review on Amazon, or join Nicole MacCarron's mailing list to receive a free short prequel to *Hazel's Shadow*. To get your free short story and to find more books by Nicole MacCarron, go to the website listed below.

You can connect with me on:

- https://nicolemaccarron.com
- https://twitter.com/MaccarronNicole
- https://www.facebook.com/maccarronnicole
- https://www.instagram.com/writersarereaders
- https://www.tiktok.com/@nicolemaccarron

www.ingramcontent.com/pod-product-compliance
Lightning Source LLC
Chambersburg PA
CBHW021307190726

48288CB00003B/731